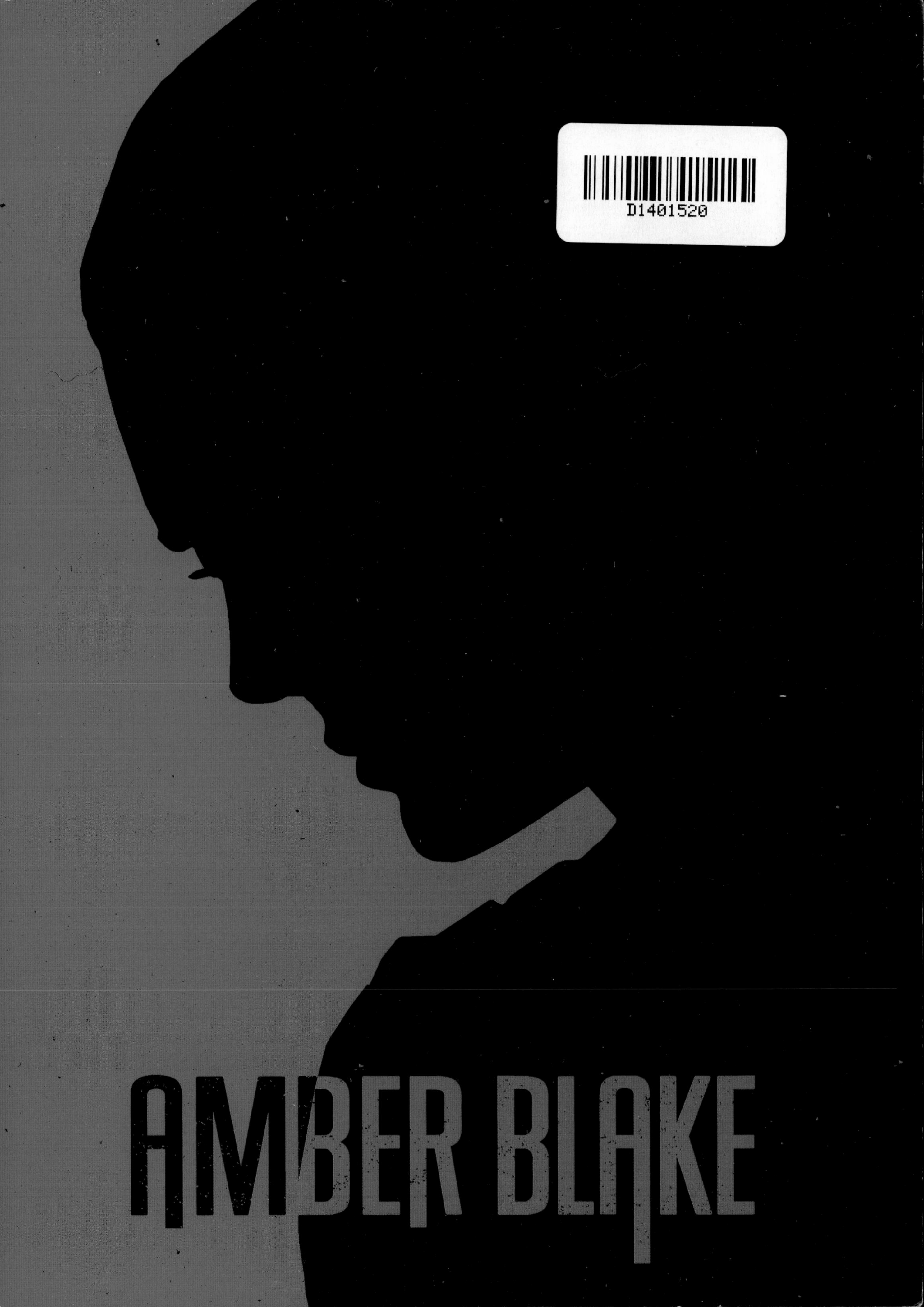
AMBER BLAKE

COLLECTION EDITORS
**JUSTIN EISINGER**
AND **ALONZO SIMON**
COLLECTION DESIGN
**SHAWN LEE**

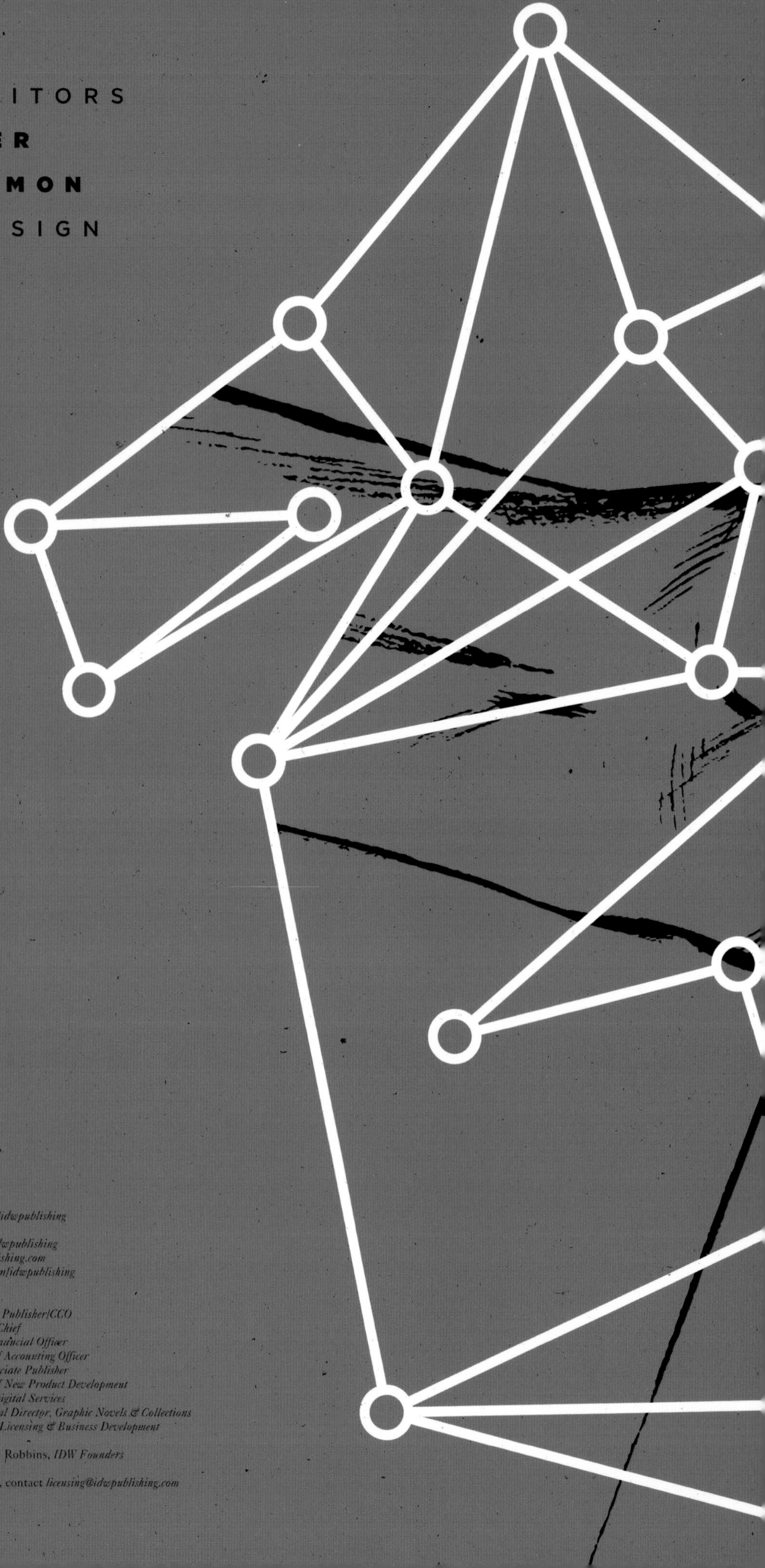

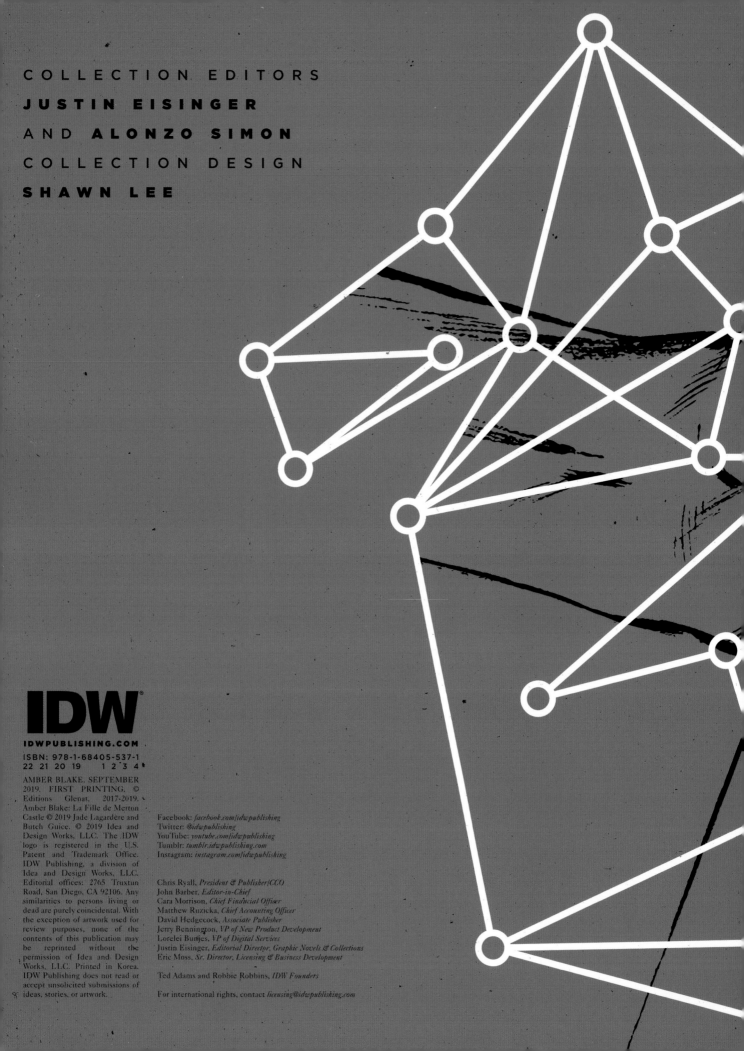

IDWPUBLISHING.COM
ISBN: 978-1-68405-537-1
22 21 20 19 1 2 3 4

AMBER BLAKE. SEPTEMBER 2019. FIRST PRINTING. 

Facebook: *facebook.com/idwpublishing*
Twitter: *@idwpublishing*
YouTube: *youtube.com/idwpublishing*
Tumblr: *tumblr.idwpublishing.com*
Instagram: *instagram.com/idwpublishing*



For international rights, contact *licensing@idwpublishing.com*

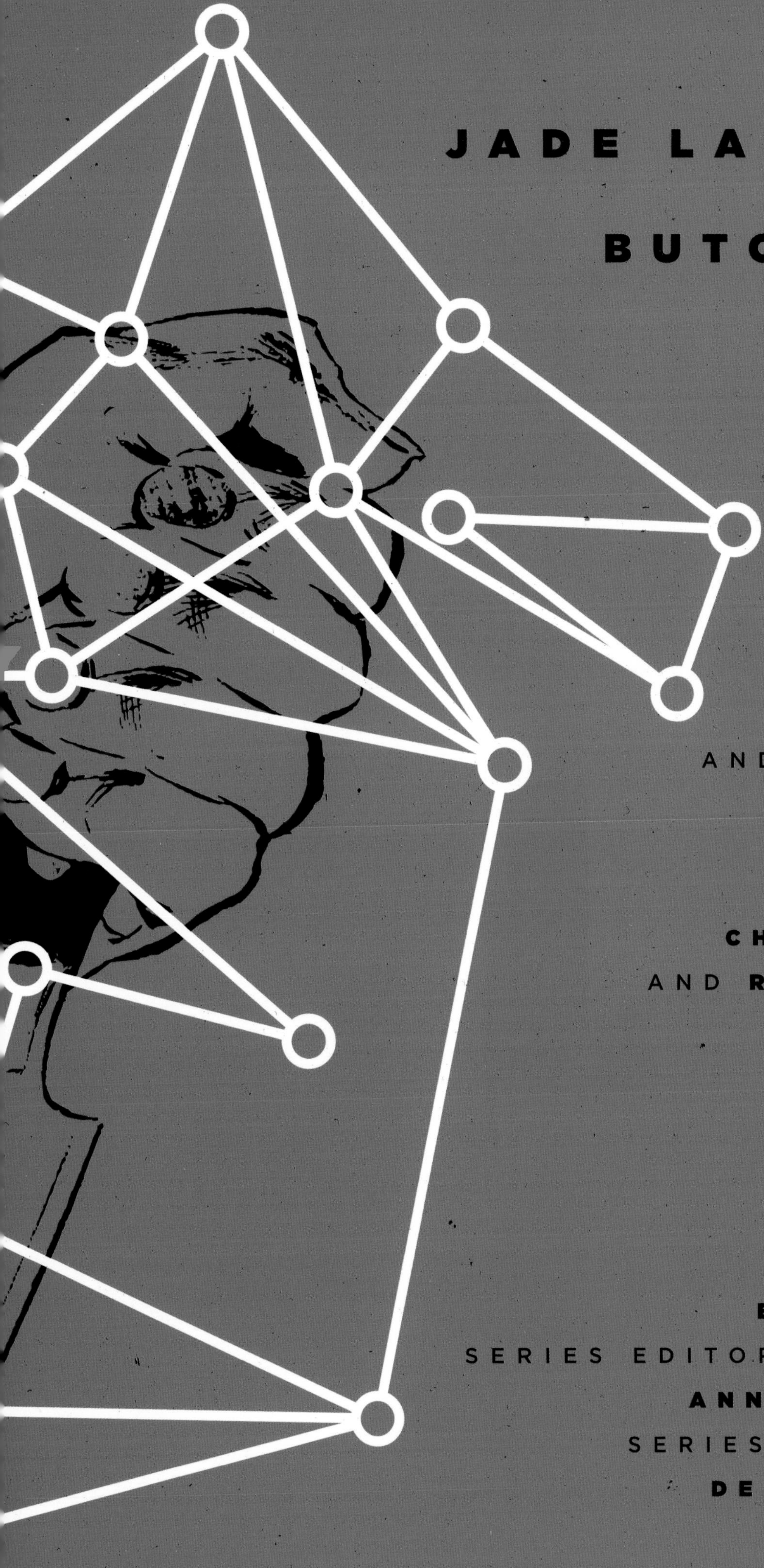

WRITTEN BY
**JADE LAGARDÉRE**
ART BY
**BUTCH GUICE**

INKS BY
**BUTCH GUICE**
AND **MIKE PERKINS**
COLORS BY
**DAN BROWN**
LETTERS BY
**CHRISTA MIESNER**
AND **ROBBIE ROBBINS**

SERIES EDITOR
**ELIZABETH BREI**
SERIES EDITORIAL ASSISTANT
**ANNI PERHEENTUPA**
SERIES GROUP EDITOR
**DENTON J. TIPTON**

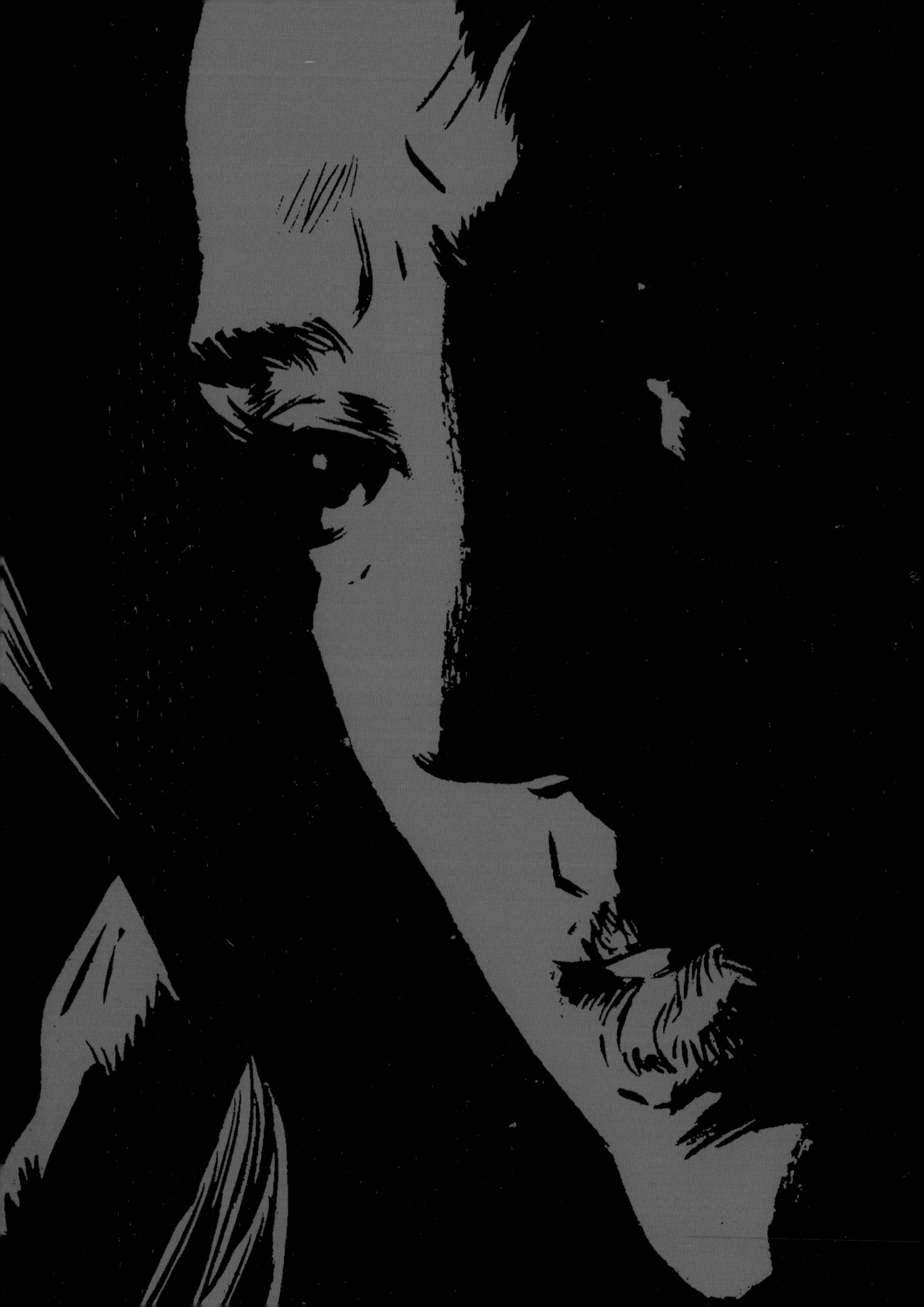

A mother's love for her children is what inspired me to create Amber Blake. I was six months pregnant with my second daughter and reflected on what it would be like for my girls to be in the world we live in today.

Memories of my own difficult childhood inspired me to create a superhero that, through her will and determination, would realize her destiny. I wanted to create a character that survived a difficult childhood marked by emotional and physical suffering, and realized her true destiny as a hero to all. I know that many girls today suffer in the same way. I want to give them hope.

Through the character of Amber Blake, I want to bring a positive message behind her story: As much as you suffer, as long as you live, keep going, fight and believe in yourself. Most of all: Love yourself as you are, as when you believe in yourself you are your own superhero.

The *Amber Blake* series gave me the ability to create a superhero whose true superpowers are her soul, her will and her tireless determination to succeed. A superhero that can push through any challenge. She stands up for justice and equality for all.

It is thanks to Butch's genius that Amber and the characters who populate her world are so vibrant and relatable.

I know that every reader will identify with and believe in Amber Blake.

I know I have. Each of you can be Amber Blake.

JADE LAGARDÈRE
Paris
2019

THE CHANNEL ISLANDS—
JERSEY, 2003

WHERE ARE
WE GOING,
MUMMY?

MY FEET
ARE REALLY
COLD.

MERTON CASTLE
ORPHANAGE

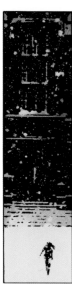

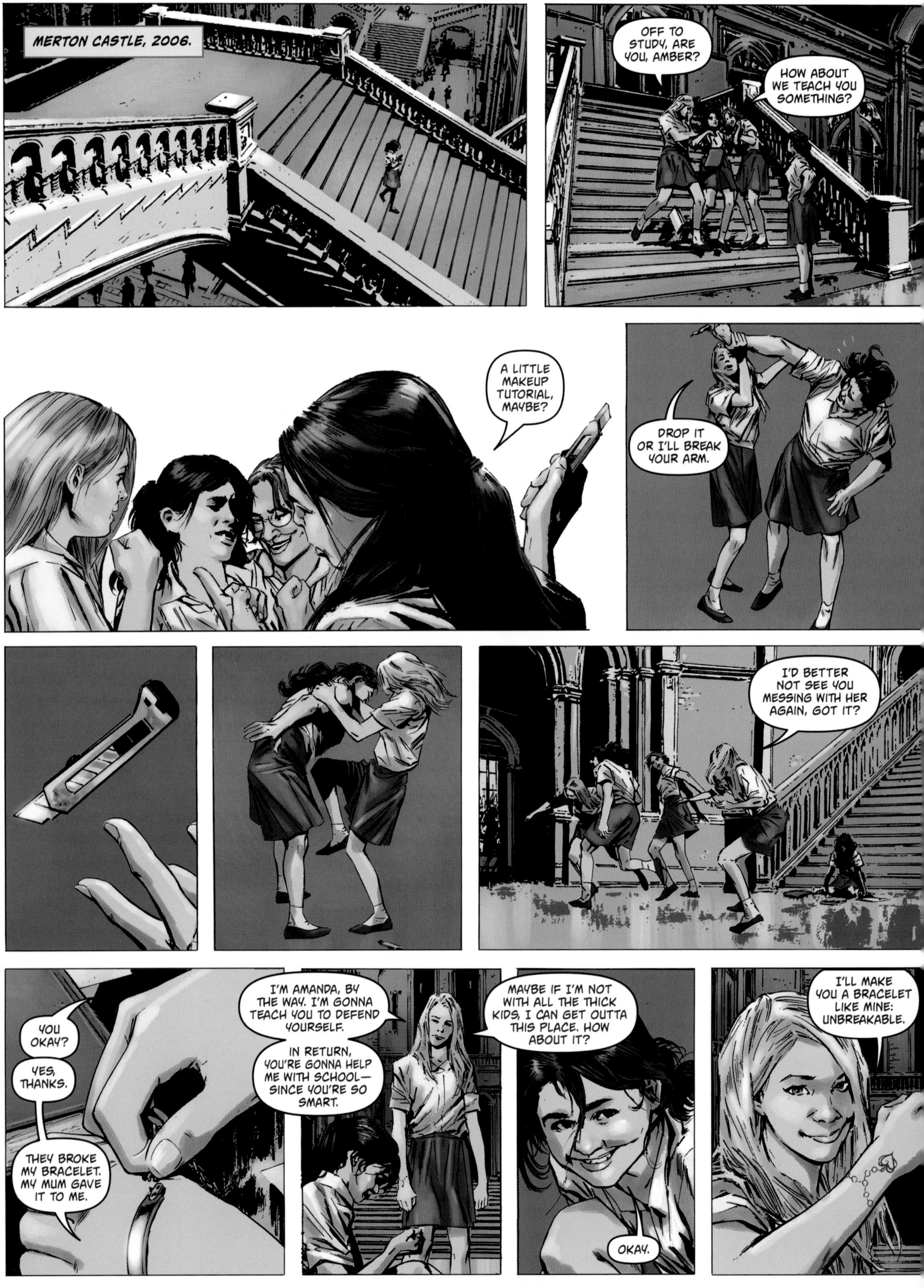
MERTON CASTLE, 2006.
OFF TO STUDY, ARE YOU, AMBER?
HOW ABOUT WE TEACH YOU SOMETHING?
A LITTLE MAKEUP TUTORIAL, MAYBE?
DROP IT OR I'LL BREAK YOUR ARM.
I'D BETTER NOT SEE YOU MESSING WITH HER AGAIN, GOT IT?
YOU OKAY?
YES, THANKS.
THEY BROKE MY BRACELET. MY MUM GAVE IT TO ME.
I'M AMANDA, BY THE WAY. I'M GONNA TEACH YOU TO DEFEND YOURSELF.
IN RETURN, YOU'RE GONNA HELP ME WITH SCHOOL— SINCE YOU'RE SO SMART.
MAYBE IF I'M NOT WITH ALL THE THICK KIDS, I CAN GET OUTTA THIS PLACE. HOW ABOUT IT?
OKAY.
I'LL MAKE YOU A BRACELET LIKE MINE: UNBREAKABLE.

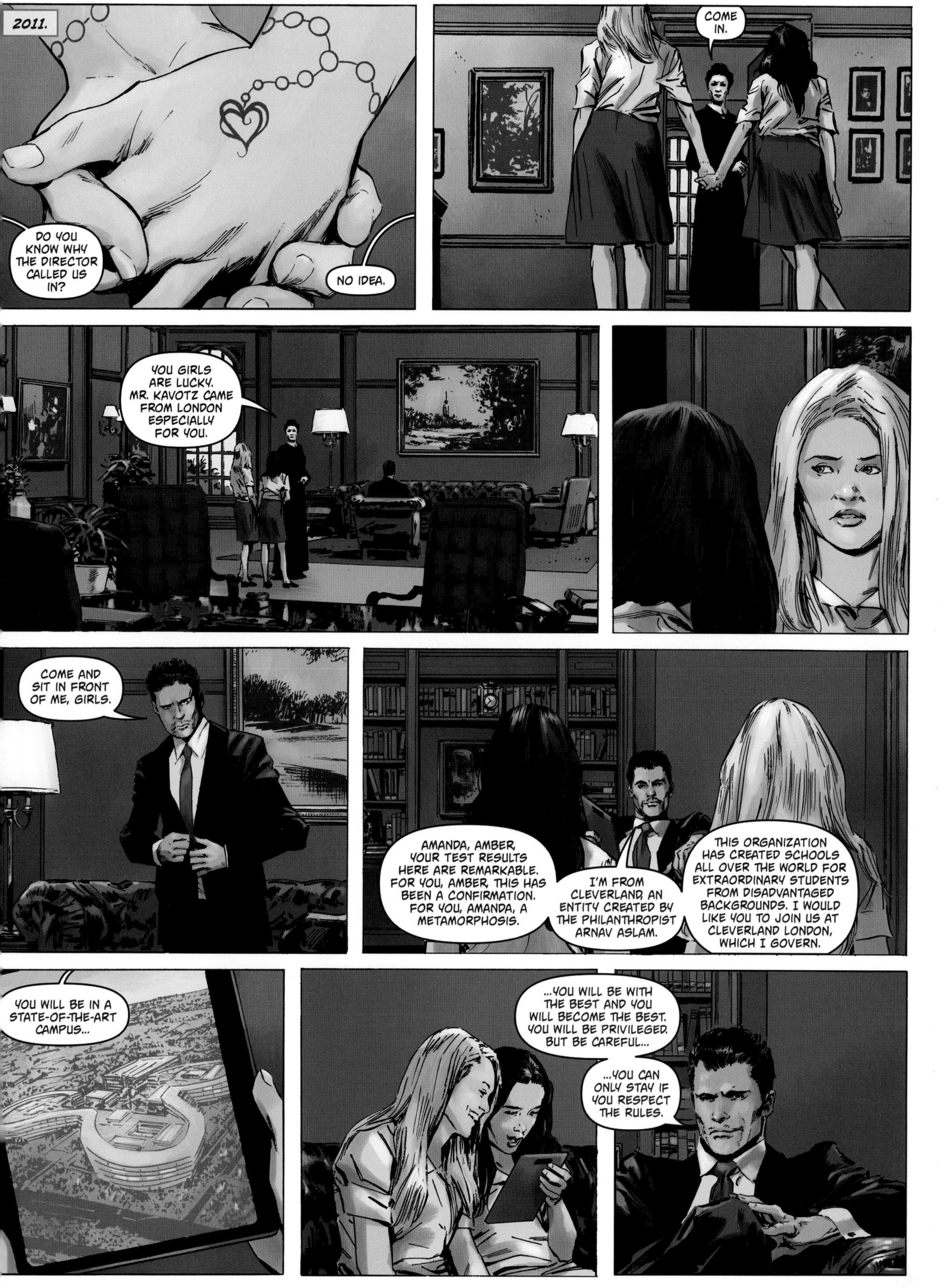
2011.
DO YOU KNOW WHY THE DIRECTOR CALLED US IN?
NO IDEA.
COME IN.
YOU GIRLS ARE LUCKY. MR. KAVOTZ CAME FROM LONDON ESPECIALLY FOR YOU.
COME AND SIT IN FRONT OF ME, GIRLS.
AMANDA, AMBER, YOUR TEST RESULTS HERE ARE REMARKABLE. FOR YOU, AMBER, THIS HAS BEEN A CONFIRMATION. FOR YOU, AMANDA, A METAMORPHOSIS.
I'M FROM CLEVERLAND, AN ENTITY CREATED BY THE PHILANTHROPIST ARNAV ASLAM.
THIS ORGANIZATION HAS CREATED SCHOOLS ALL OVER THE WORLD FOR EXTRAORDINARY STUDENTS FROM DISADVANTAGED BACKGROUNDS. I WOULD LIKE YOU TO JOIN US AT CLEVERLAND LONDON, WHICH I GOVERN.
YOU WILL BE IN A STATE-OF-THE-ART CAMPUS...
...YOU WILL BE WITH THE BEST AND YOU WILL BECOME THE BEST. YOU WILL BE PRIVILEGED. BUT BE CAREFUL...
...YOU CAN ONLY STAY IF YOU RESPECT THE RULES.

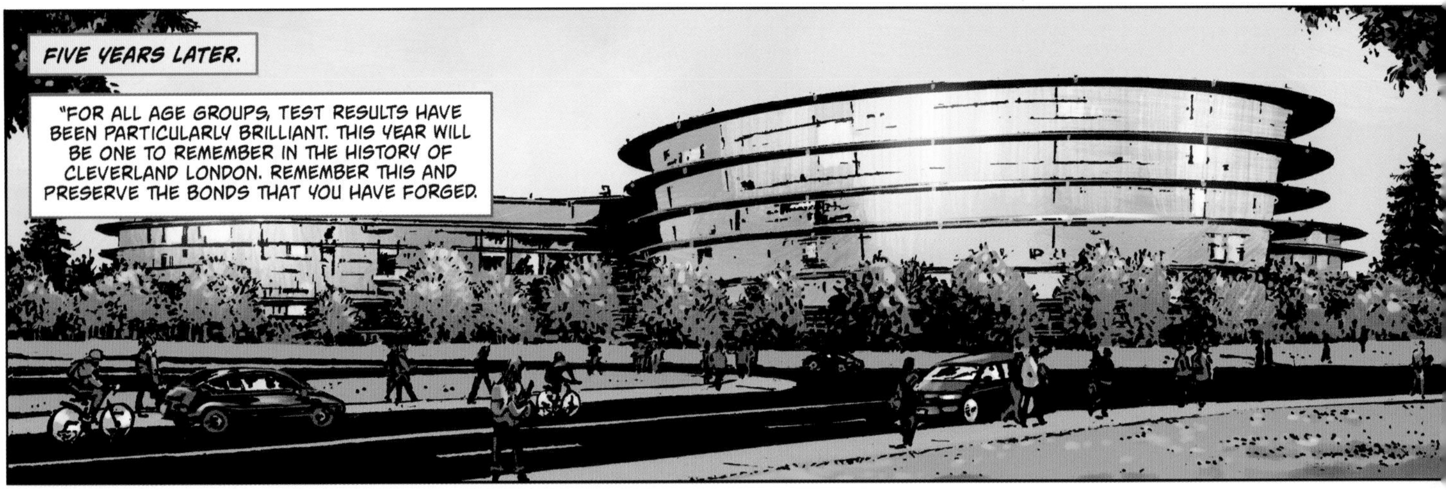
FIVE YEARS LATER.
"FOR ALL AGE GROUPS, TEST RESULTS HAVE BEEN PARTICULARLY BRILLIANT. THIS YEAR WILL BE ONE TO REMEMBER IN THE HISTORY OF CLEVERLAND LONDON. REMEMBER THIS AND PRESERVE THE BONDS THAT YOU HAVE FORGED.

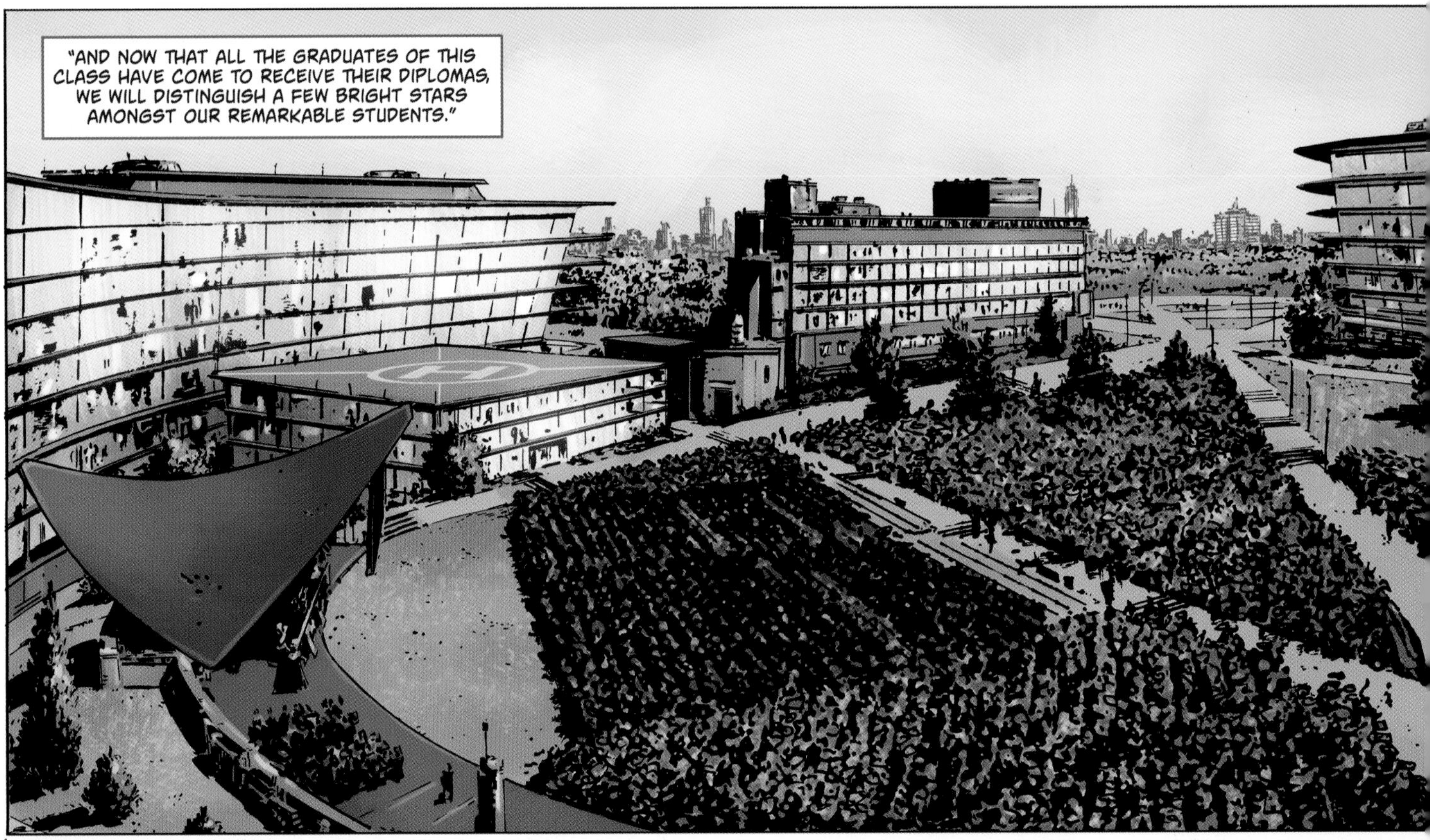
"AND NOW THAT ALL THE GRADUATES OF THIS CLASS HAVE COME TO RECEIVE THEIR DIPLOMAS, WE WILL DISTINGUISH A FEW BRIGHT STARS AMONGST OUR REMARKABLE STUDENTS."

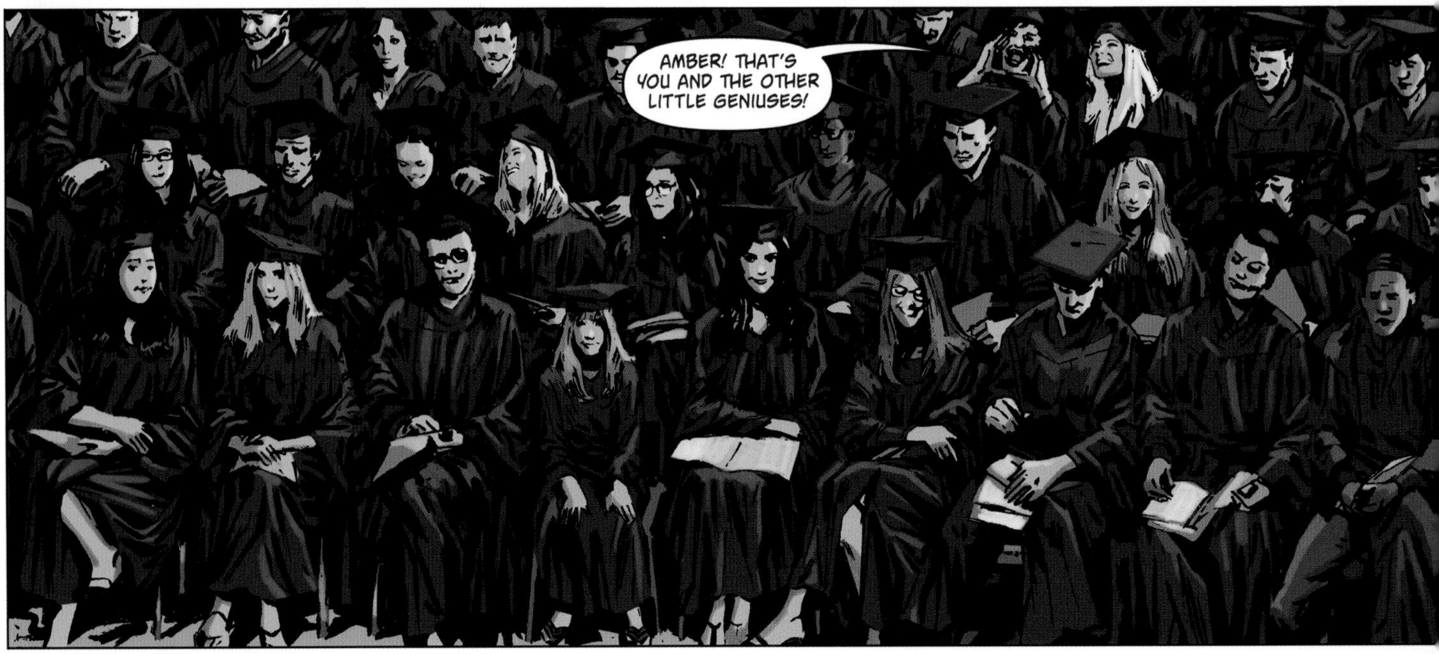
AMBER! THAT'S YOU AND THE OTHER LITTLE GENIUSES!

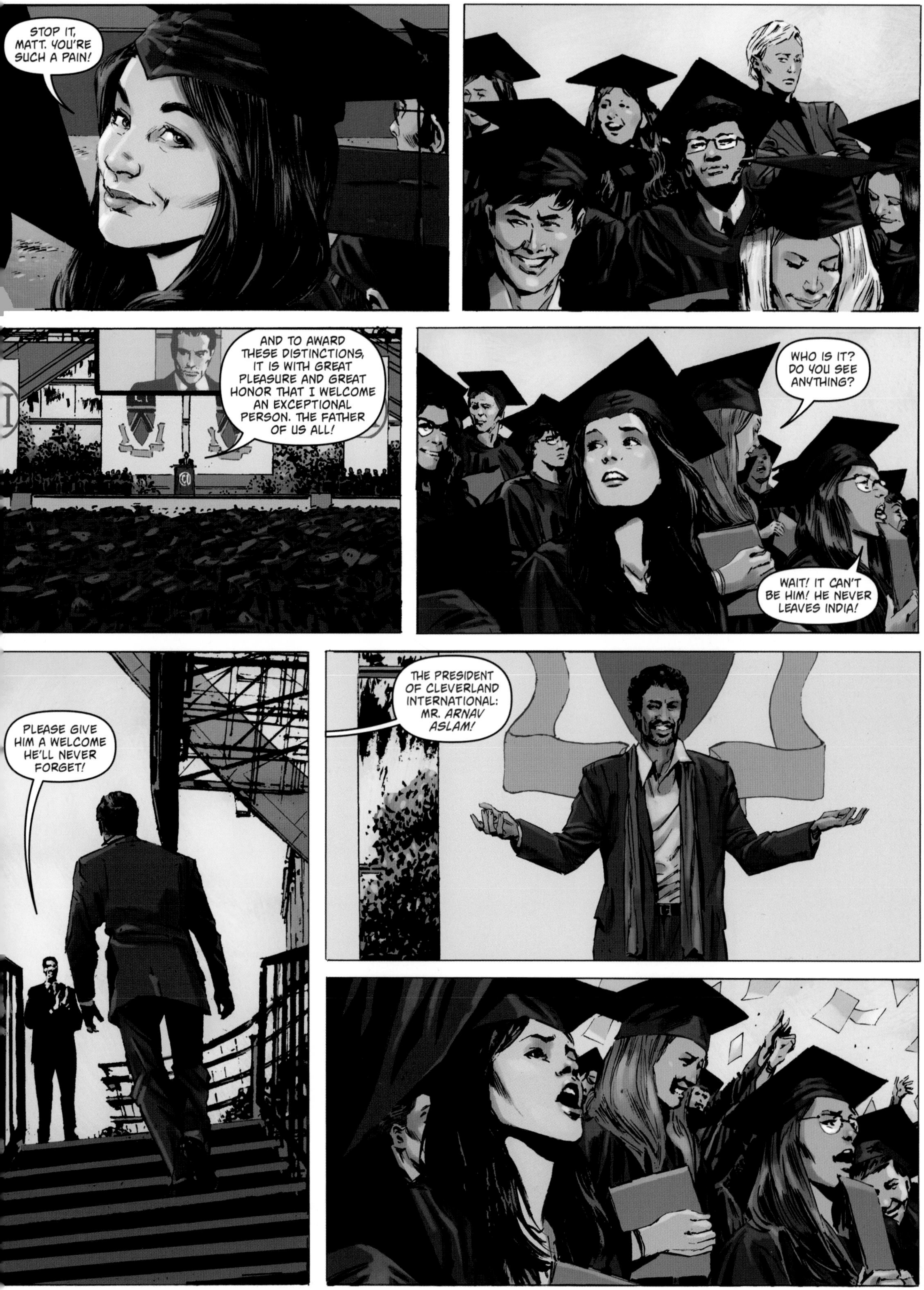
STOP IT, MATT. YOU'RE SUCH A PAIN!
AND TO AWARD THESE DISTINCTIONS, IT IS WITH GREAT PLEASURE AND GREAT HONOR THAT I WELCOME AN EXCEPTIONAL PERSON. THE FATHER OF US ALL!
WHO IS IT? DO YOU SEE ANYTHING?
WAIT! IT CAN'T BE HIM! HE NEVER LEAVES INDIA!
PLEASE GIVE HIM A WELCOME HE'LL NEVER FORGET!
THE PRESIDENT OF CLEVERLAND INTERNATIONAL: MR. ARNAV ASLAM!

FOR HER EXCEPTIONAL AND PRECOCIOUS RESULTS AND FOR HER NEVER-FAILING PERSONAL INVESTMENT ON CAMPUS, I CALL AMBER ANDERSON!

CONGRATULATIONS, DARLING!

THANK YOU, MR. ASLAM. I AM VERY HONORED.

THE HONOR IS MINE. CONGRATULATIONS ON YOUR WORK AND YOUR TALENT, AMBER.

EACH SUCCESS LIKE YOURS GIVES ME SO MUCH JOY.

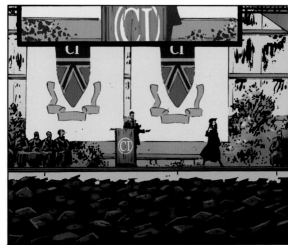

YOU SEE WHEN WE RESPECT THE RULES...

AND BECAUSE MERIT ISN'T BASED ON AGE, I NOW CALL ALICE FROST!

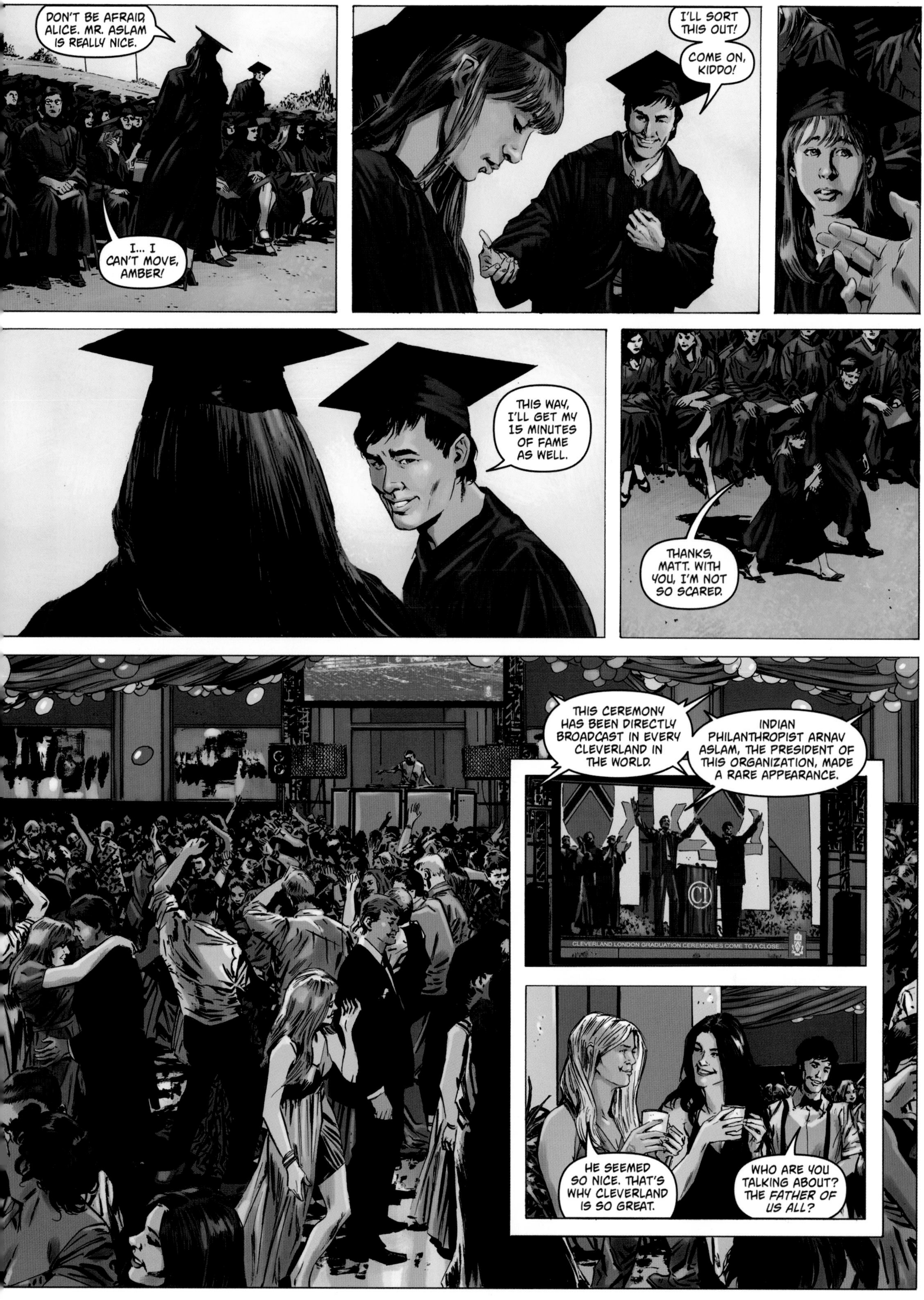
DON'T BE AFRAID, ALICE. MR. ASLAM IS REALLY NICE.
I... I CAN'T MOVE, AMBER!
I'LL SORT THIS OUT!
COME ON, KIDDO!
THIS WAY, I'LL GET MY 15 MINUTES OF FAME AS WELL.
THANKS, MATT. WITH YOU, I'M NOT SO SCARED.
THIS CEREMONY HAS BEEN DIRECTLY BROADCAST IN EVERY CLEVERLAND IN THE WORLD.
INDIAN PHILANTHROPIST ARNAV ASLAM, THE PRESIDENT OF THIS ORGANIZATION, MADE A RARE APPEARANCE.
CLEVERLAND LONDON GRADUATION CEREMONIES COME TO A CLOSE
HE SEEMED SO NICE. THAT'S WHY CLEVERLAND IS SO GREAT.
WHO ARE YOU TALKING ABOUT? THE *FATHER OF US ALL*?

TO CLOSE THIS CEREMONY, A MESSAGE FROM CAMILA DOREGO, PRESIDENT OF ARGENTINA. FROM THE SLUMS OF ROSARIO...

...FORMER STUDENT OF CLEVERLAND BUENOS-AIRES, SHE IS ONE OF THE BRIGHTEST STORIES OF SUCCESS IN ARNAV ASLAM'S EDUCATIONAL PROGRAM.

I'M NOT GOING TO LECTURE YOU. YOU ALREADY KNOW SO MANY THINGS. INSTEAD I WILL SAY THIS—

PERSEVERE. TAKE ADVANTAGE OF THE EXCEPTIONAL STUDIES THAT CLEVERLAND HAS TO OFFER, OF THE HUMAN WARMTH WHICH IS ITS BACKBONE, AND ABOVE ALL, THE RULES YOU WILL LEARN TO RESPECT.

CONGRATULATIONS AND GOOD EVENING.

...CAMILA DOREGO, LIVE FROM THE PRESIDENTIAL OFFICES OF ARGENTINA, AND FORMER S

IF I COULD HAVE A QUARTER OF HER SUCCESS!

YOU'RE REALLY BRILLIANT, MATT. YOU SHOULD HAVE HAD YOUR PLACE ON THE FIRST ROW AS WELL.

BUT I'M NOT AS GOOD-LOOKING AS YOU, DEAR AMANDA.

YOU'RE GORGEOUS.

AND YOUR LITTLE TECHNOLOGY BREAKTHROUGH SHOULD MAKE YOU THE MASTER OF THE WORLD, SHOULDN'T IT?

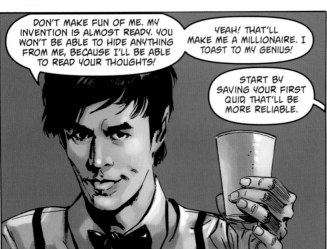

DON'T MAKE FUN OF ME. MY INVENTION IS ALMOST READY. YOU WON'T BE ABLE TO HIDE ANYTHING FROM ME, BECAUSE I'LL BE ABLE TO READ YOUR THOUGHTS!

YEAH! THAT'LL MAKE ME A MILLIONAIRE. I TOAST TO MY GENIUS!

START BY SAVING YOUR FIRST QUID, THAT'LL BE MORE RELIABLE.

I HAVE LEARNED FIVE LANGUAGES HERE. I'M GOING TO TRAVEL THROUGH EVERY COUNTRY IN THE WORLD AND EARN TONS OF MONEY AS A MODEL.

I TOAST TO MY LINGUISTIC GENIUS AND MY PERFECT BODY!

I WOULD LIKE TO DO SOMETHING DIFFERENT.

I WANT TO BECOME A LAWYER AND DEFEND THOSE WHO CAN'T DEFEND THEMSELVES, THOSE WHO ARE TOO WEAK, OR TOO YOUNG...

I WILL COME TO THE AID OF ABUSED CHILDREN, WHEREVER THEY ARE IN THE WORLD.

HIRE ME AS YOUR TECHNICAL CONSULTANT. ON THE SUBJECT OF ABUSED CHILDREN, I SURELY KNOW MORE THAN YOU.

AND THAT WAY I'LL DO SOMETHING USEFUL TOO.

WHY DID HE REACT LIKE THAT?

HE NEVER TALKS ABOUT HIS PAST—BUT IT MUST HAVE BEEN TERRIBLE.

OH? IS THERE A CONTEST FOR WHO'S FELT THE MOST MISERY? CAN THEY RANK US THAT WAY TOO?

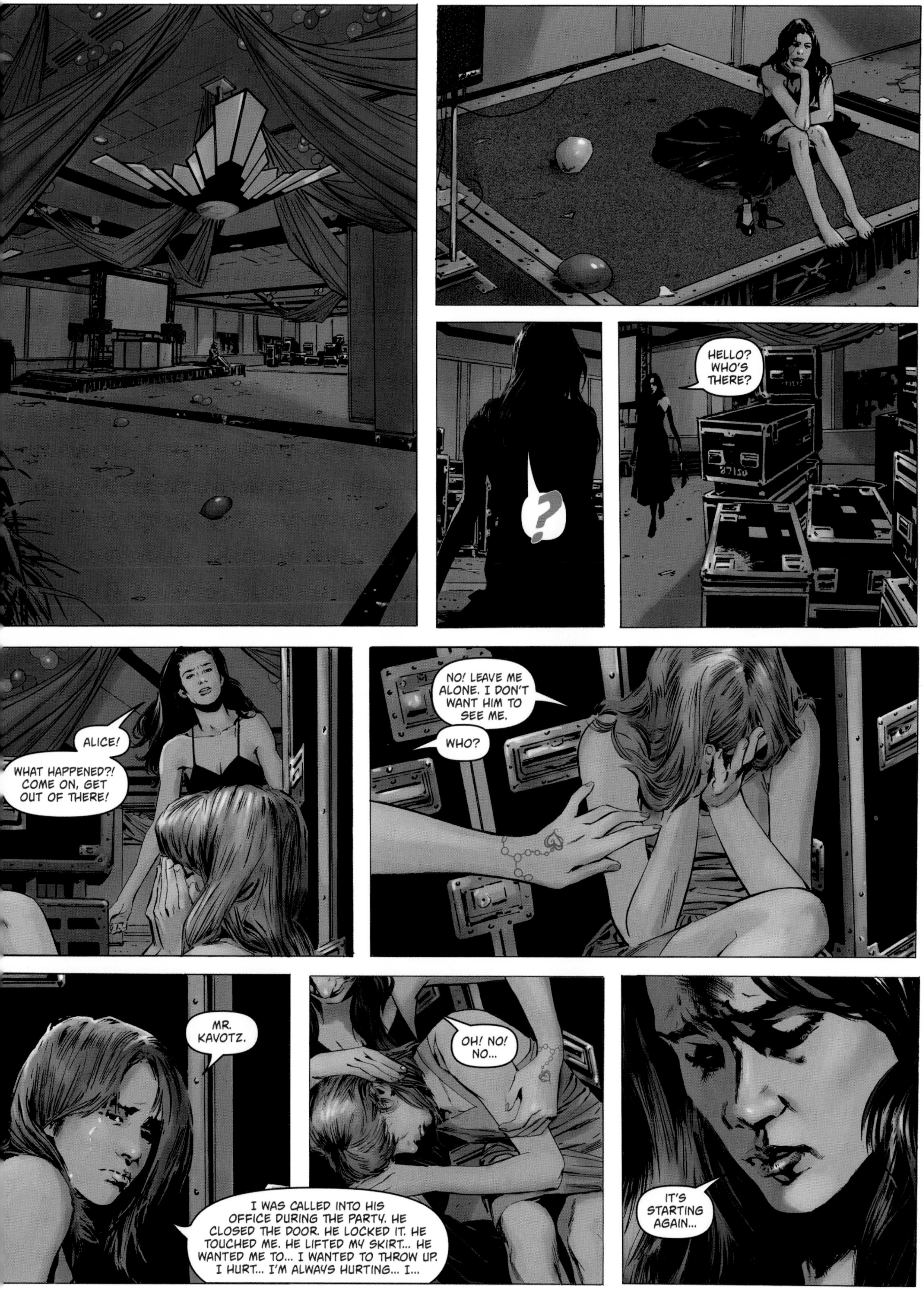
?
HELLO? WHO'S THERE?
ALICE!
WHAT HAPPENED?! COME ON, GET OUT OF THERE!
NO! LEAVE ME ALONE. I DON'T WANT HIM TO SEE ME.
WHO?
MR. KAVOTZ.
OH! NO! NO...
I WAS CALLED INTO HIS OFFICE DURING THE PARTY. HE CLOSED THE DOOR. HE LOCKED IT. HE TOUCHED ME. HE LIFTED MY SKIRT... HE WANTED ME TO... I WANTED TO THROW UP. I HURT... I'M ALWAYS HURTING... I...
IT'S STARTING AGAIN...

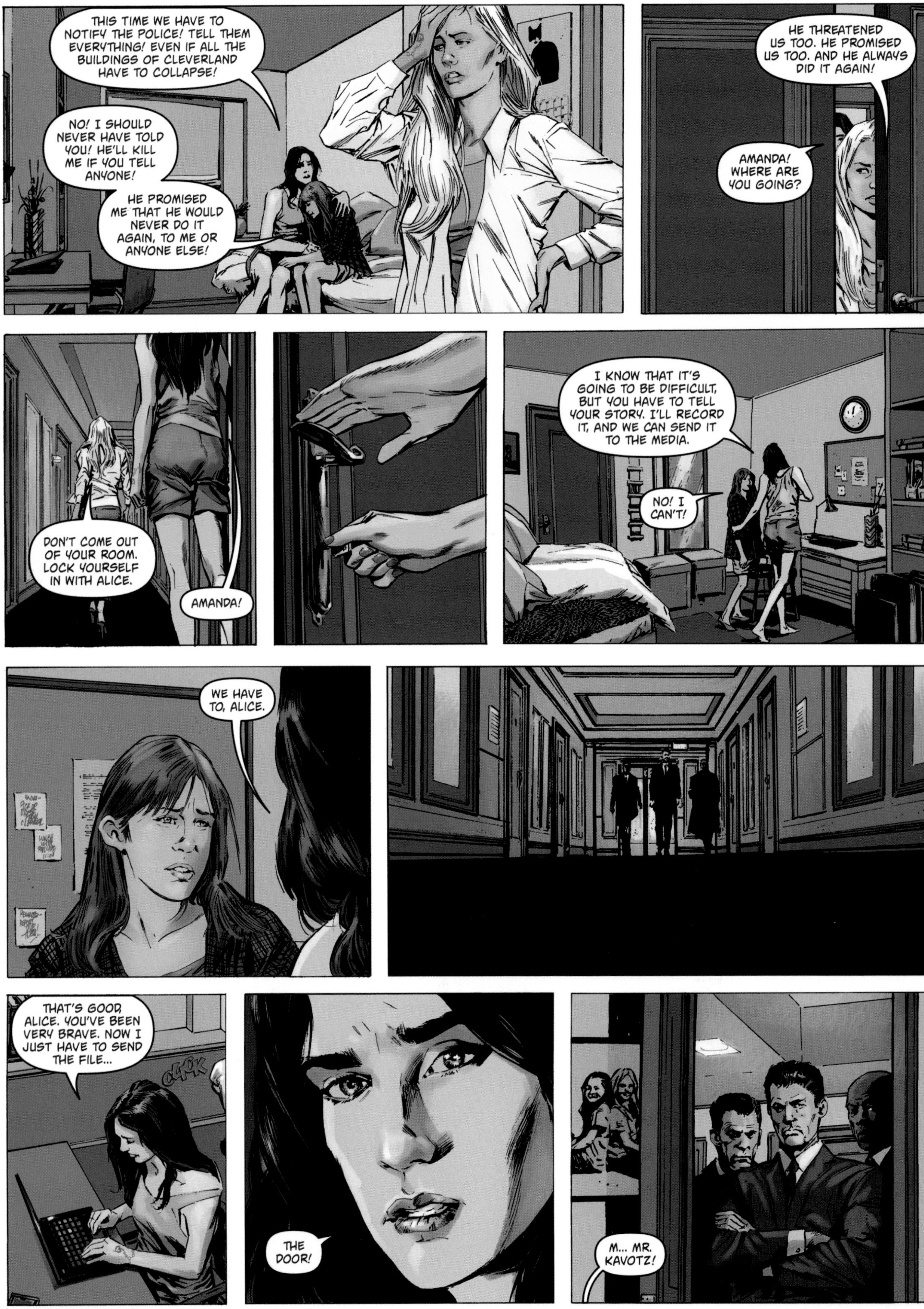

THIS TIME WE HAVE TO NOTIFY THE POLICE! TELL THEM EVERYTHING! EVEN IF ALL THE BUILDINGS OF CLEVERLAND HAVE TO COLLAPSE!
NO! I SHOULD NEVER HAVE TOLD YOU! HE'LL KILL ME IF YOU TELL ANYONE!
HE PROMISED ME THAT HE WOULD NEVER DO IT AGAIN, TO ME OR ANYONE ELSE!
HE THREATENED US TOO. HE PROMISED US TOO. AND HE ALWAYS DID IT AGAIN!
AMANDA! WHERE ARE YOU GOING?
DON'T COME OUT OF YOUR ROOM. LOCK YOURSELF IN WITH ALICE.
AMANDA!
I KNOW THAT IT'S GOING TO BE DIFFICULT, BUT YOU HAVE TO TELL YOUR STORY. I'LL RECORD IT, AND WE CAN SEND IT TO THE MEDIA.
NO! I CAN'T!
WE HAVE TO, ALICE.
THAT'S GOOD, ALICE. YOU'VE BEEN VERY BRAVE. NOW I JUST HAVE TO SEND THE FILE...
CLICK
THE DOOR!
M... MR. KAVOTZ!

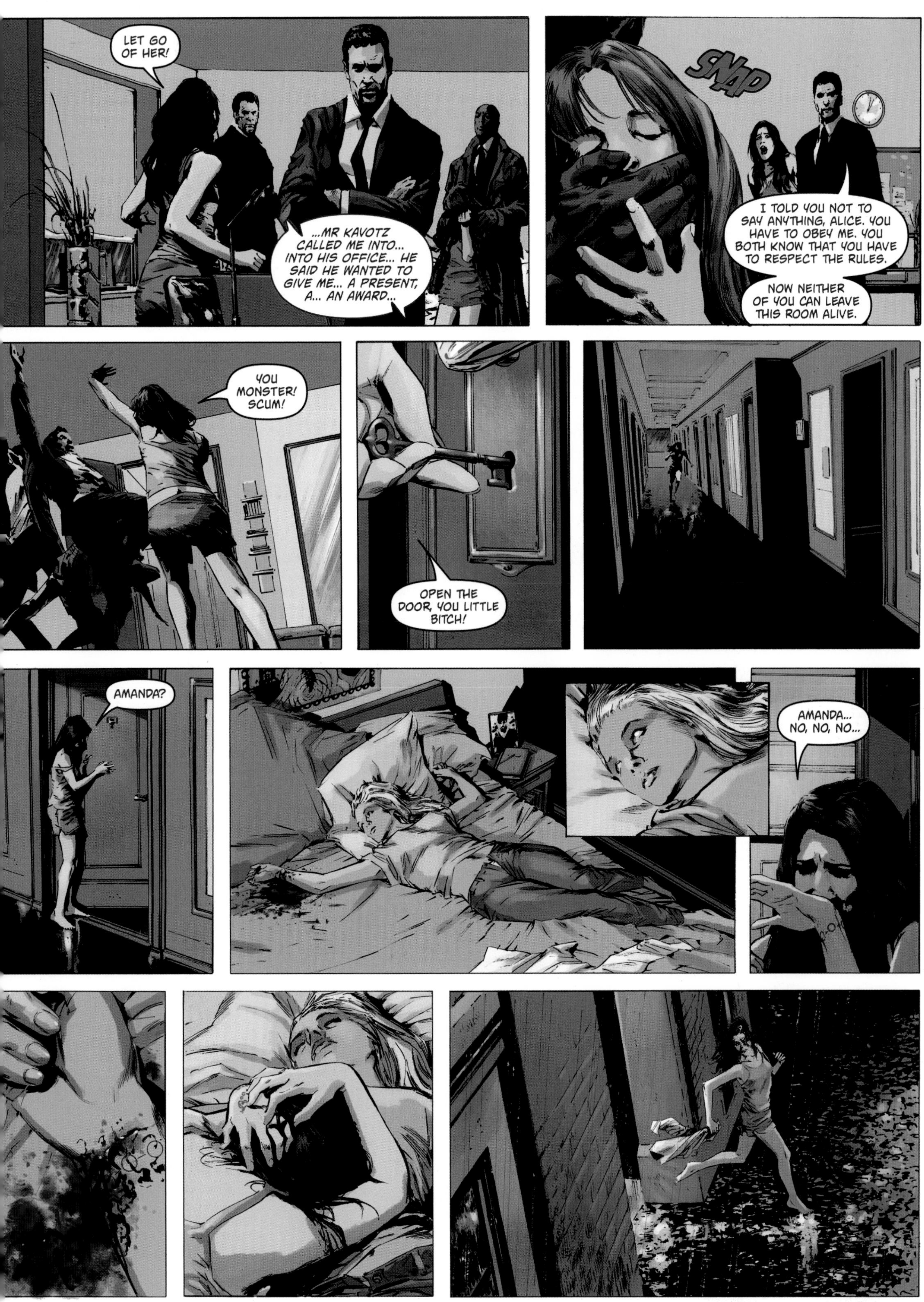
LET GO OF HER!
...MR KAVOTZ CALLED ME INTO... INTO HIS OFFICE... HE SAID HE WANTED TO GIVE ME... A PRESENT, A... AN AWARD...
SNAP
I TOLD YOU NOT TO SAY ANYTHING, ALICE. YOU HAVE TO OBEY ME. YOU BOTH KNOW THAT YOU HAVE TO RESPECT THE RULES.
NOW NEITHER OF YOU CAN LEAVE THIS ROOM ALIVE.
YOU MONSTER! SCUM!
OPEN THE DOOR, YOU LITTLE BITCH!
AMANDA?
AMANDA... NO, NO, NO...

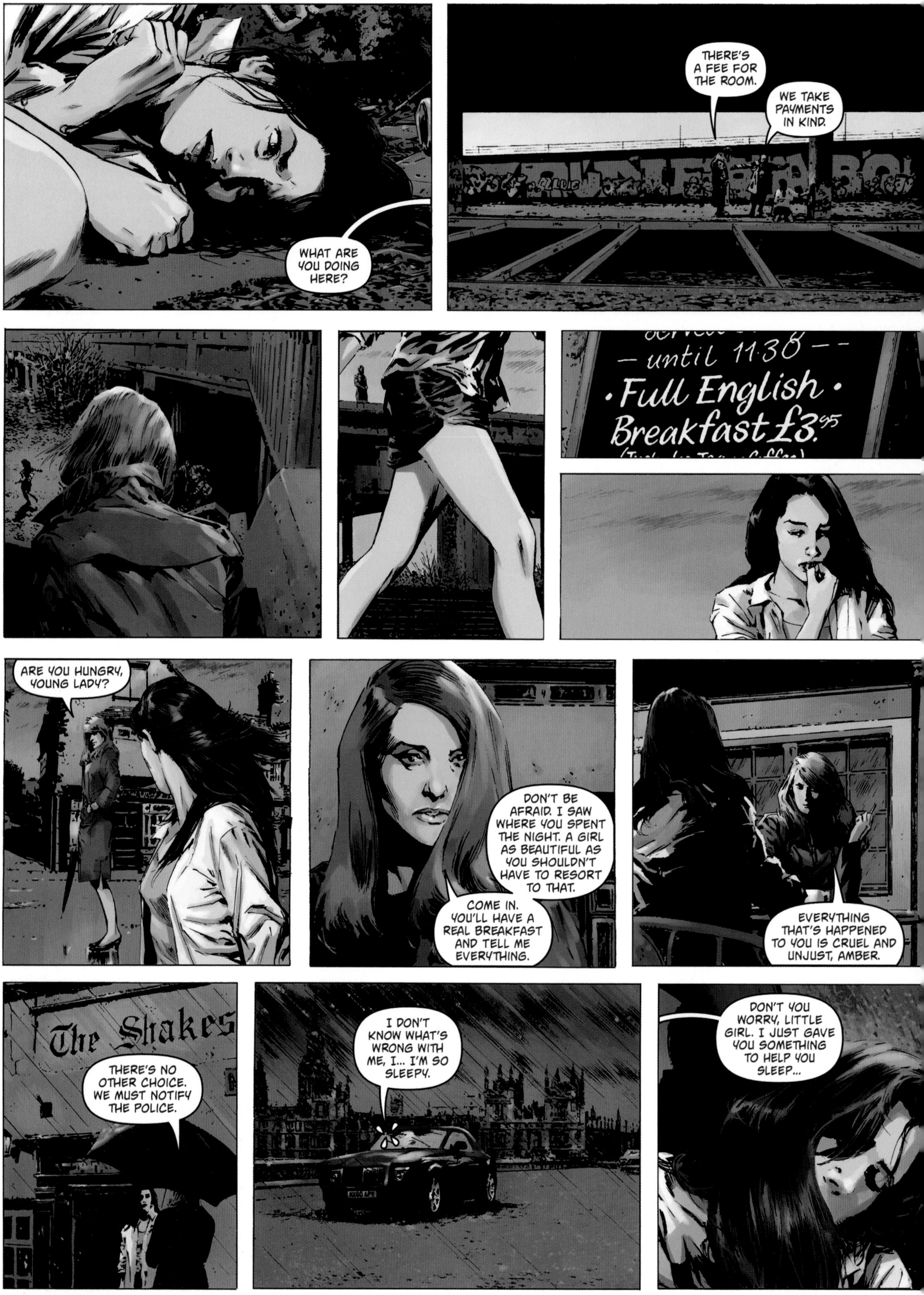
WHAT ARE YOU DOING HERE?
THERE'S A FEE FOR THE ROOM.
WE TAKE PAYMENTS IN KIND.
until 11·30
· Full English ·
Breakfast £3.95
ARE YOU HUNGRY, YOUNG LADY?
DON'T BE AFRAID. I SAW WHERE YOU SPENT THE NIGHT. A GIRL AS BEAUTIFUL AS YOU SHOULDN'T HAVE TO RESORT TO THAT.
COME IN. YOU'LL HAVE A REAL BREAKFAST AND TELL ME EVERYTHING.
EVERYTHING THAT'S HAPPENED TO YOU IS CRUEL AND UNJUST, AMBER.
The Shakes
THERE'S NO OTHER CHOICE. WE MUST NOTIFY THE POLICE.
I DON'T KNOW WHAT'S WRONG WITH ME, I... I'M SO SLEEPY.
DON'T YOU WORRY, LITTLE GIRL. I JUST GAVE YOU SOMETHING TO HELP YOU SLEEP...

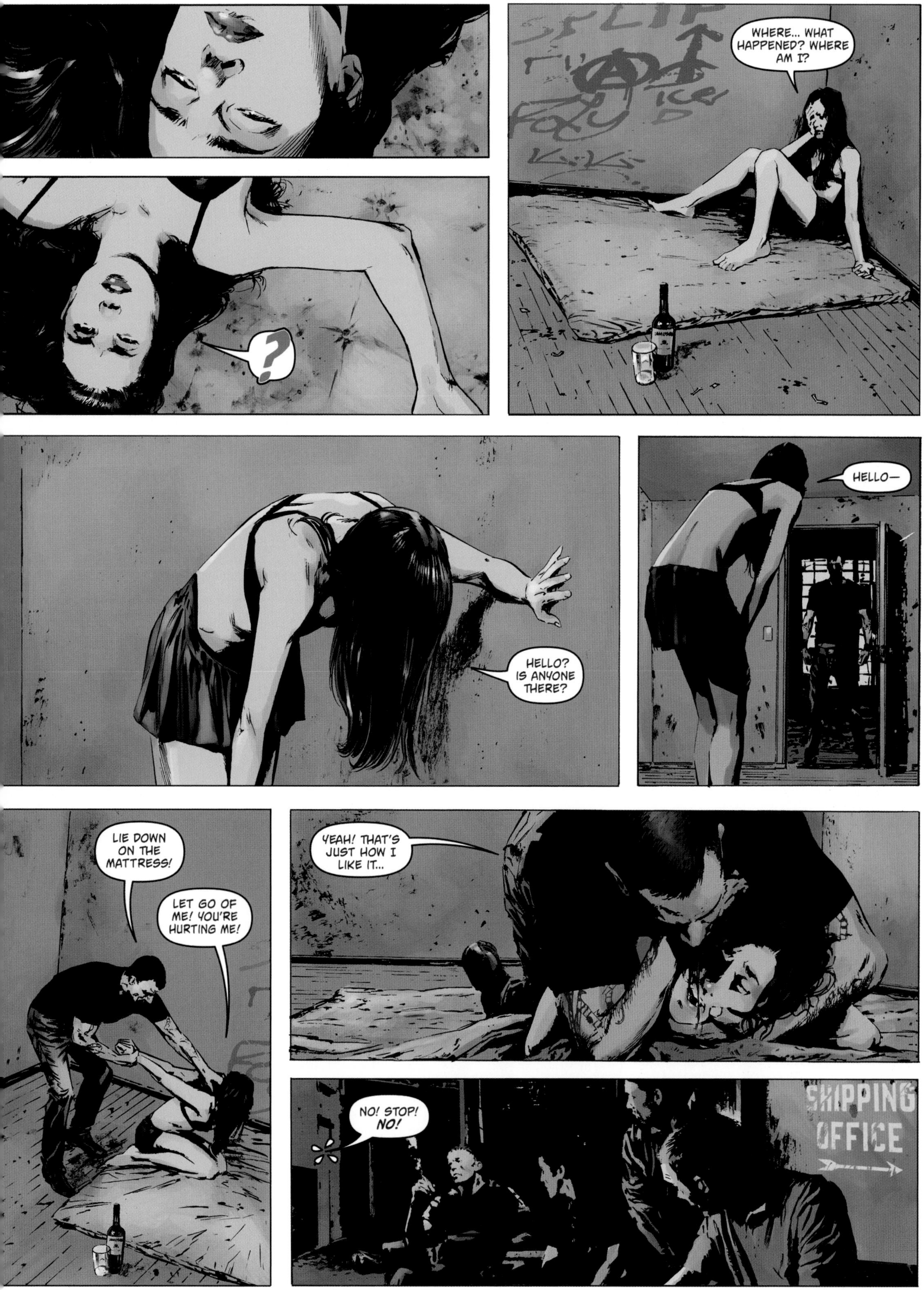
?
WHERE... WHAT HAPPENED? WHERE AM I?
HELLO? IS ANYONE THERE?
HELLO—
LIE DOWN ON THE MATTRESS!
LET GO OF ME! YOU'RE HURTING ME!
YEAH! THAT'S JUST HOW I LIKE IT...
NO! STOP! NO!
SHIPPING OFFICE

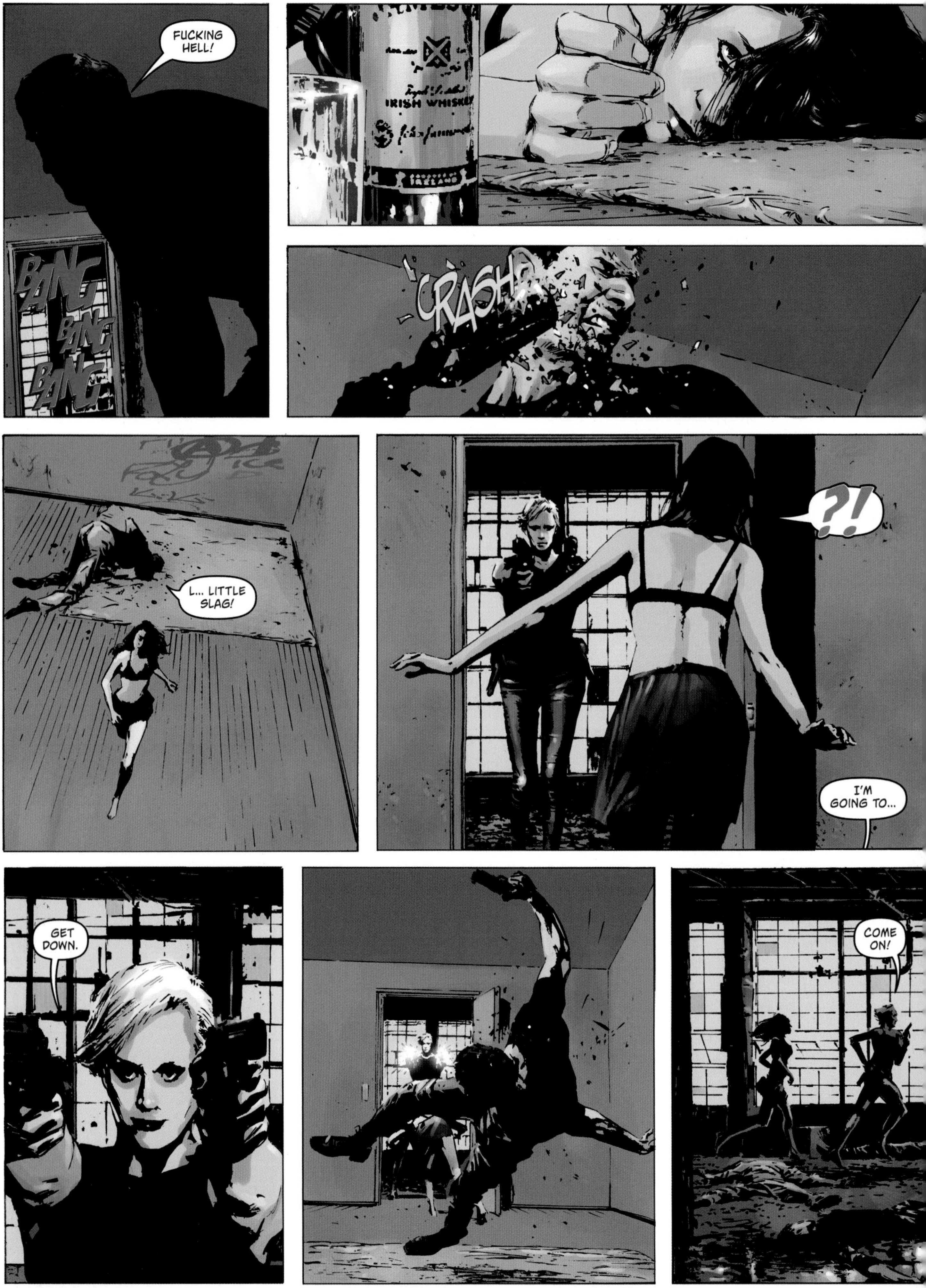
FUCKING HELL!
BANG BANG BANG BANG
IRISH WHISKEY
CRASH
L... LITTLE SLAG!
?!
I'M GOING TO...
GET DOWN.
COME ON!

CAREFUL!

TAKE THIS REVOLVER. I'LL HAVE A HARD TIME USING IT.

THROUGH HERE!

IS THIS THE WAY OUT?

I HOPE SO. IF NOT, THE ONLY WAY OUT IS THROUGH THE MORGUE.

I WOULD HAVE LIKED TO GIVE YOU AN EDUCATION, BUT SADLY FOR YOU, NOW YOU'RE JUST GOING TO DIE.

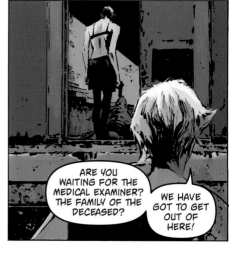

ARE YOU WAITING FOR THE MEDICAL EXAMINER? THE FAMILY OF THE DECEASED?

WE HAVE GOT TO GET OUT OF HERE!

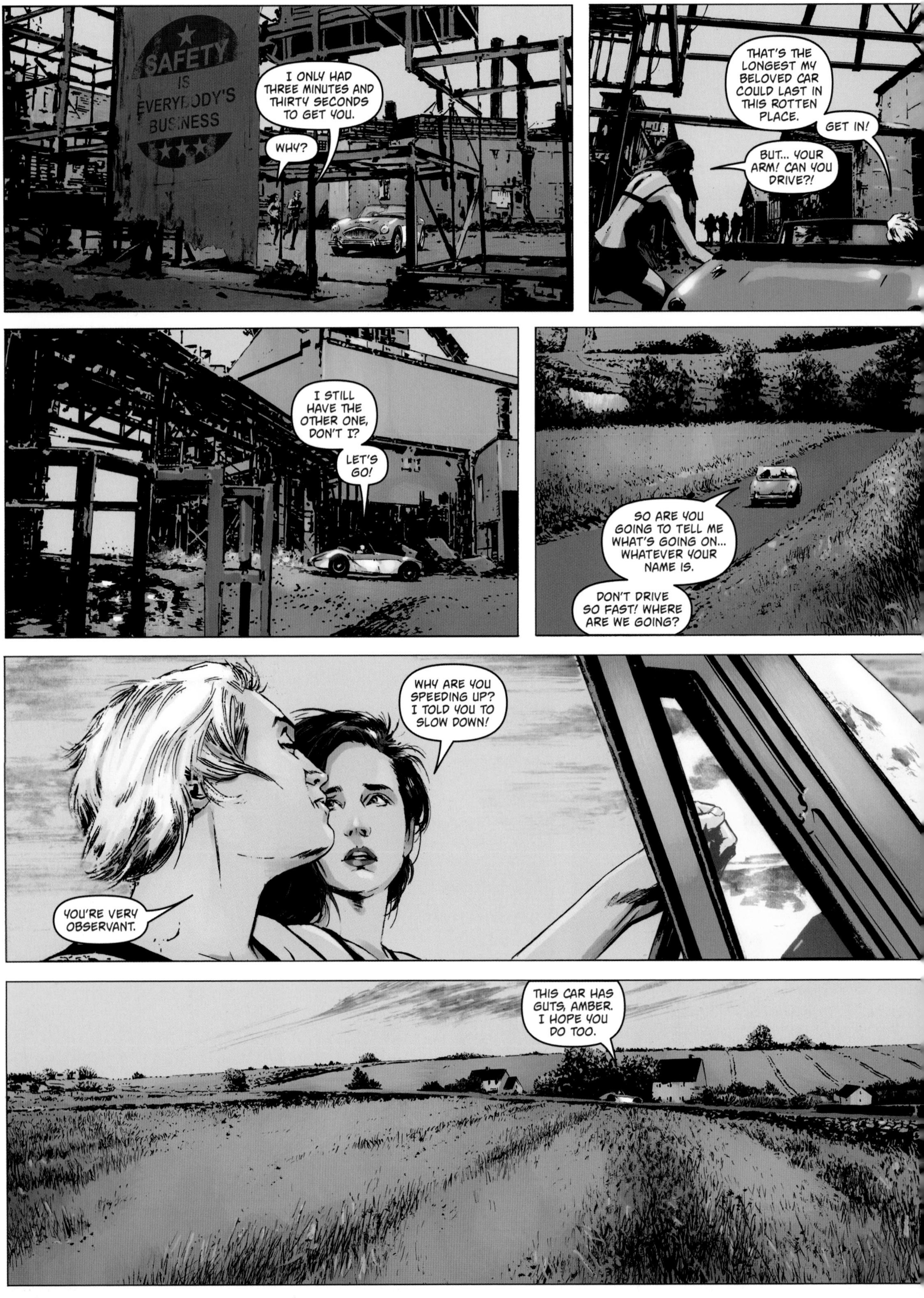
SAFETY IS EVERYBODY'S BUSINESS
I ONLY HAD THREE MINUTES AND THIRTY SECONDS TO GET YOU.
WHY?
THAT'S THE LONGEST MY BELOVED CAR COULD LAST IN THIS ROTTEN PLACE.
GET IN!
BUT... YOUR ARM! CAN YOU DRIVE?!
I STILL HAVE THE OTHER ONE, DON'T I?
LET'S GO!
SO ARE YOU GOING TO TELL ME WHAT'S GOING ON... WHATEVER YOUR NAME IS.
DON'T DRIVE SO FAST! WHERE ARE WE GOING?
WHY ARE YOU SPEEDING UP? I TOLD YOU TO SLOW DOWN!
YOU'RE VERY OBSERVANT.
THIS CAR HAS GUTS, AMBER. I HOPE YOU DO TOO.

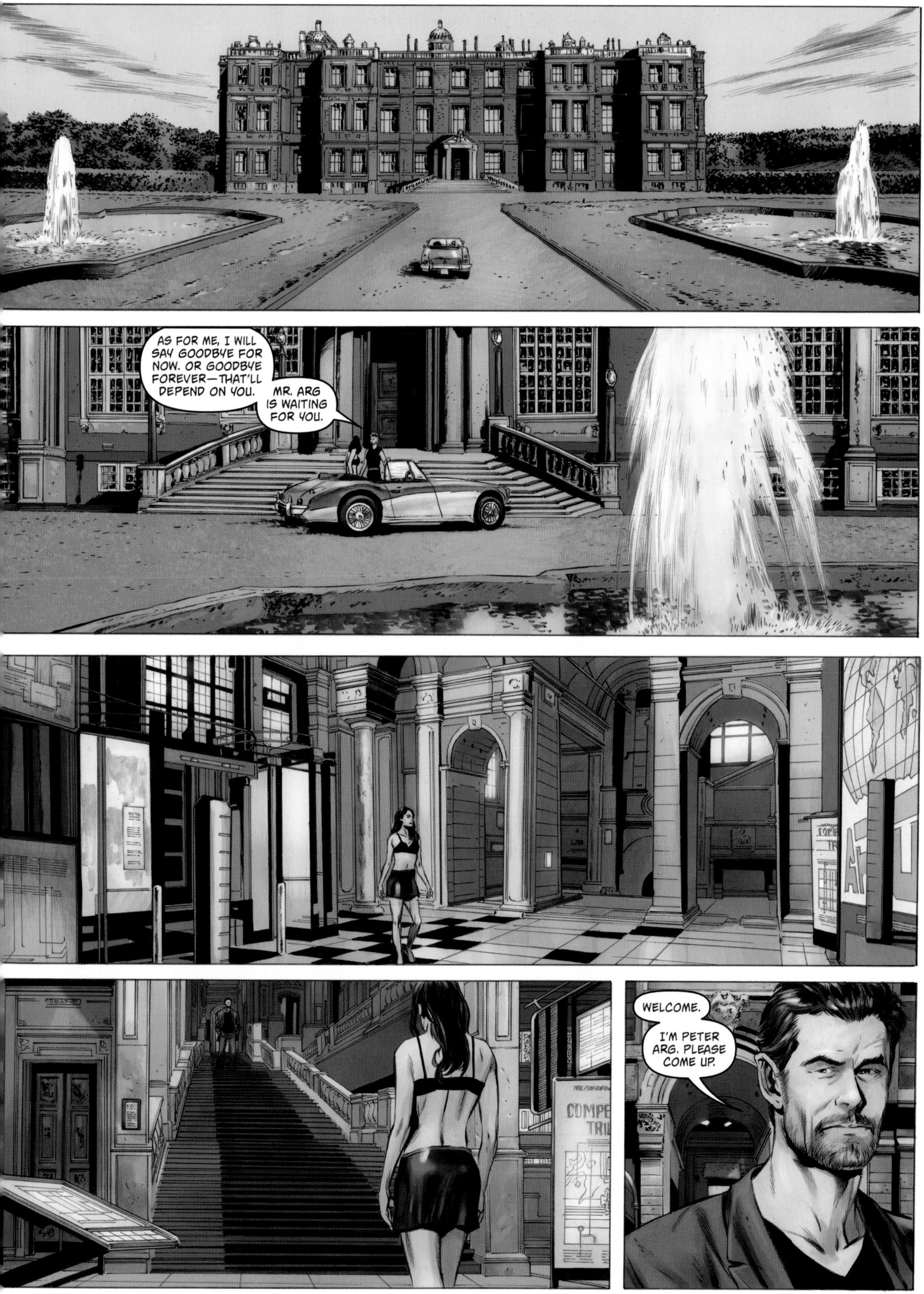
AS FOR ME, I WILL SAY GOODBYE FOR NOW. OR GOODBYE FOREVER—THAT'LL DEPEND ON YOU.
MR. ARG IS WAITING FOR YOU.
WELCOME.
I'M PETER ARG. PLEASE COME UP.

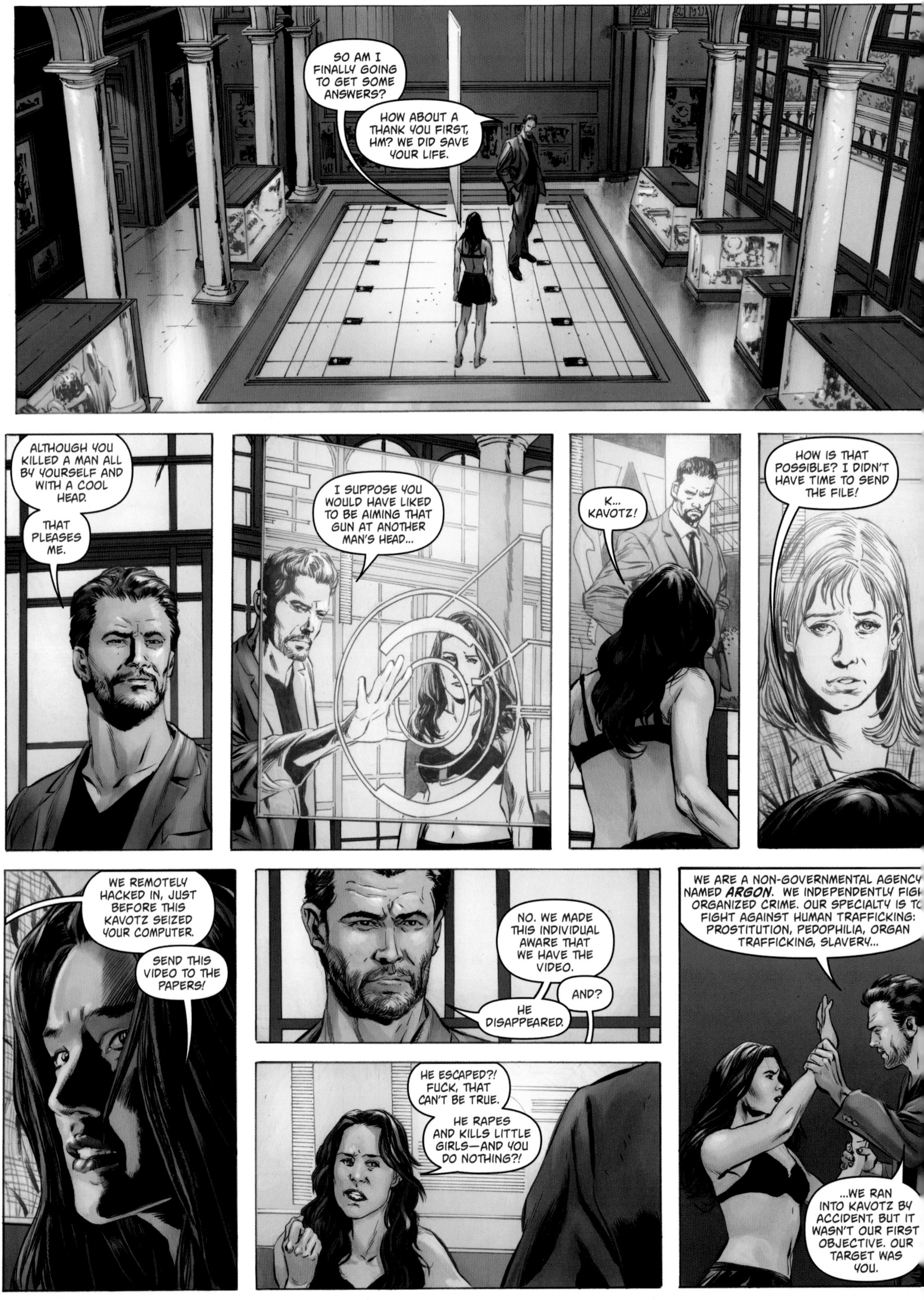
SO AM I FINALLY GOING TO GET SOME ANSWERS?
HOW ABOUT A THANK YOU FIRST, HM? WE DID SAVE YOUR LIFE.
ALTHOUGH YOU KILLED A MAN ALL BY YOURSELF AND WITH A COOL HEAD.
THAT PLEASES ME.
I SUPPOSE YOU WOULD HAVE LIKED TO BE AIMING THAT GUN AT ANOTHER MAN'S HEAD...
K... KAVOTZ!
HOW IS THAT POSSIBLE? I DIDN'T HAVE TIME TO SEND THE FILE!
WE REMOTELY HACKED IN, JUST BEFORE THIS KAVOTZ SEIZED YOUR COMPUTER.
SEND THIS VIDEO TO THE PAPERS!
NO. WE MADE THIS INDIVIDUAL AWARE THAT WE HAVE THE VIDEO.
AND?
HE DISAPPEARED.
HE ESCAPED?! FUCK, THAT CAN'T BE TRUE.
HE RAPES AND KILLS LITTLE GIRLS—AND YOU DO NOTHING?!
WE ARE A NON-GOVERNMENTAL AGENCY NAMED ARGON. WE INDEPENDENTLY FIGHT ORGANIZED CRIME. OUR SPECIALTY IS TO FIGHT AGAINST HUMAN TRAFFICKING: PROSTITUTION, PEDOPHILIA, ORGAN TRAFFICKING, SLAVERY...
...WE RAN INTO KAVOTZ BY ACCIDENT, BUT IT WASN'T OUR FIRST OBJECTIVE. OUR TARGET WAS YOU.

"WE'VE BEEN FOLLOWING YOU FOR A LONG TIME, ALONG WITH SEVERAL OTHER PRECOCIOUS STUDENTS ALL OVER THE COUNTRY.

"WE'VE FOLLOWED PRACTICALLY EVERY STEP YOU'VE TAKEN, AMBER.

CLEVER
PHENON
TOP HO

LONDON REPORT

AMBER BLAKE,
at the world renowned
took top swim honors
for young ladies eight
Great Britain Open Inv
held at the Roach Swir

Miss Blake, broke not

"OUR AGENCY RECRUITS THE BEST. WE WANT TO HIRE YOU."

YOU'VE KNOWN ALL MY SECRETS ALL THESE YEARS... AND AMANDA—YOU COULDN'T SAVE HER?

AND AN AGENCY? SO WHAT—YOU'RE A HUMANITARIAN MI6? WHAT A JOKE.

I NEED SOME AIR

I'M SORRY ABOUT WHAT HAPPENED TO YOU. UNFORTUNATELY, I CAN'T CHANGE THE PAST. BUT I CAN HELP YOU CHANGE YOUR FUTURE.

FOR EXAMPLE, YOU'LL LEARN AN INTENSIVE FORM OF TOP SPEED DRIVING. OLGA MOIR GAVE YOU A SMALL GLIMPSE OF THE ADVANTAGES THAT THAT CAN REPRESENT WHEN SHE RESCUED YOU TODAY.

YOU'LL MASTER MARTIAL ARTS, FIREARMS, BLADES, PARACHUTING, AND CLIMBING, HOW TO CRACK CONFIDENTIAL INFORMATION, LANGUAGES THAT YOU DON'T ALREADY KNOW. AND THAT'S JUST THE BEGINNING.

TO PROVE TO YOU THAT WE REALLY RECRUIT THE BEST, KNOW THAT WE HAVE SOLICITED ANOTHER STUDENT FROM CLEVERLAND LONDON: MATT BOLAN.

MATT?

JOIN US AND I PROMISE YOU THAT, THANKS TO ARGON, THANKS TO YOU, THERE WILL BE FEWER MEN LIKE KAVOTZ ON EARTH.

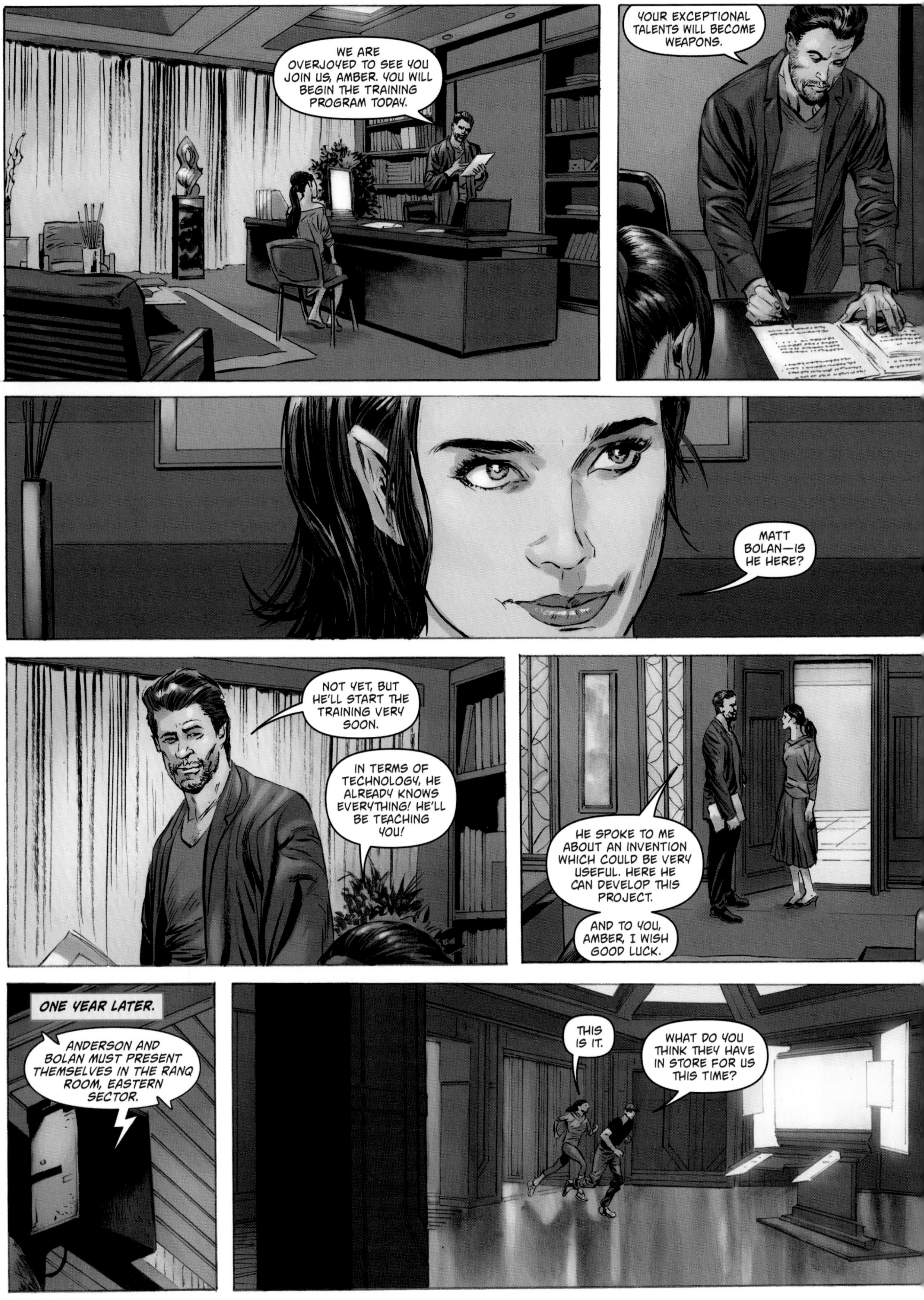
WE ARE OVERJOYED TO SEE YOU JOIN US, AMBER. YOU WILL BEGIN THE TRAINING PROGRAM TODAY.
YOUR EXCEPTIONAL TALENTS WILL BECOME WEAPONS.
MATT BOLAN—IS HE HERE?
NOT YET, BUT HE'LL START THE TRAINING VERY SOON.
IN TERMS OF TECHNOLOGY, HE ALREADY KNOWS EVERYTHING! HE'LL BE TEACHING YOU!
HE SPOKE TO ME ABOUT AN INVENTION WHICH COULD BE VERY USEFUL. HERE HE CAN DEVELOP THIS PROJECT.
AND TO YOU, AMBER, I WISH GOOD LUCK.
ONE YEAR LATER.
ANDERSON AND BOLAN MUST PRESENT THEMSELVES IN THE RANQ ROOM, EASTERN SECTOR.
THIS IS IT.
WHAT DO YOU THINK THEY HAVE IN STORE FOR US THIS TIME?

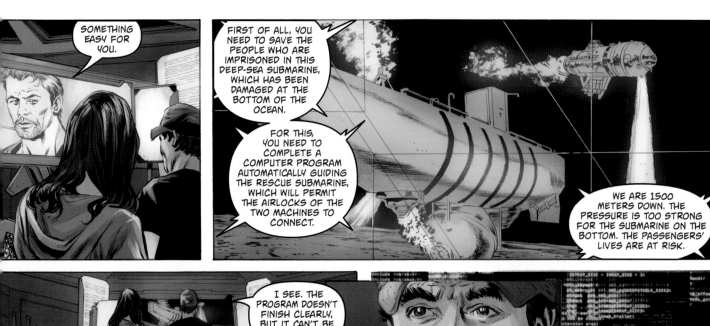

SOMETHING EASY FOR YOU.

FIRST OF ALL, YOU NEED TO SAVE THE PEOPLE WHO ARE IMPRISONED IN THIS DEEP-SEA SUBMARINE, WHICH HAS BEEN DAMAGED AT THE BOTTOM OF THE OCEAN.

FOR THIS, YOU NEED TO COMPLETE A COMPUTER PROGRAM AUTOMATICALLY GUIDING THE RESCUE SUBMARINE, WHICH WILL PERMIT THE AIRLOCKS OF THE TWO MACHINES TO CONNECT.

WE ARE 1500 METERS DOWN. THE PRESSURE IS TOO STRONG FOR THE SUBMARINE ON THE BOTTOM. THE PASSENGERS' LIVES ARE AT RISK.

I SEE. THE PROGRAM DOESN'T FINISH CLEARLY, BUT IT CAN'T BE IMPOSSIBLE.

IT MUST BE HIDING SOMETHING.

WHAT WAS THAT NOISE?

CRAAACK

THE WALL! IT'S CRUMBLING!

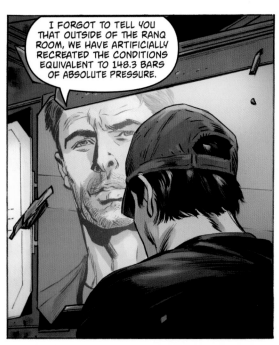

I FORGOT TO TELL YOU THAT OUTSIDE OF THE RANQ ROOM, WE HAVE ARTIFICIALLY RECREATED THE CONDITIONS EQUIVALENT TO 148.3 BARS OF ABSOLUTE PRESSURE.

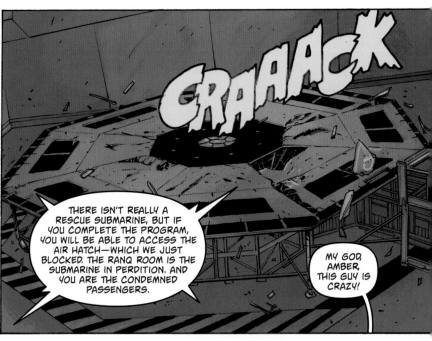

CRAAACK

THERE ISN'T REALLY A RESCUE SUBMARINE, BUT IF YOU COMPLETE THE PROGRAM, YOU WILL BE ABLE TO ACCESS THE AIR HATCH—WHICH WE JUST BLOCKED. THE RANQ ROOM IS THE SUBMARINE IN PERDITION. AND YOU ARE THE CONDEMNED PASSENGERS.

MY GOD, AMBER, THIS GUY IS CRAZY!

FOCUS, MATT. START OVER FROM THE BEGINNING. YOU SAID THAT IT WOULD BE EASY TO COMPLETE THE PROGRAM.

YEAH, WELL, EASY...

DO IT!

OKAY, OKAY!

BUT... THERE'S A PROBLEM.

THE BEGINNING OF THE PROGRAM ERASES ITSELF AS SOON AS I TYPE THE LAST LINES OF CODE!

WE NEED TO MEMORIZE ALL THE LINES OF CODE BEFORE THEY'RE ERASED.

I'VE GOT THEM.

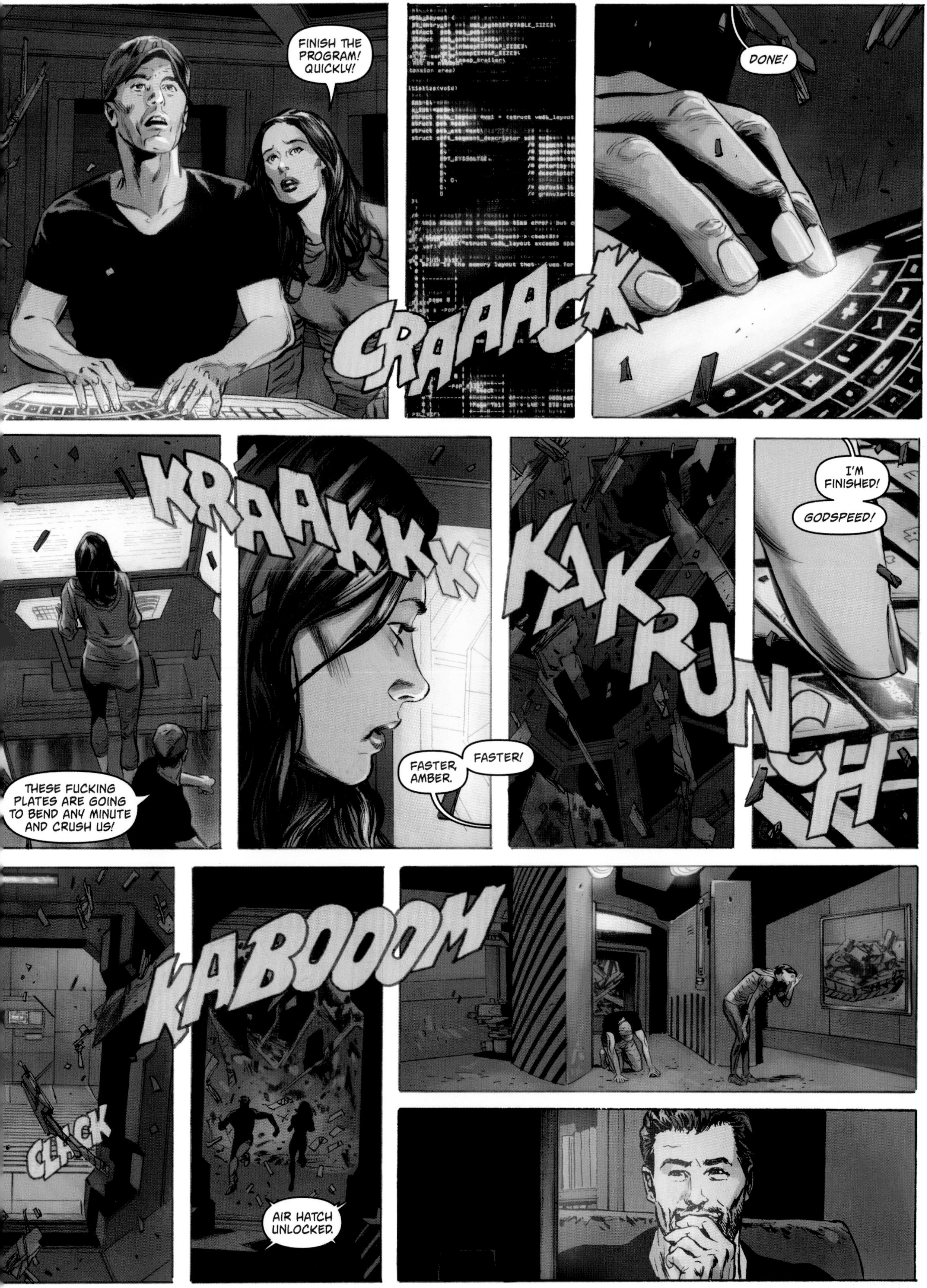
FINISH THE PROGRAM! QUICKLY!
CRAAACK
DONE!
KRAAKKK
THESE FUCKING PLATES ARE GOING TO BEND ANY MINUTE AND CRUSH US!
FASTER, AMBER.
FASTER!
KAKRUNCH
I'M FINISHED!
GODSPEED!
KABOOOM
CLACK
AIR HATCH UNLOCKED.

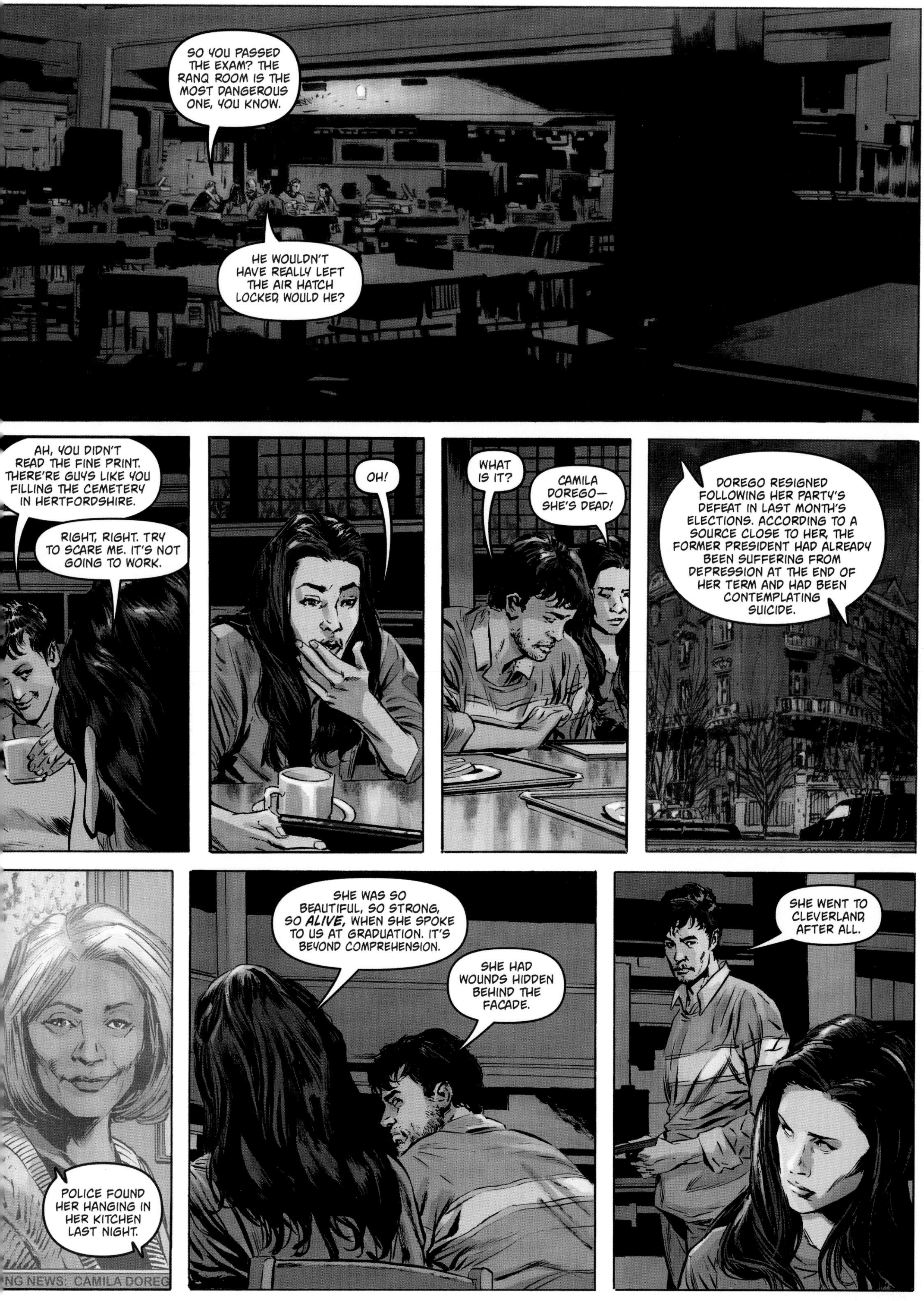
SO YOU PASSED THE EXAM? THE RANQ ROOM IS THE MOST DANGEROUS ONE, YOU KNOW.
HE WOULDN'T HAVE REALLY LEFT THE AIR HATCH LOCKED, WOULD HE?
AH, YOU DIDN'T READ THE FINE PRINT. THERE'RE GUYS LIKE YOU FILLING THE CEMETERY IN HERTFORDSHIRE.
RIGHT, RIGHT. TRY TO SCARE ME. IT'S NOT GOING TO WORK.
OH!
WHAT IS IT?
CAMILA DOREGO— SHE'S DEAD!
DOREGO RESIGNED FOLLOWING HER PARTY'S DEFEAT IN LAST MONTH'S ELECTIONS. ACCORDING TO A SOURCE CLOSE TO HER, THE FORMER PRESIDENT HAD ALREADY BEEN SUFFERING FROM DEPRESSION AT THE END OF HER TERM AND HAD BEEN CONTEMPLATING SUICIDE.
POLICE FOUND HER HANGING IN HER KITCHEN LAST NIGHT.
NG NEWS: CAMILA DOREG
SHE WAS SO BEAUTIFUL, SO STRONG, SO *ALIVE,* WHEN SHE SPOKE TO US AT GRADUATION. IT'S BEYOND COMPREHENSION.
SHE HAD WOUNDS HIDDEN BEHIND THE FACADE.
SHE WENT TO CLEVERLAND, AFTER ALL.

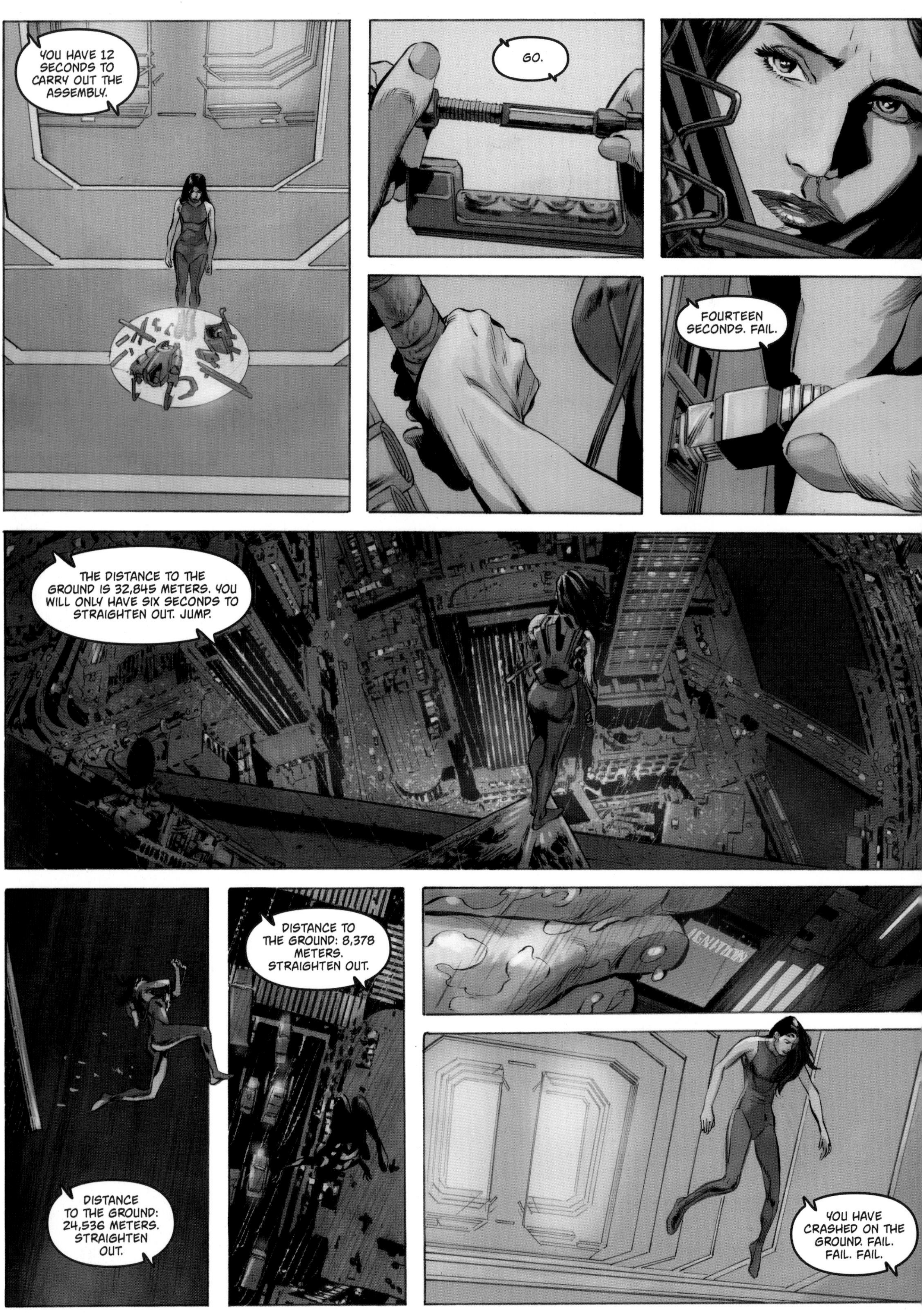
YOU HAVE 12 SECONDS TO CARRY OUT THE ASSEMBLY.
GO.
FOURTEEN SECONDS. FAIL.
THE DISTANCE TO THE GROUND IS 32,845 METERS. YOU WILL ONLY HAVE SIX SECONDS TO STRAIGHTEN OUT. JUMP.
DISTANCE TO THE GROUND: 24,536 METERS. STRAIGHTEN OUT.
DISTANCE TO THE GROUND: 8,378 METERS. STRAIGHTEN OUT.
YOU HAVE CRASHED ON THE GROUND. FAIL. FAIL. FAIL.

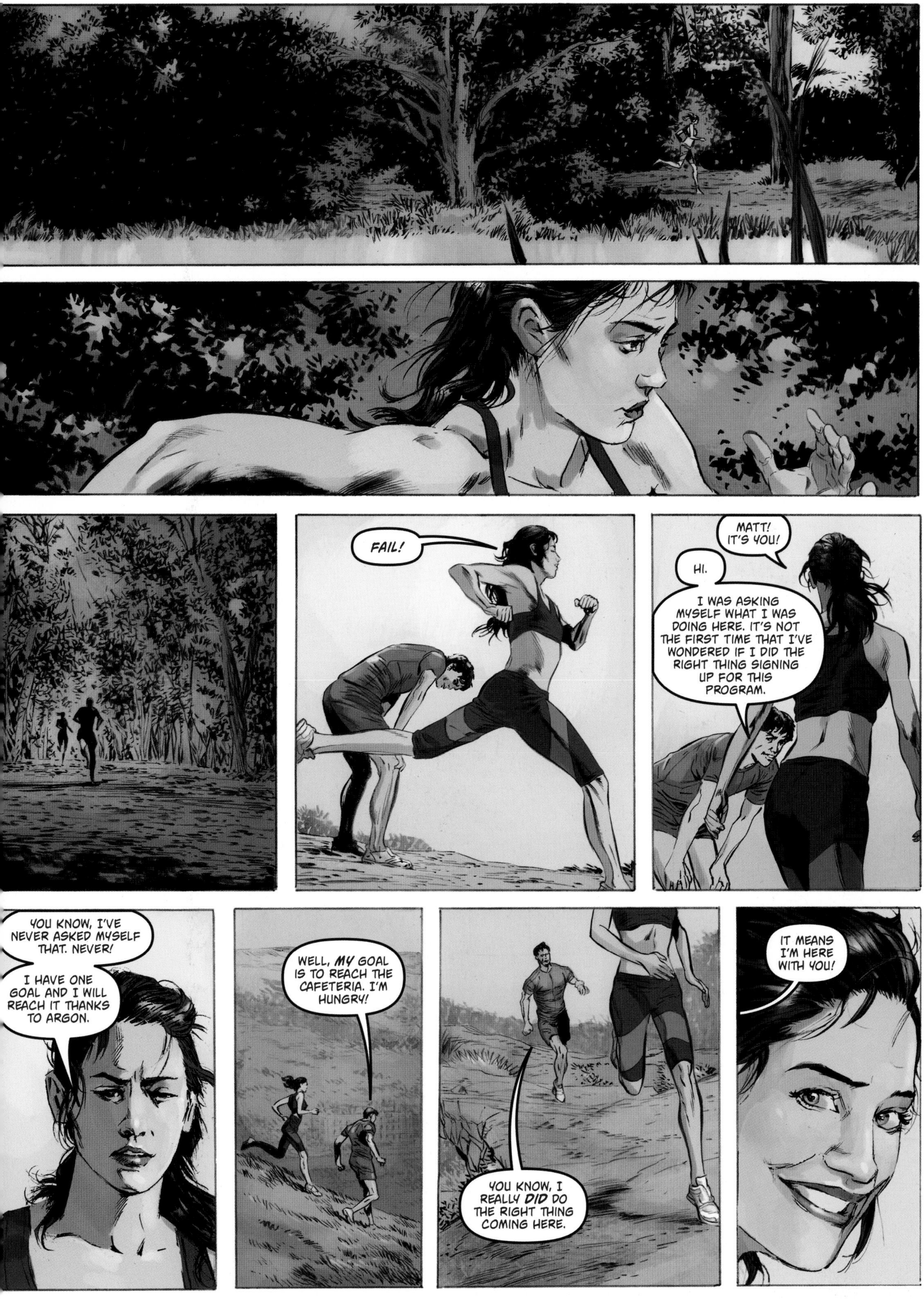
FAIL!
MATT! IT'S YOU!
HI.
I WAS ASKING MYSELF WHAT I WAS DOING HERE. IT'S NOT THE FIRST TIME THAT I'VE WONDERED IF I DID THE RIGHT THING SIGNING UP FOR THIS PROGRAM.
YOU KNOW, I'VE NEVER ASKED MYSELF THAT. NEVER!
I HAVE ONE GOAL AND I WILL REACH IT THANKS TO ARGON.
WELL, MY GOAL IS TO REACH THE CAFETERIA. I'M HUNGRY!
YOU KNOW, I REALLY DID DO THE RIGHT THING COMING HERE.
IT MEANS I'M HERE WITH YOU!

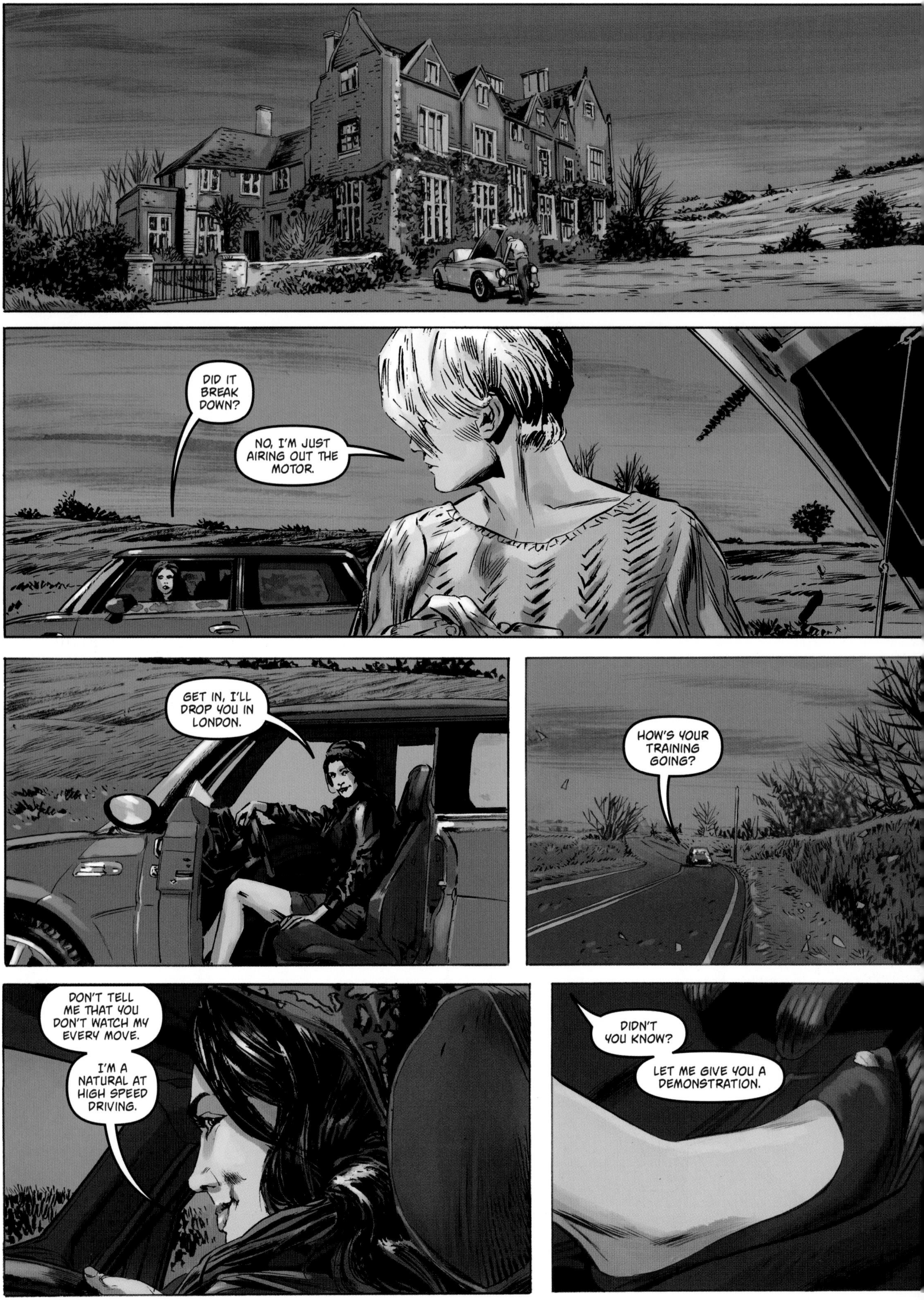
DID IT BREAK DOWN?
NO, I'M JUST AIRING OUT THE MOTOR.
GET IN, I'LL DROP YOU IN LONDON.
HOW'S YOUR TRAINING GOING?
DON'T TELL ME THAT YOU DON'T WATCH MY EVERY MOVE.
I'M A NATURAL AT HIGH SPEED DRIVING.
DIDN'T YOU KNOW?
LET ME GIVE YOU A DEMONSTRATION.

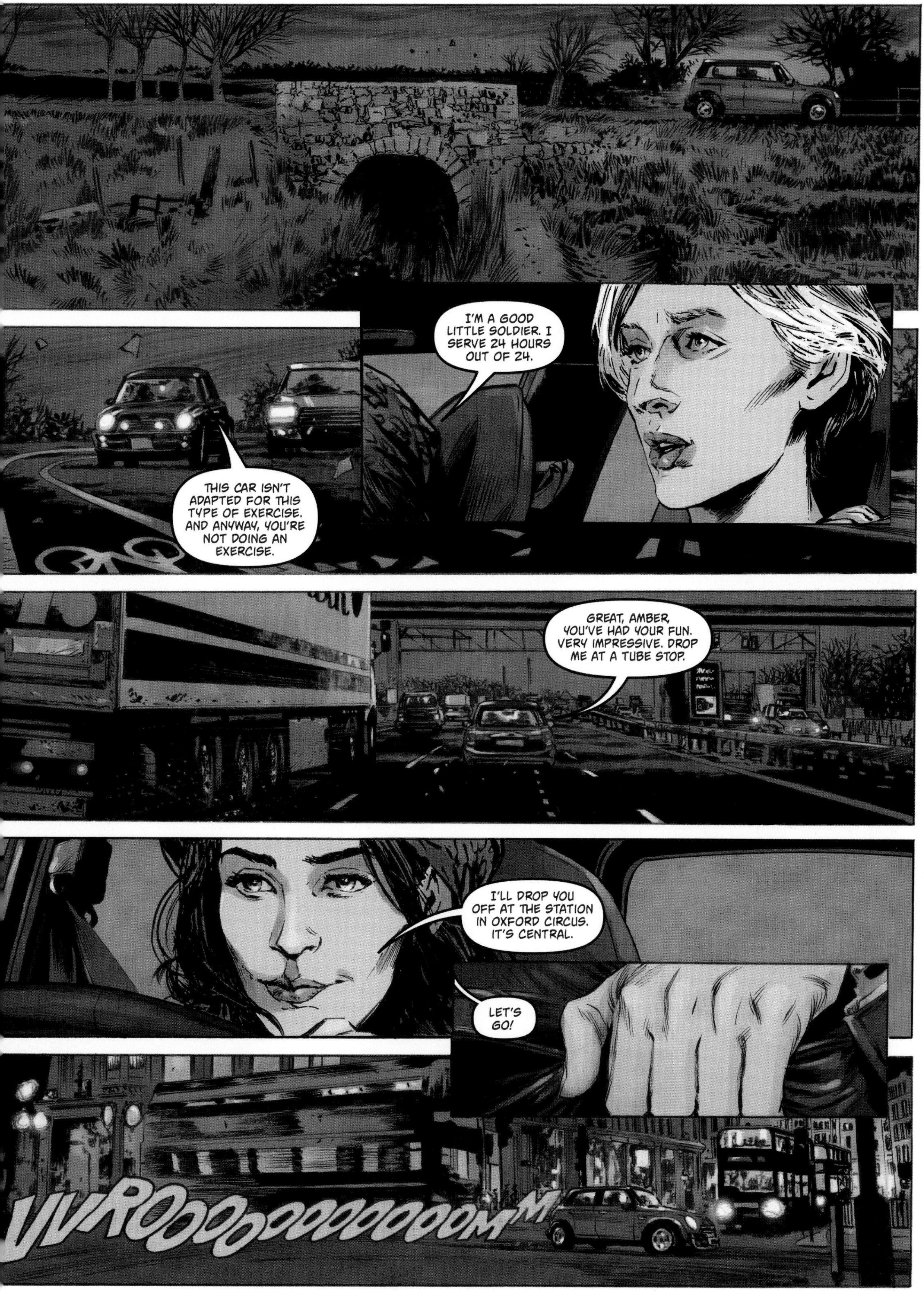
I'M A GOOD LITTLE SOLDIER. I SERVE 24 HOURS OUT OF 24.
THIS CAR ISN'T ADAPTED FOR THIS TYPE OF EXERCISE. AND ANYWAY, YOU'RE NOT DOING AN EXERCISE.
GREAT, AMBER, YOU'VE HAD YOUR FUN. VERY IMPRESSIVE. DROP ME AT A TUBE STOP.
I'LL DROP YOU OFF AT THE STATION IN OXFORD CIRCUS. IT'S CENTRAL.
LET'S GO!
VVROOOOOOOOOOOOMM

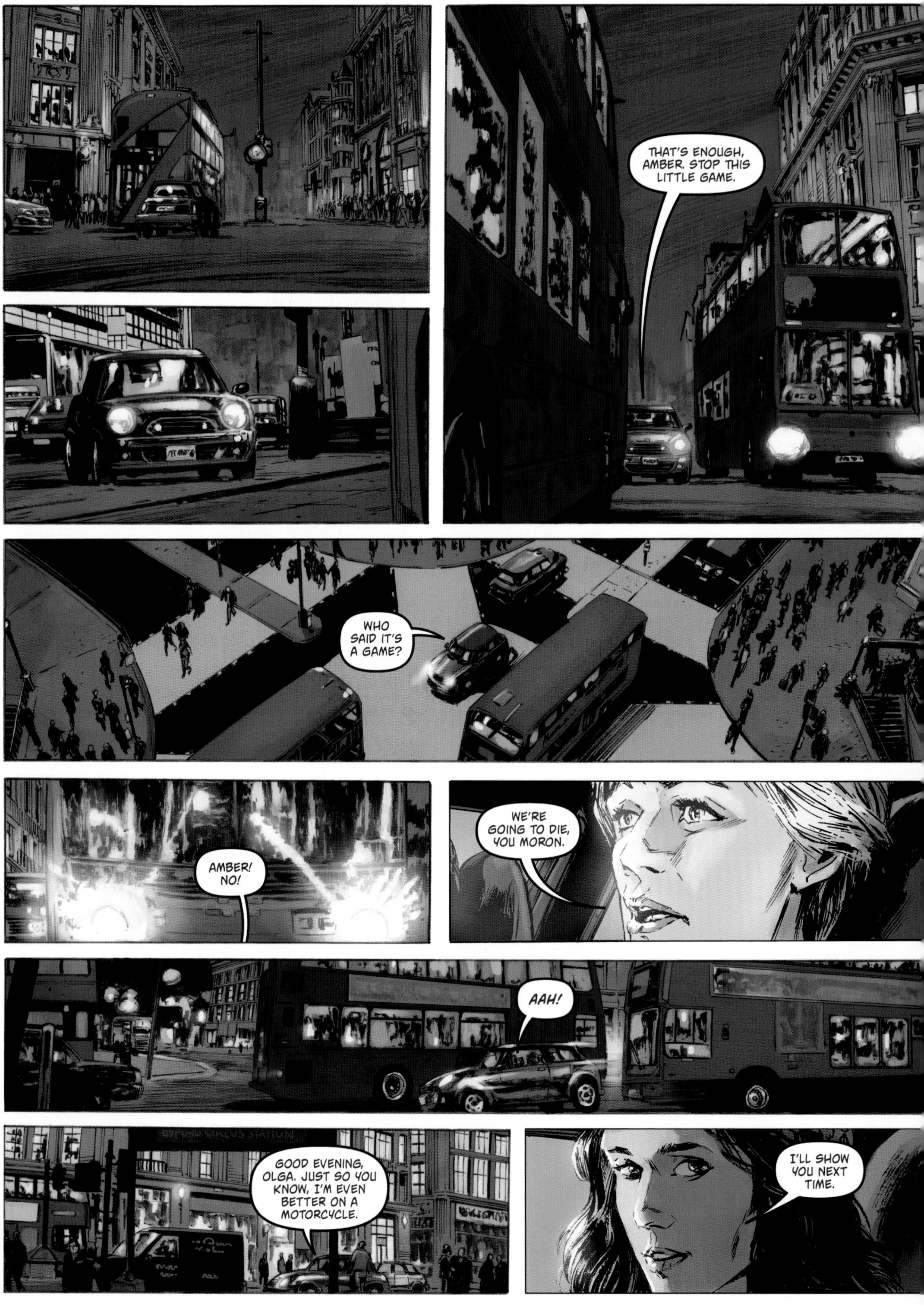
THAT'S ENOUGH, AMBER. STOP THIS LITTLE GAME.
WHO SAID IT'S A GAME?
AMBER! NO!
WE'RE GOING TO DIE, YOU MORON.
AAH!
GOOD EVENING, OLGA. JUST SO YOU KNOW, I'M EVEN BETTER ON A MOTORCYCLE.
I'LL SHOW YOU NEXT TIME.

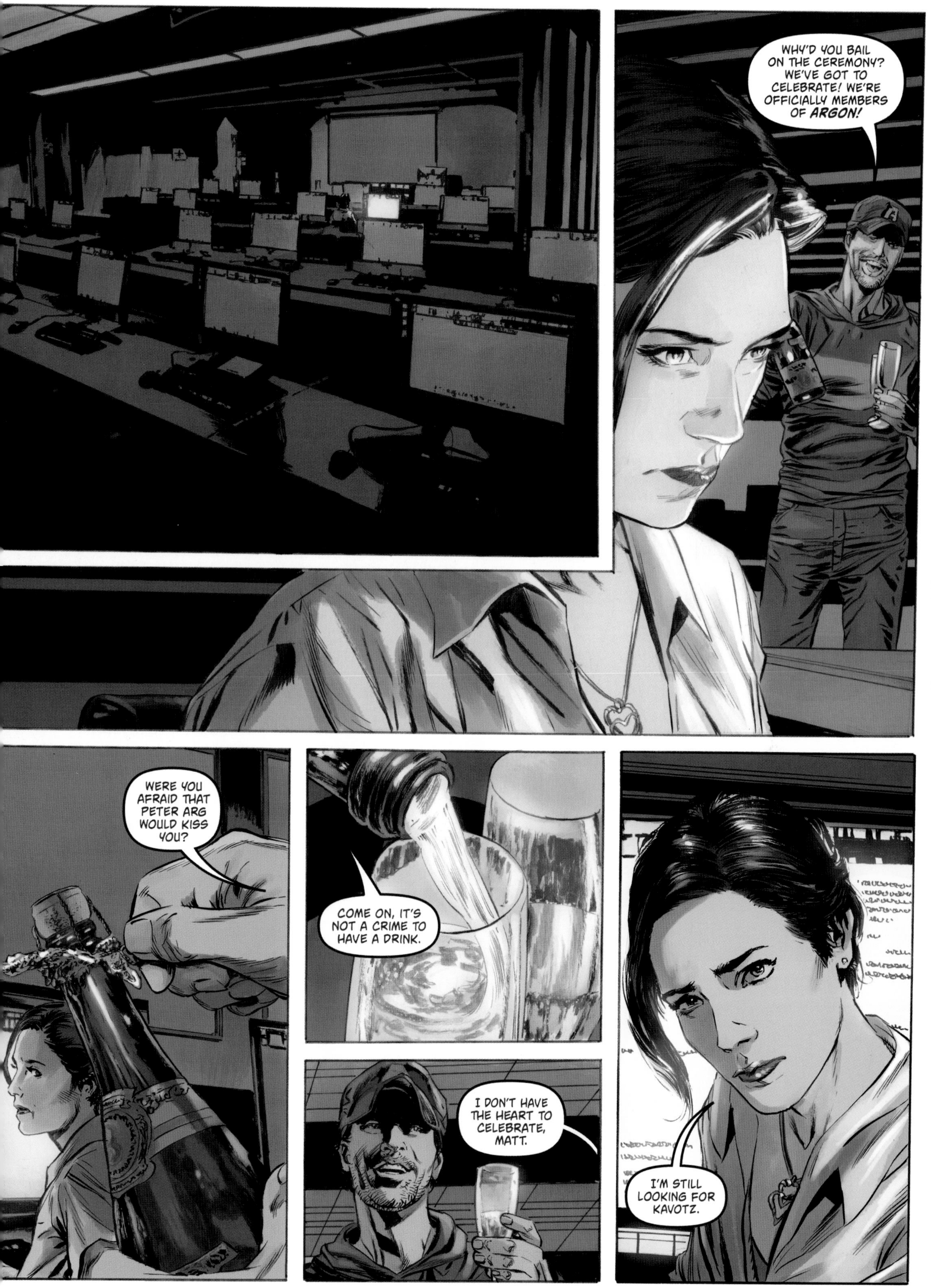
WHY'D YOU BAIL ON THE CEREMONY? WE'VE GOT TO CELEBRATE! WE'RE OFFICIALLY MEMBERS OF ARGON!
WERE YOU AFRAID THAT PETER ARG WOULD KISS YOU?
COME ON, IT'S NOT A CRIME TO HAVE A DRINK.
I DON'T HAVE THE HEART TO CELEBRATE, MATT.
I'M STILL LOOKING FOR KAVOTZ.

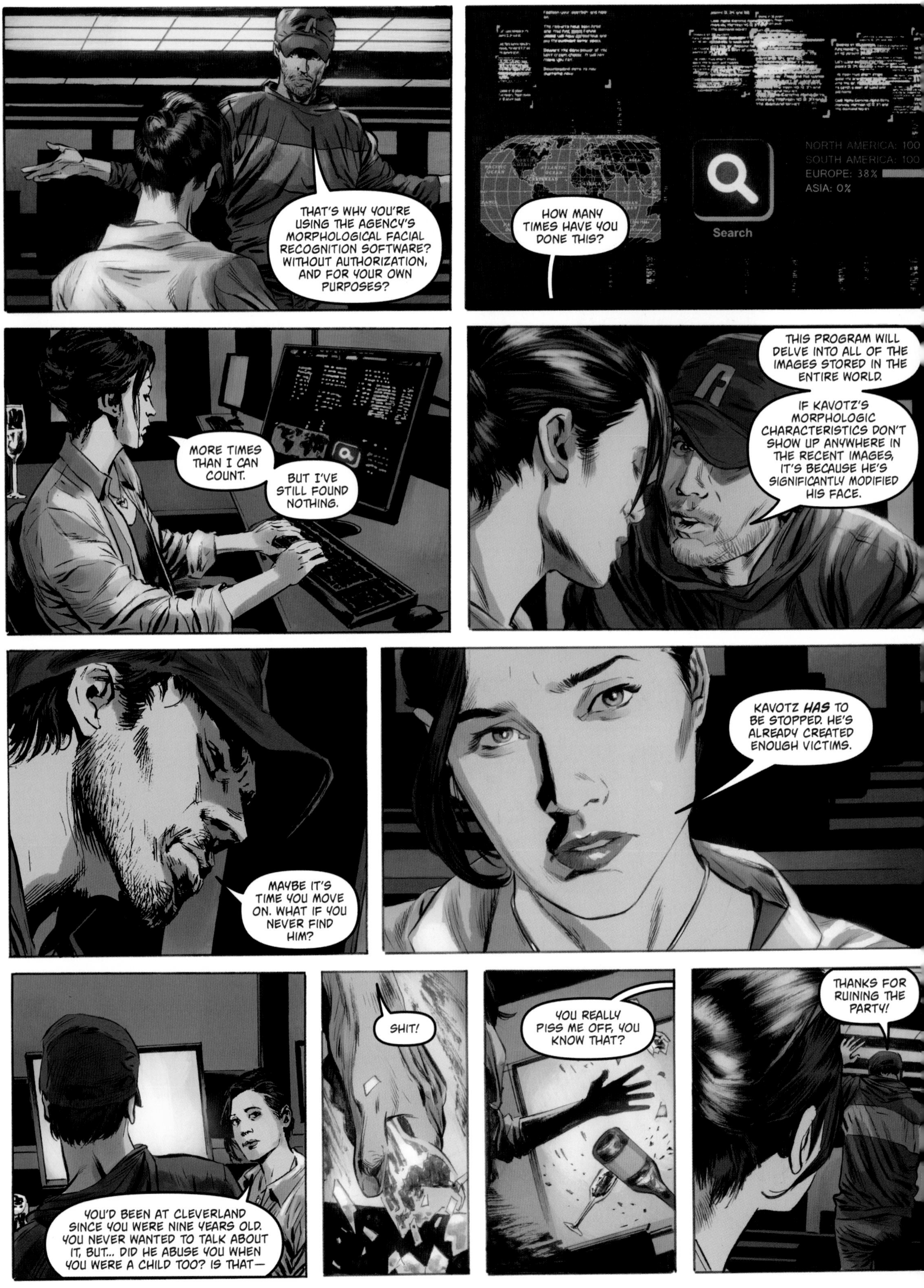
THAT'S WHY YOU'RE USING THE AGENCY'S MORPHOLOGICAL FACIAL RECOGNITION SOFTWARE? WITHOUT AUTHORIZATION, AND FOR YOUR OWN PURPOSES?
HOW MANY TIMES HAVE YOU DONE THIS?
Search
NORTH AMERICA: 100
SOUTH AMERICA: 100
EUROPE: 38%
ASIA: 0%
MORE TIMES THAN I CAN COUNT.
BUT I'VE STILL FOUND NOTHING.
THIS PROGRAM WILL DELVE INTO ALL OF THE IMAGES STORED IN THE ENTIRE WORLD.
IF KAVOTZ'S MORPHOLOGIC CHARACTERISTICS DON'T SHOW UP ANYWHERE IN THE RECENT IMAGES, IT'S BECAUSE HE'S SIGNIFICANTLY MODIFIED HIS FACE.
MAYBE IT'S TIME YOU MOVE ON. WHAT IF YOU NEVER FIND HIM?
KAVOTZ **HAS** TO BE STOPPED. HE'S ALREADY CREATED ENOUGH VICTIMS.
YOU'D BEEN AT CLEVERLAND SINCE YOU WERE NINE YEARS OLD. YOU NEVER WANTED TO TALK ABOUT IT, BUT... DID HE ABUSE YOU WHEN YOU WERE A CHILD TOO? IS THAT—
SHIT!
YOU REALLY PISS ME OFF, YOU KNOW THAT?
THANKS FOR RUINING THE PARTY!

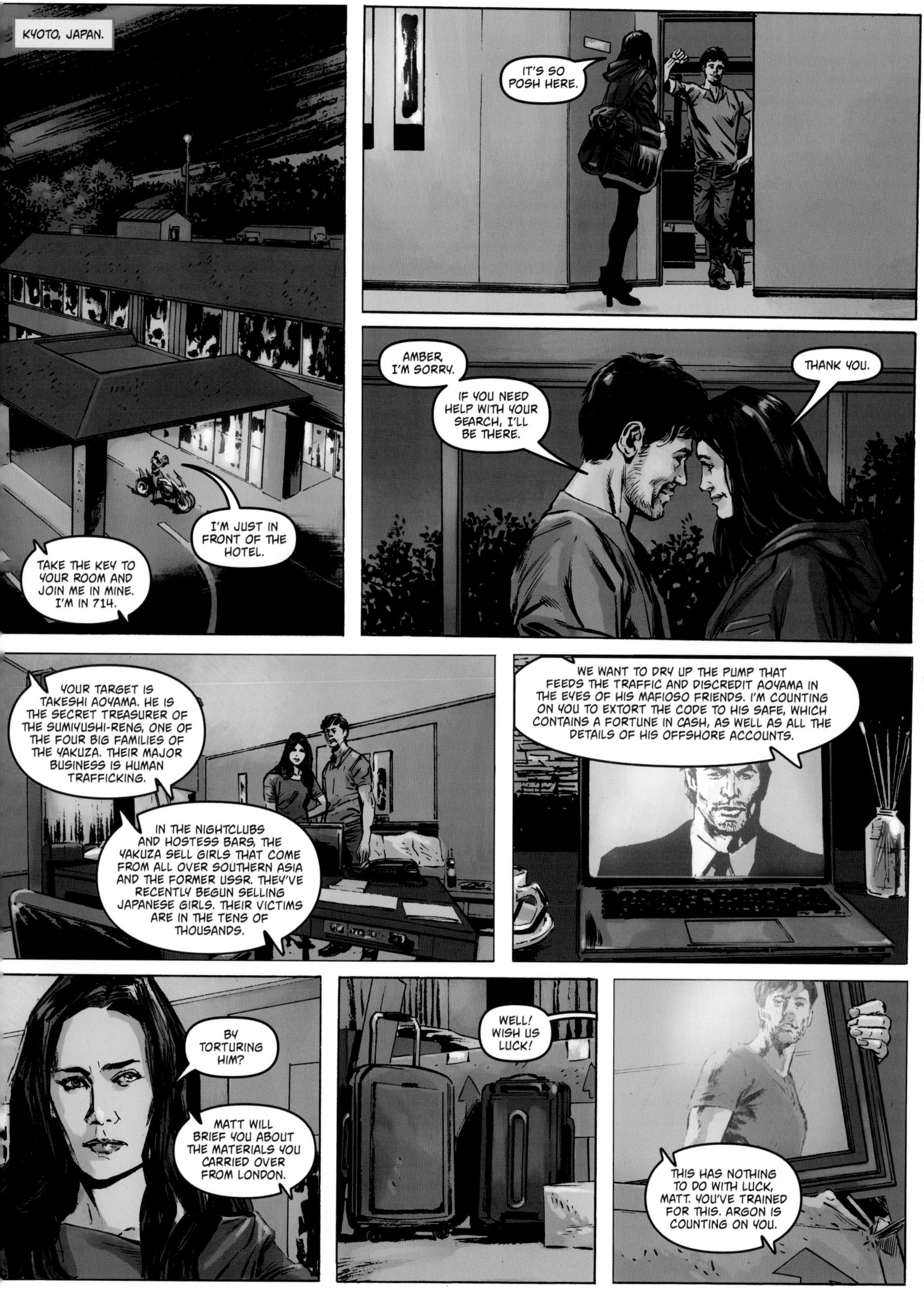
KYOTO, JAPAN.
I'M JUST IN FRONT OF THE HOTEL.
TAKE THE KEY TO YOUR ROOM AND JOIN ME IN MINE. I'M IN 714.
IT'S SO POSH HERE.
AMBER, I'M SORRY.
IF YOU NEED HELP WITH YOUR SEARCH, I'LL BE THERE.
THANK YOU.
YOUR TARGET IS TAKESHI AOYAMA. HE IS THE SECRET TREASURER OF THE SUMIYUSHI-RENG, ONE OF THE FOUR BIG FAMILIES OF THE YAKUZA. THEIR MAJOR BUSINESS IS HUMAN TRAFFICKING.
IN THE NIGHTCLUBS AND HOSTESS BARS, THE YAKUZA SELL GIRLS THAT COME FROM ALL OVER SOUTHERN ASIA AND THE FORMER USSR. THEY'VE RECENTLY BEGUN SELLING JAPANESE GIRLS. THEIR VICTIMS ARE IN THE TENS OF THOUSANDS.
WE WANT TO DRY UP THE PUMP THAT FEEDS THE TRAFFIC AND DISCREDIT AOYAMA IN THE EYES OF HIS MAFIOSO FRIENDS. I'M COUNTING ON YOU TO EXTORT THE CODE TO HIS SAFE, WHICH CONTAINS A FORTUNE IN CASH, AS WELL AS ALL THE DETAILS OF HIS OFFSHORE ACCOUNTS.
BY TORTURING HIM?
MATT WILL BRIEF YOU ABOUT THE MATERIALS YOU CARRIED OVER FROM LONDON.
WELL! WISH US LUCK!
THIS HAS NOTHING TO DO WITH LUCK, MATT. YOU'VE TRAINED FOR THIS. ARGON IS COUNTING ON YOU.

WE'VE SECURED THIS ROOM. DO YOU UNDERSTAND WHAT YOU HAVE TO DO, AMBER?

YES, HE'LL SIT HERE. HE'LL BE CLOSE TO THE MIRROR FOR THE INTERVIEW. YOU HAVE THE QUESTIONS?

NO, YOU'LL HAVE TO WING IT. BUT HE CAN'T HIDE ANYTHING FROM US. HE'LL TELL US EVERYTHING WE WANT TO KNOW.

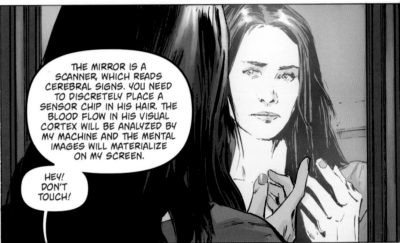

THE MIRROR IS A SCANNER, WHICH READS CEREBRAL SIGNS. YOU NEED TO DISCRETELY PLACE A SENSOR CHIP IN HIS HAIR. THE BLOOD FLOW IN HIS VISUAL CORTEX WILL BE ANALYZED BY MY MACHINE AND THE MENTAL IMAGES WILL MATERIALIZE ON MY SCREEN.

HEY! DON'T TOUCH!

WE'LL DO A TEST. I'LL PUT THE CAPTOR IN YOUR HAIR.

THINK REALLY HARD ABOUT SOMETHING, ANYTHING.

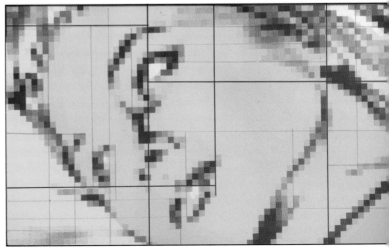

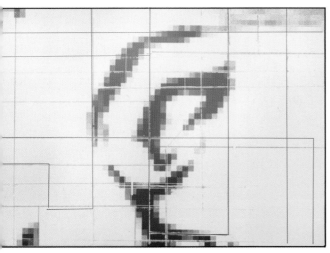

AMANDA...

I CAN'T BELIEVE IT WORKS—IT'S INCREDIBLE.

YEAH. MAYBE YOU COULD THINK ABOUT SOMETHING A LITTLE HAPPIER NEXT TIME.

COME ON, YOU COULD THINK ABOUT ME!

I NEVER THINK ABOUT YOU.

IS THAT SO?

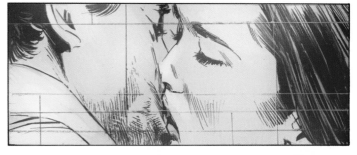

Save

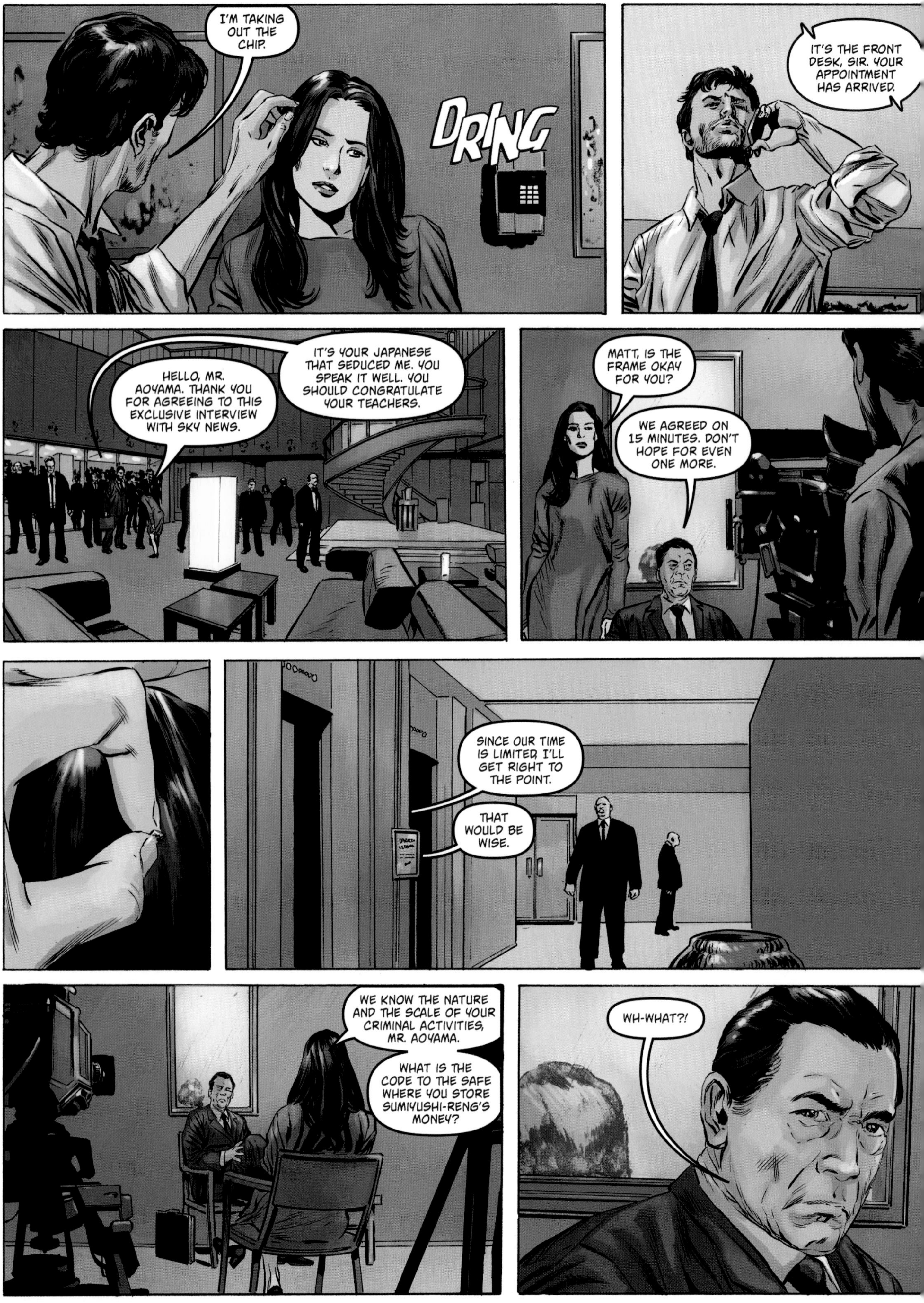
I'M TAKING OUT THE CHIP.
DRING
IT'S THE FRONT DESK, SIR. YOUR APPOINTMENT HAS ARRIVED.
HELLO, MR. AOYAMA. THANK YOU FOR AGREEING TO THIS EXCLUSIVE INTERVIEW WITH SKY NEWS.
IT'S YOUR JAPANESE THAT SEDUCED ME. YOU SPEAK IT WELL. YOU SHOULD CONGRATULATE YOUR TEACHERS.
MATT, IS THE FRAME OKAY FOR YOU?
WE AGREED ON 15 MINUTES. DON'T HOPE FOR EVEN ONE MORE.
SINCE OUR TIME IS LIMITED, I'LL GET RIGHT TO THE POINT.
THAT WOULD BE WISE.
WE KNOW THE NATURE AND THE SCALE OF YOUR CRIMINAL ACTIVITIES, MR. AOYAMA.
WHAT IS THE CODE TO THE SAFE WHERE YOU STORE SUMIYUSHI-RENG'S MONEY?
WH-WHAT?!

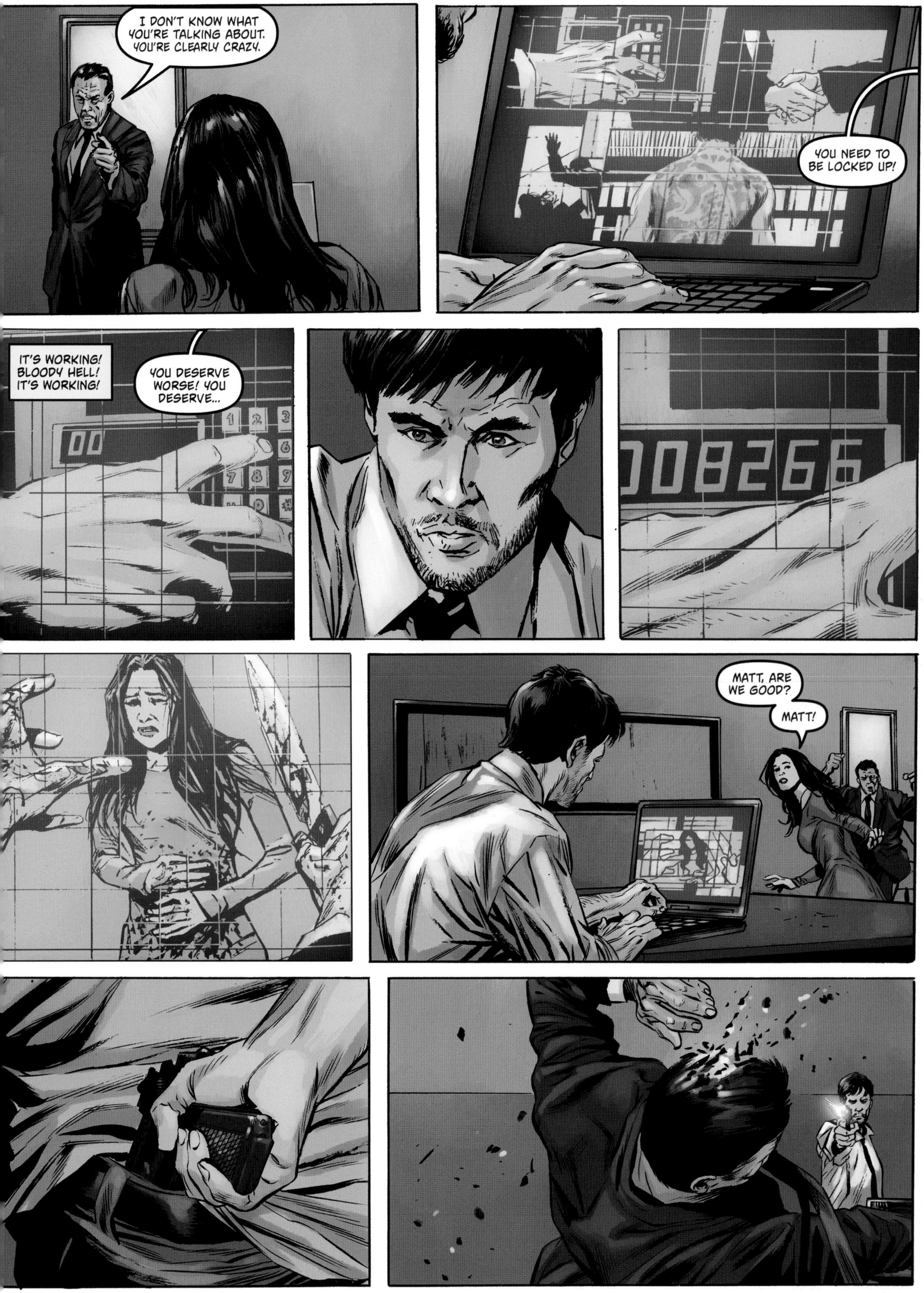
I DON'T KNOW WHAT YOU'RE TALKING ABOUT. YOU'RE CLEARLY CRAZY.
YOU NEED TO BE LOCKED UP!
IT'S WORKING! BLOODY HELL! IT'S WORKING!
YOU DESERVE WORSE! YOU DESERVE...
MATT, ARE WE GOOD?
MATT!

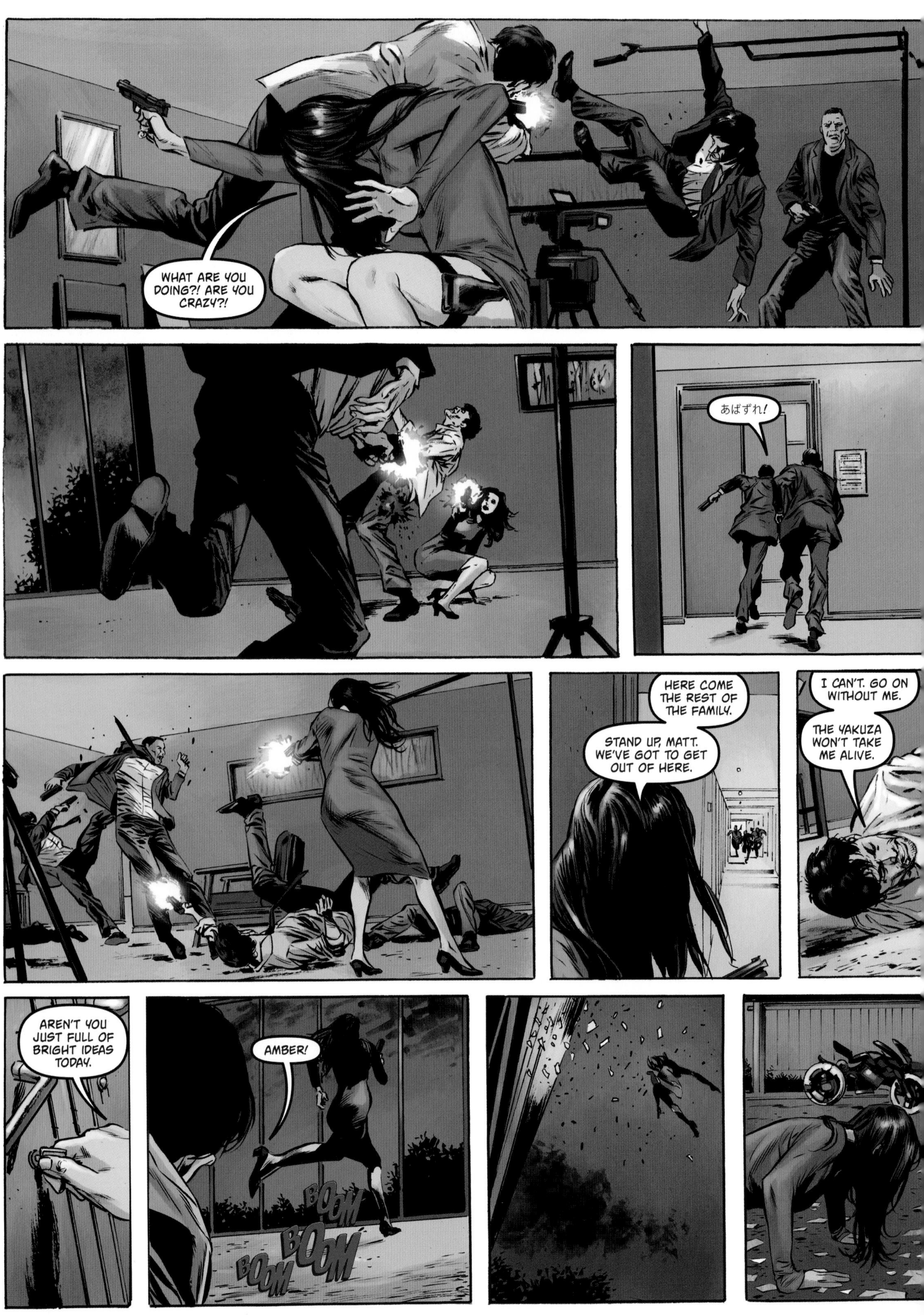
WHAT ARE YOU DOING?! ARE YOU CRAZY?!
あばずれ!
HERE COME THE REST OF THE FAMILY.
STAND UP, MATT. WE'VE GOT TO GET OUT OF HERE.
I CAN'T. GO ON WITHOUT ME.
THE YAKUZA WON'T TAKE ME ALIVE.
AREN'T YOU JUST FULL OF BRIGHT IDEAS TODAY.
AMBER!
BOOM
BOOM
BOOM

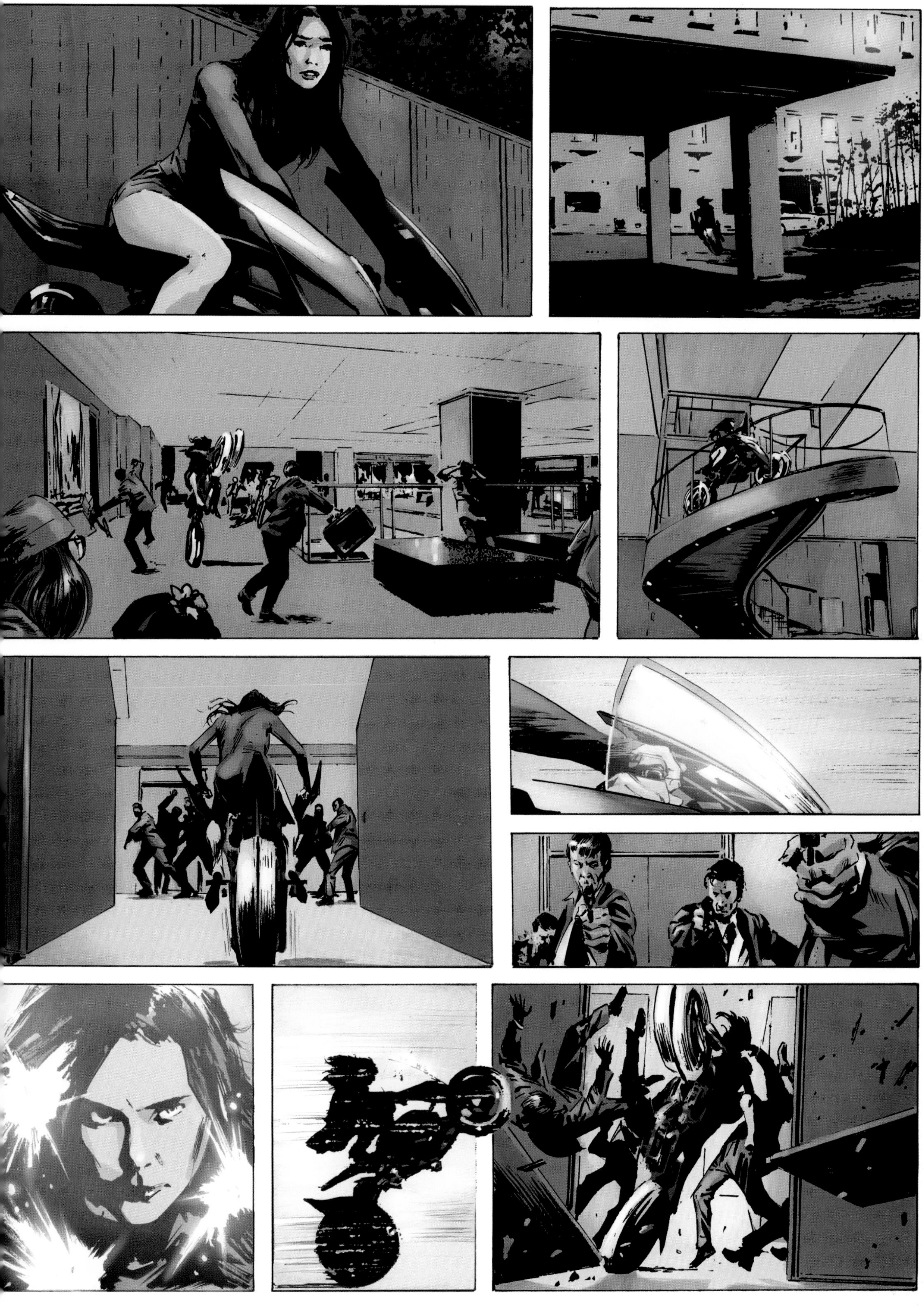

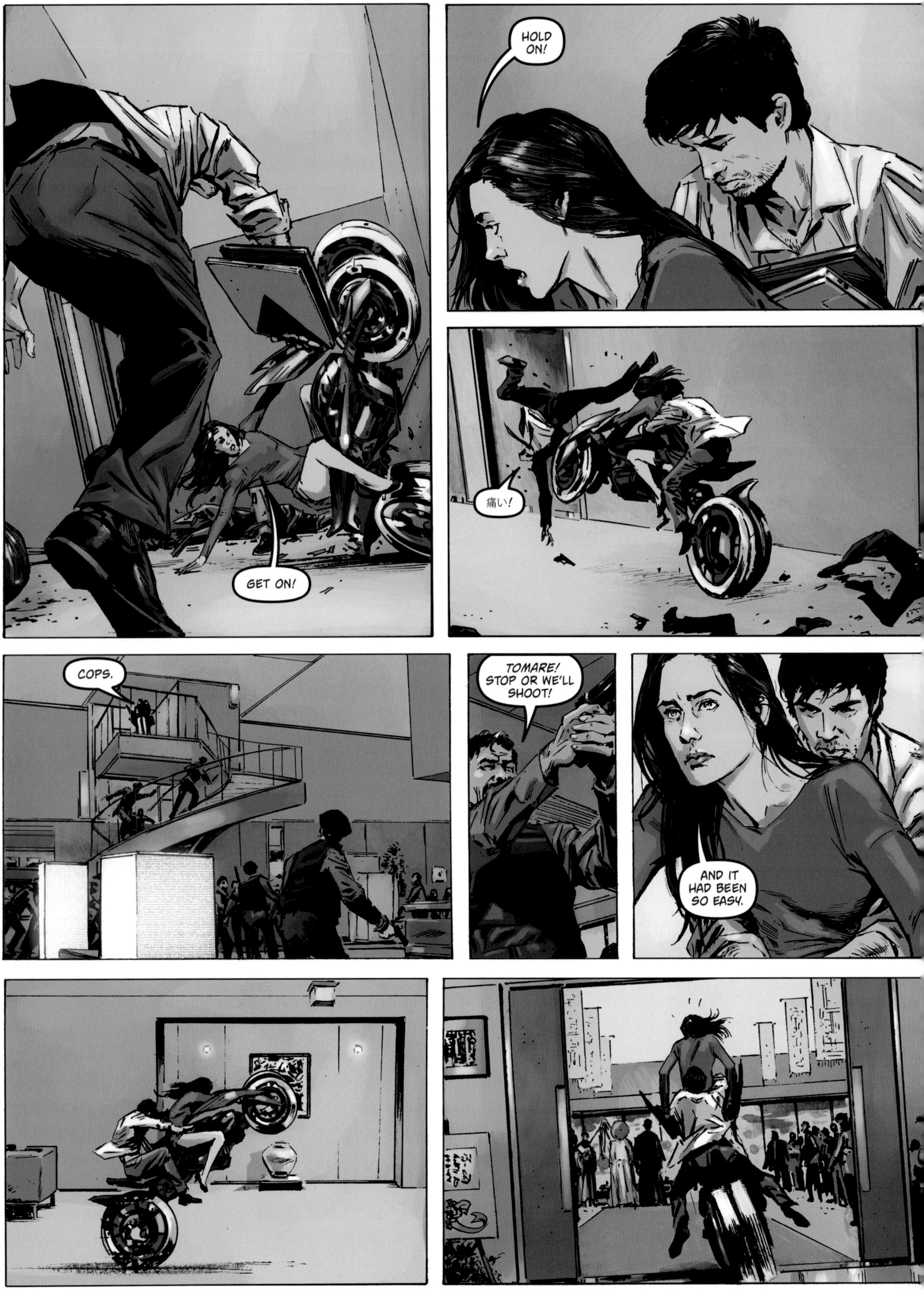
HOLD ON!
GET ON!
痛い!
COPS.
TOMARE! STOP OR WE'LL SHOOT!
AND IT HAD BEEN SO EASY.

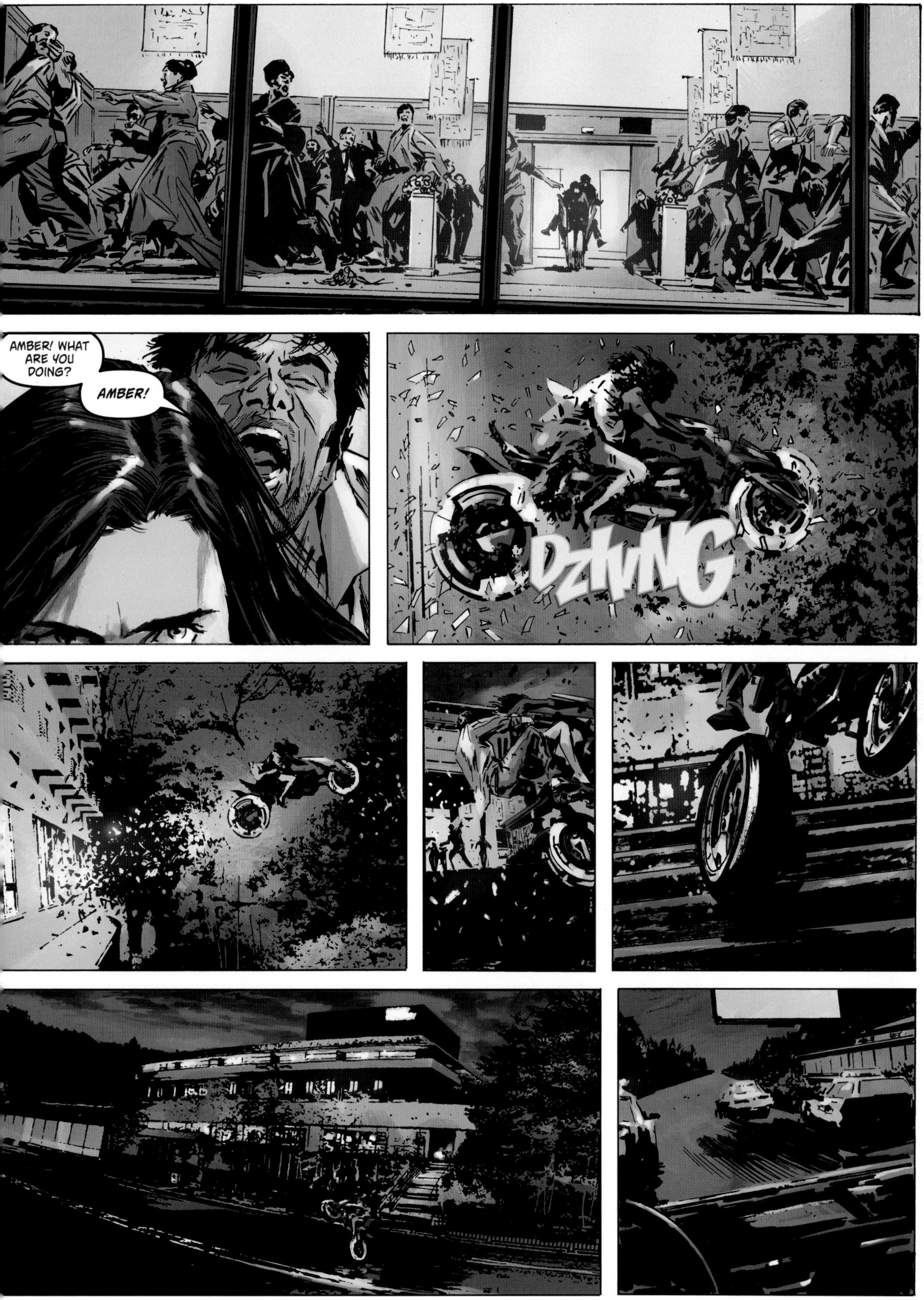

AMBER! WHAT ARE YOU DOING?
AMBER!
DZIVNG

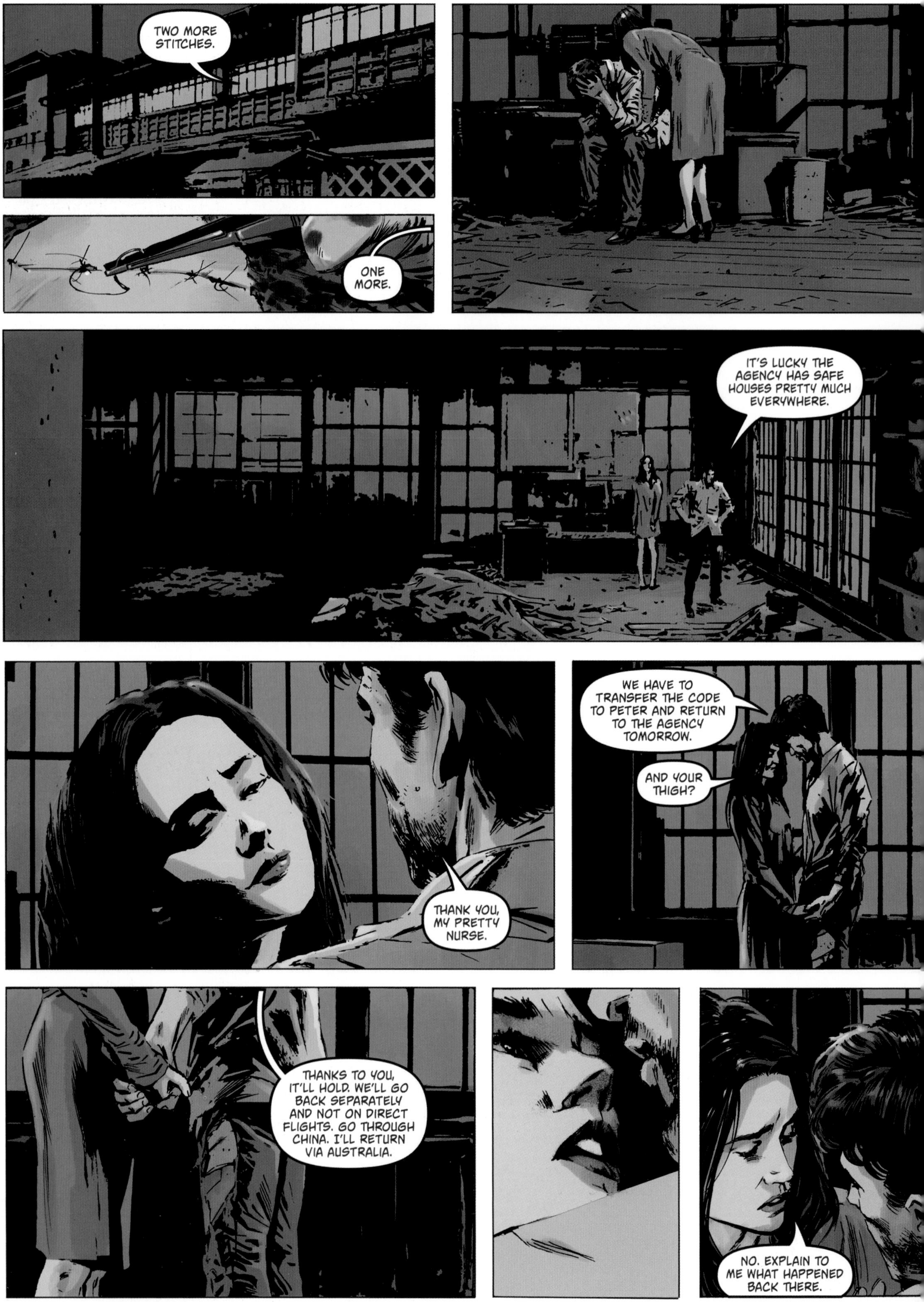
TWO MORE STITCHES.
ONE MORE.
IT'S LUCKY THE AGENCY HAS SAFE HOUSES PRETTY MUCH EVERYWHERE.
THANK YOU, MY PRETTY NURSE.
WE HAVE TO TRANSFER THE CODE TO PETER AND RETURN TO THE AGENCY TOMORROW.
AND YOUR THIGH?
THANKS TO YOU, IT'LL HOLD. WE'LL GO BACK SEPARATELY AND NOT ON DIRECT FLIGHTS. GO THROUGH CHINA. I'LL RETURN VIA AUSTRALIA.
NO. EXPLAIN TO ME WHAT HAPPENED BACK THERE.

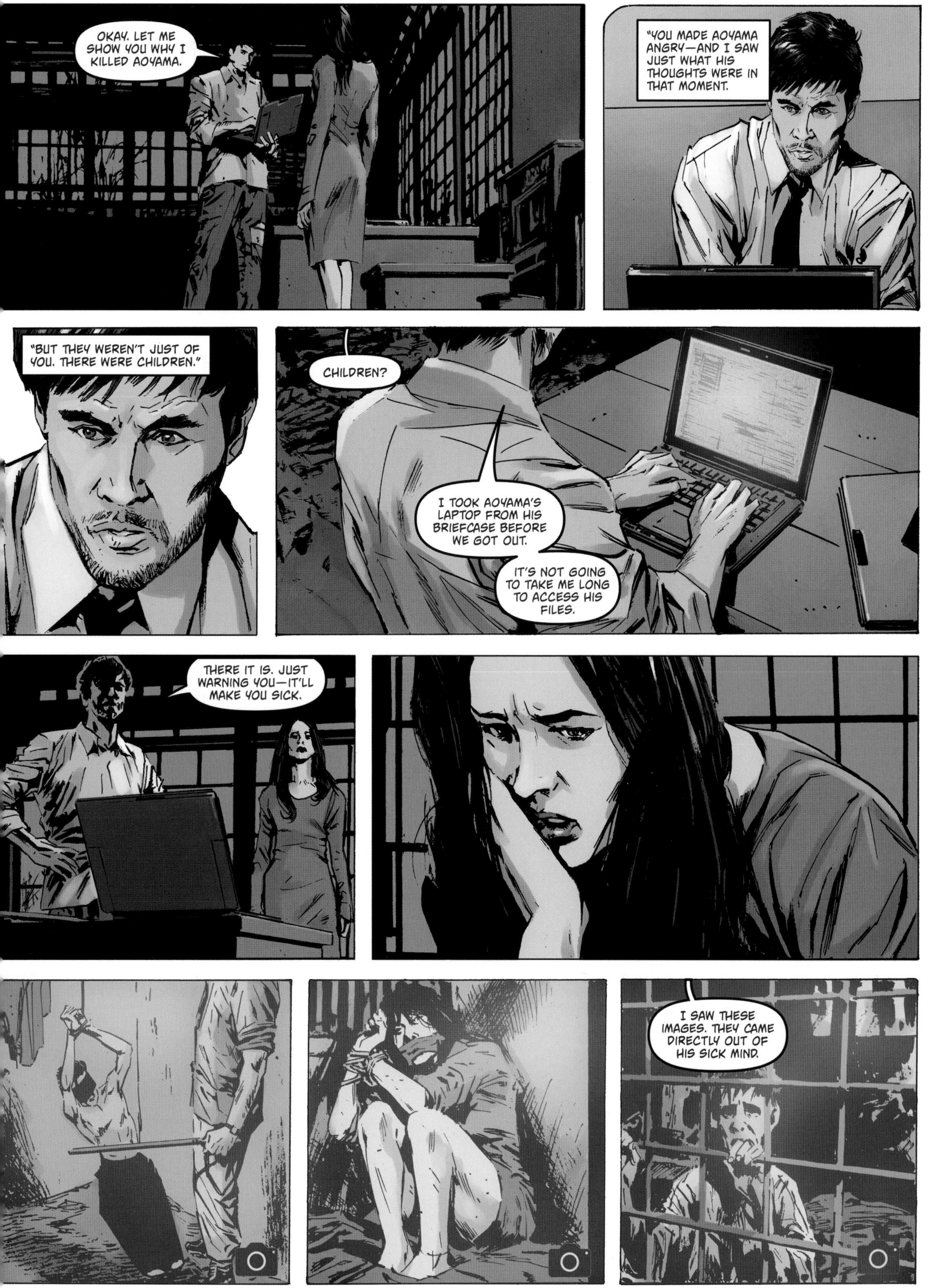

OKAY. LET ME SHOW YOU WHY I KILLED AOYAMA.
"YOU MADE AOYAMA ANGRY—AND I SAW JUST WHAT HIS THOUGHTS WERE IN THAT MOMENT.
"BUT THEY WEREN'T JUST OF YOU. THERE WERE CHILDREN."
CHILDREN?
I TOOK AOYAMA'S LAPTOP FROM HIS BRIEFCASE BEFORE WE GOT OUT.
IT'S NOT GOING TO TAKE ME LONG TO ACCESS HIS FILES.
THERE IT IS. JUST WARNING YOU—IT'LL MAKE YOU SICK.
I SAW THESE IMAGES. THEY CAME DIRECTLY OUT OF HIS SICK MIND.

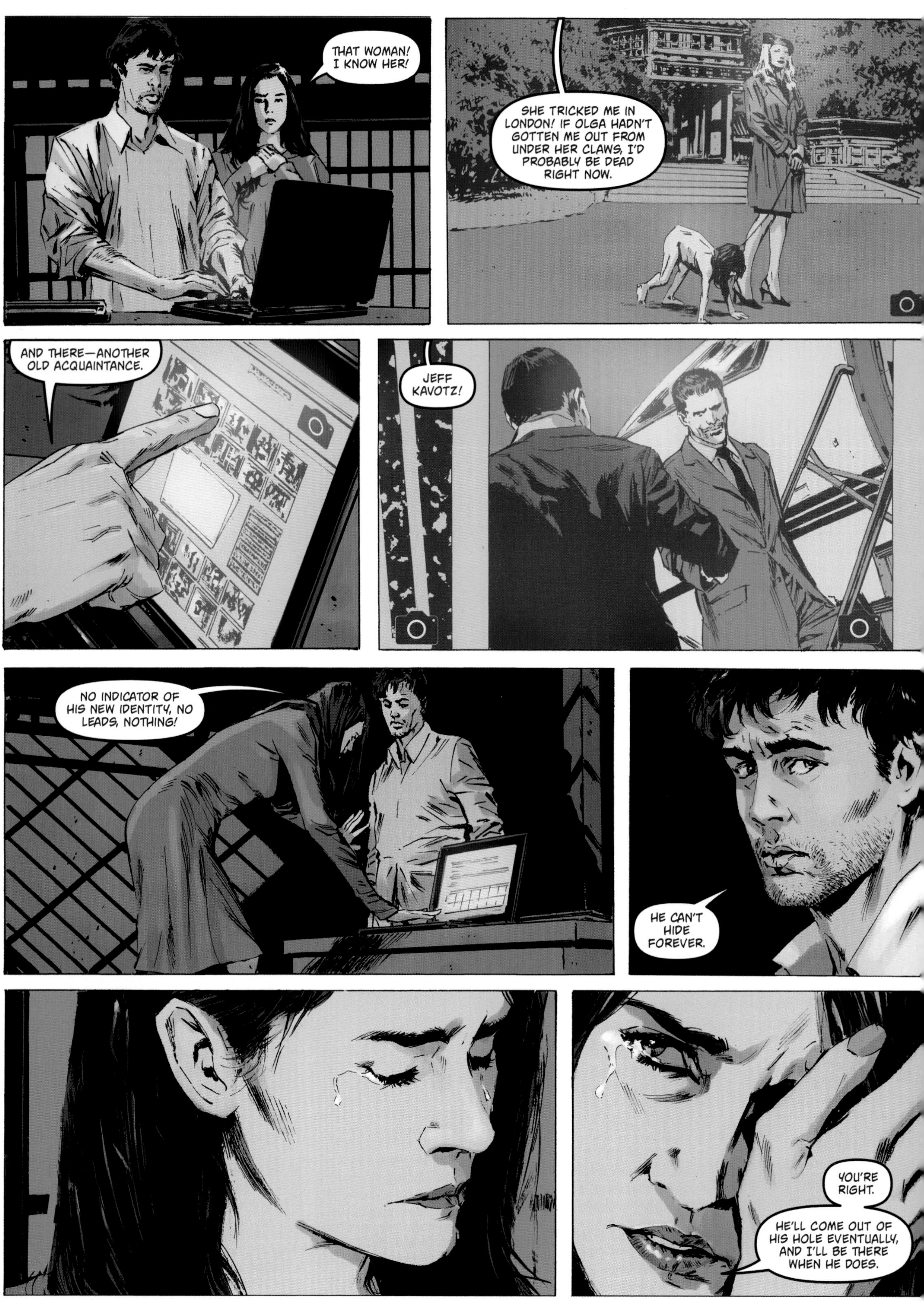
THAT WOMAN! I KNOW HER!
SHE TRICKED ME IN LONDON! IF OLGA HADN'T GOTTEN ME OUT FROM UNDER HER CLAWS, I'D PROBABLY BE DEAD RIGHT NOW.
AND THERE—ANOTHER OLD ACQUAINTANCE.
JEFF KAVOTZ!
NO INDICATOR OF HIS NEW IDENTITY, NO LEADS, NOTHING!
HE CAN'T HIDE FOREVER.
YOU'RE RIGHT.
HE'LL COME OUT OF HIS HOLE EVENTUALLY, AND I'LL BE THERE WHEN HE DOES.

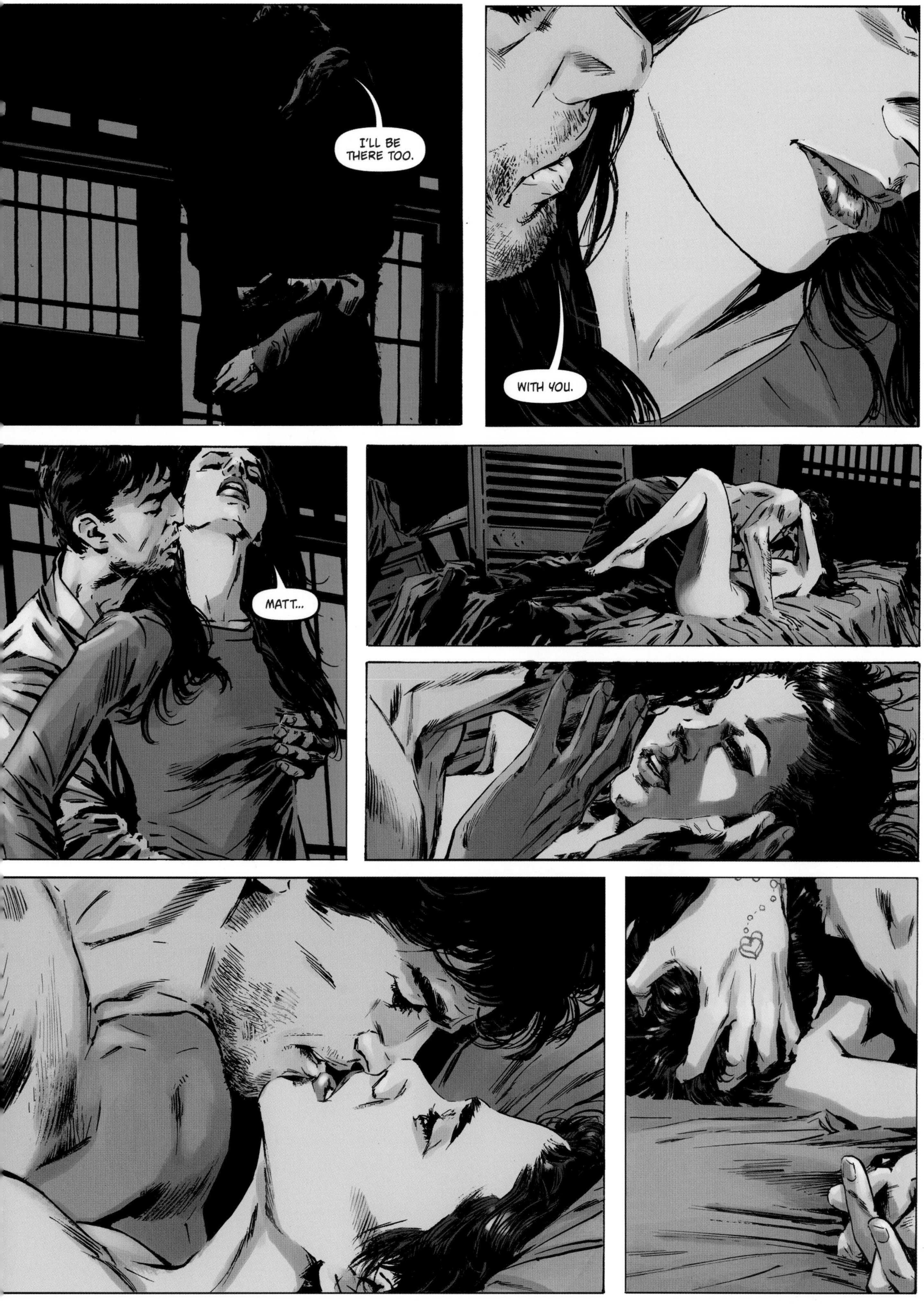
I'LL BE THERE TOO.
WITH YOU.
MATT...

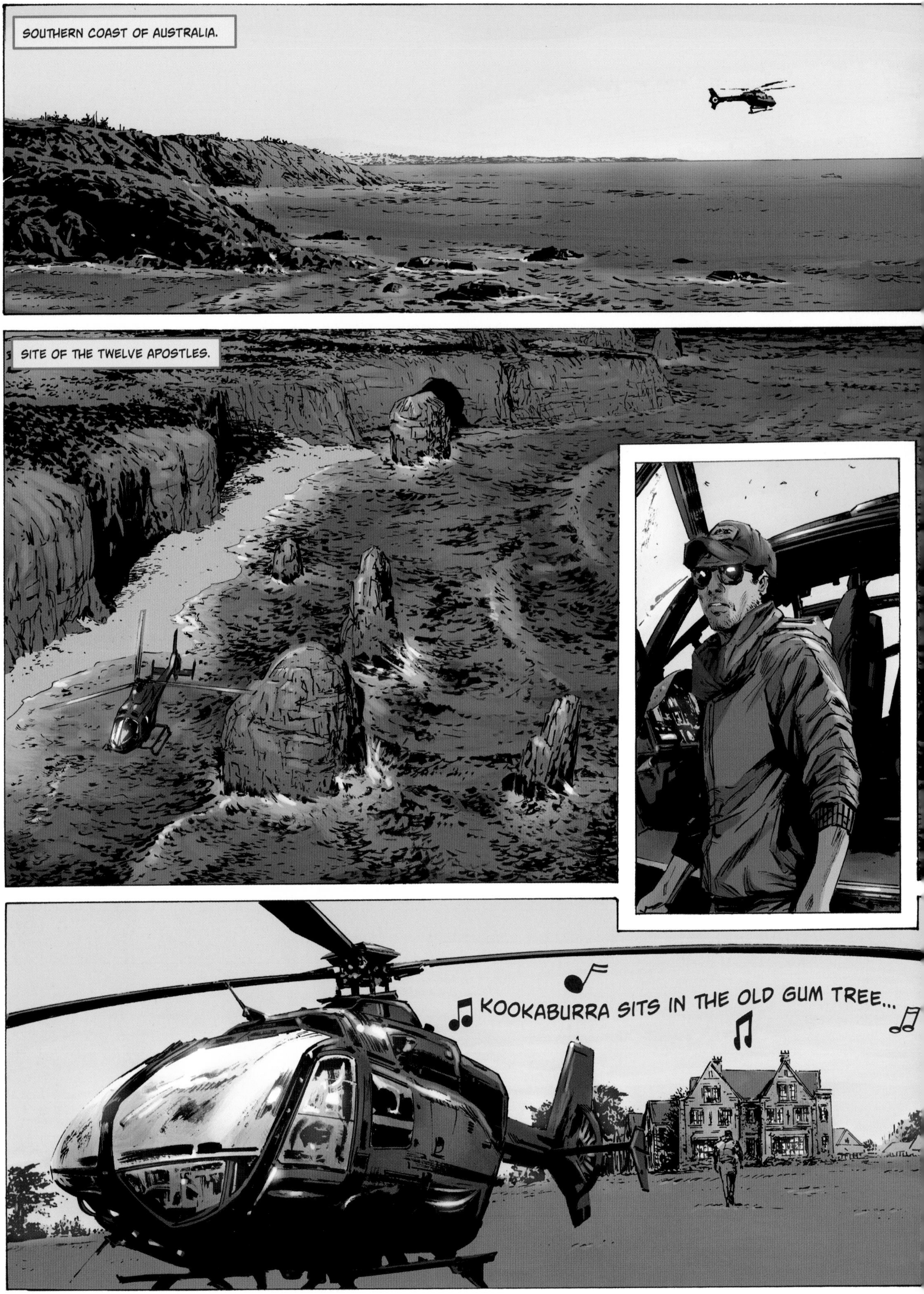
SOUTHERN COAST OF AUSTRALIA.
SITE OF THE TWELVE APOSTLES.
KOOKABURRA SITS IN THE OLD GUM TREE...

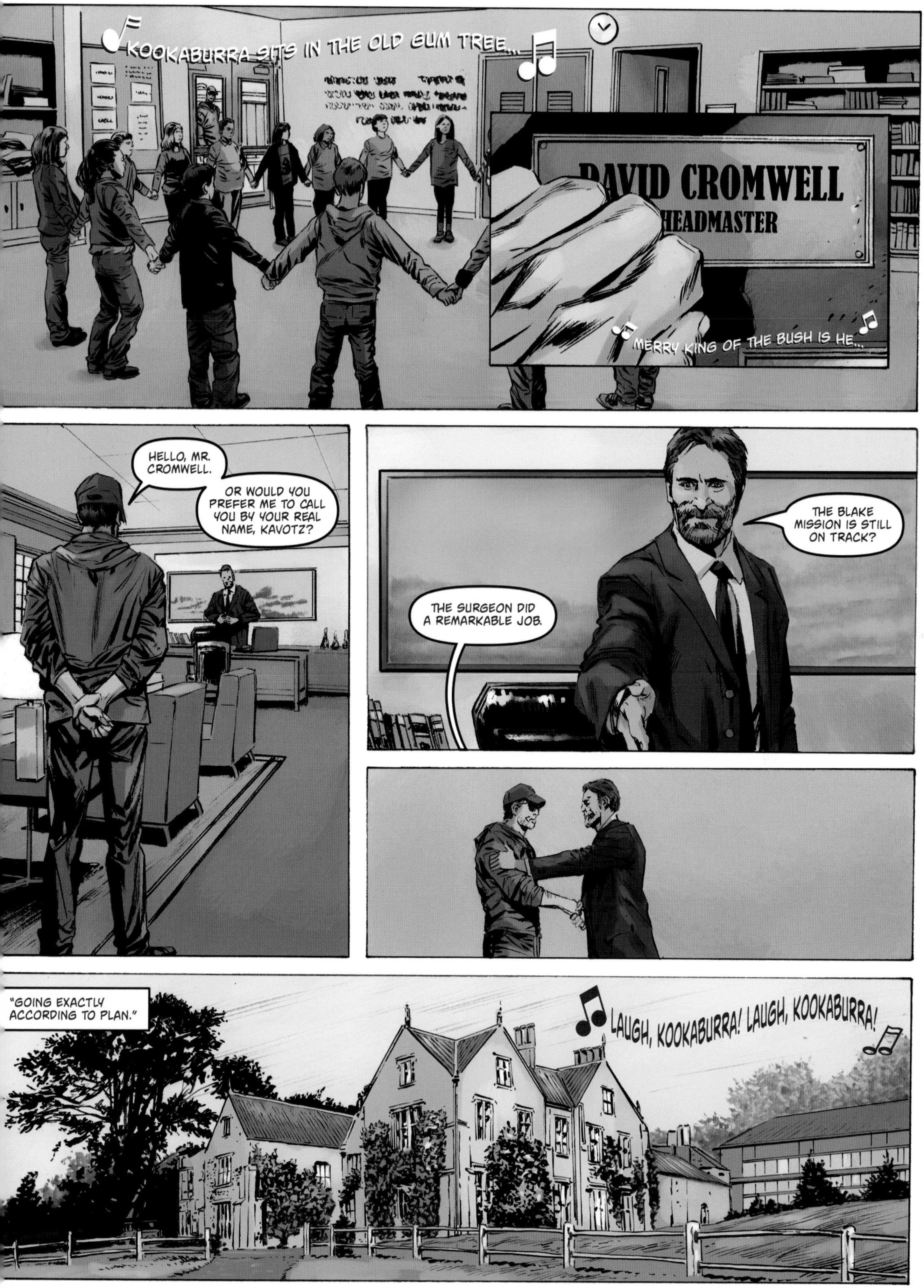
KOOKABURRA SITS IN THE OLD GUM TREE...
DAVID CROMWELL
HEADMASTER
MERRY KING OF THE BUSH IS HE...
HELLO, MR. CROMWELL.
OR WOULD YOU PREFER ME TO CALL YOU BY YOUR REAL NAME, KAVOTZ?
THE BLAKE MISSION IS STILL ON TRACK?
THE SURGEON DID A REMARKABLE JOB.
"GOING EXACTLY ACCORDING TO PLAN."
LAUGH, KOOKABURRA! LAUGH, KOOKABURRA!

"YOUR FIRST MISSION HAS BEEN A CATASTROPHIC FAILURE! WHEN YOU SCREW SOMETHING UP, YOU REALLY DON'T DO IT HALFWAY, DO YOU?"

THE CODE TO AOYAMA'S SAFE WAS WORTHLESS. HE CHANGED IT JUST AS YOU ASSASSINATED HIM! OUR SECOND TEAM IN KYOTO COULDN'T DO ANYTHING!

IT'S MY FAULT, MR. ARG. THINGS GOT OUT OF HAND BECAUSE OF ME.

SHUT IT, BOLAN!

IF THAT'S WHAT YOU CALL "GETTING OUT OF HAND," I DON'T EVEN WANT TO KNOW WHAT YOU THINK "FAILURE" LOOKS LIKE.

YOU SHIP OFF TO NEW YORK IN ONE WEEK. IT'S IN YOUR BEST INTEREST TO DO BETTER BY THEN.

РОССИЙСКАЯ ФЕ[ЕРАЦИЯ

ПАСПОРТ/ PASSPORT

BLAKE, HERE IS YOUR COVER. YOU'RE A MODEL. YOU HAVE A PHOTO SHOOT IN LONDON TOMORROW. IN THE MEANTIME, WE WILL SEND 'YOUR' PORTFOLIO TO AN AMERICAN AGENCY CALLED TWO MODELS, WHICH IS A LEGAL FRONT FOR A NETWORK OF DRUG TRAFFICKING AND PROSTITUTION.

YOU'LL DEPART FOR NEW YORK WITH BOLAN NEXT TUESDAY.

22.12.2[

МИД РОССИ[

P<RUSKUCHENKO<<<<IRINA<<<<<<<<<<<<<<<<<
0972151<<2RUS2002118F521028 5<<<<<<<<<<

VERA, GIVE THEM THE FILE.

NEITHER OF YOU SHOULD ASSUME YOU'VE GOT A PERMANENT CONTRACT AT ARGON.

IF YOUR NEXT MISSION DOESN'T CONVINCE ME, IT WILL BE YOUR LAST!

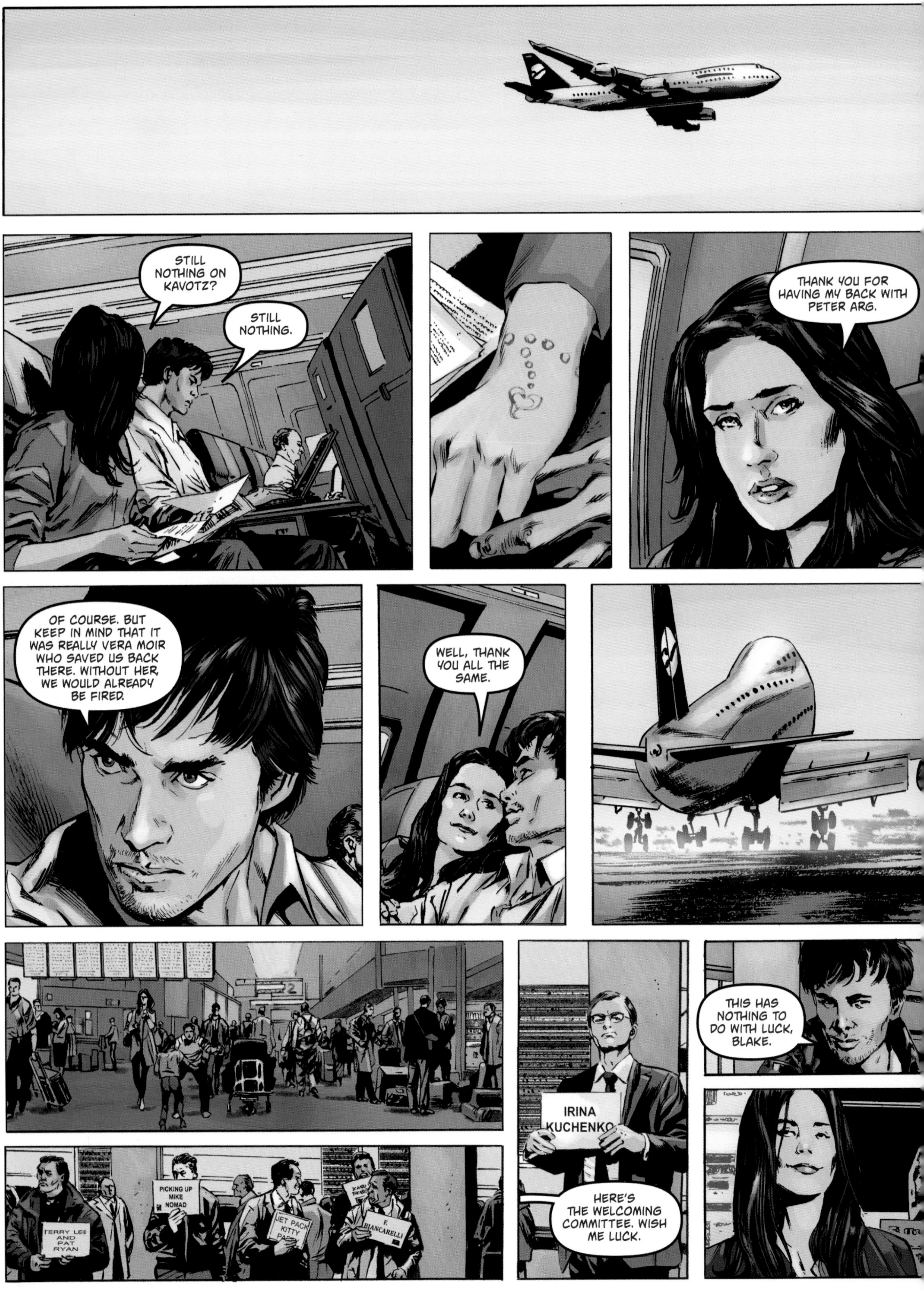
STILL NOTHING ON KAVOTZ?
STILL NOTHING.
THANK YOU FOR HAVING MY BACK WITH PETER ARG.
OF COURSE. BUT KEEP IN MIND THAT IT WAS REALLY VERA MOIR WHO SAVED US BACK THERE. WITHOUT HER, WE WOULD ALREADY BE FIRED.
WELL, THANK YOU ALL THE SAME.
TERRY LEE AND PAT RYAN
PICKING UP MIKE NOMAD
JET PACK KITTY
F. BIANCARELLI
IRINA KUCHENKO
HERE'S THE WELCOMING COMMITTEE. WISH ME LUCK.
THIS HAS NOTHING TO DO WITH LUCK, BLAKE.

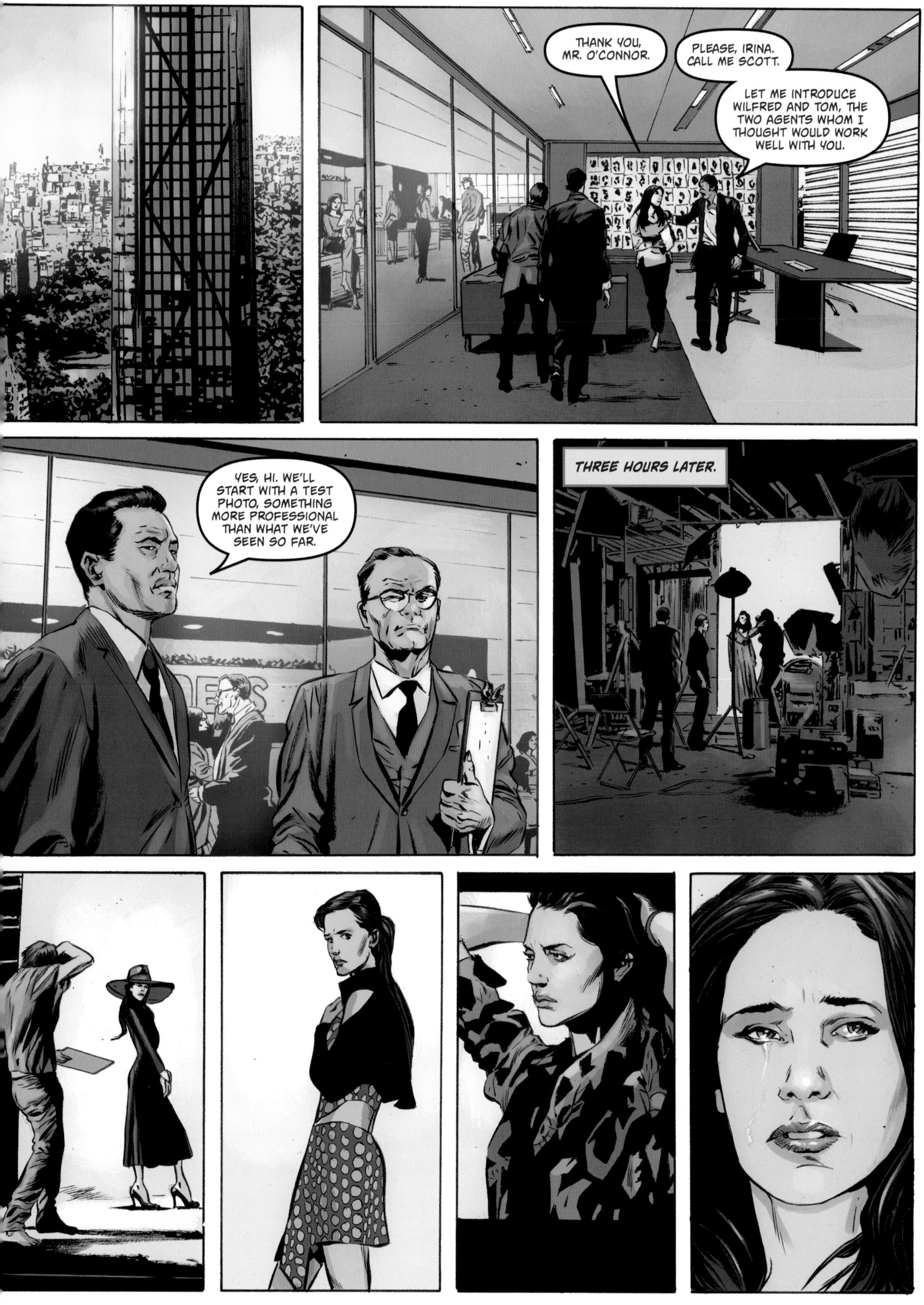
THANK YOU, MR. O'CONNOR.
PLEASE, IRINA. CALL ME SCOTT.
LET ME INTRODUCE WILFRED AND TOM, THE TWO AGENTS WHOM I THOUGHT WOULD WORK WELL WITH YOU.
YES, HI. WE'LL START WITH A TEST PHOTO, SOMETHING MORE PROFESSIONAL THAN WHAT WE'VE SEEN SO FAR.
THREE HOURS LATER.

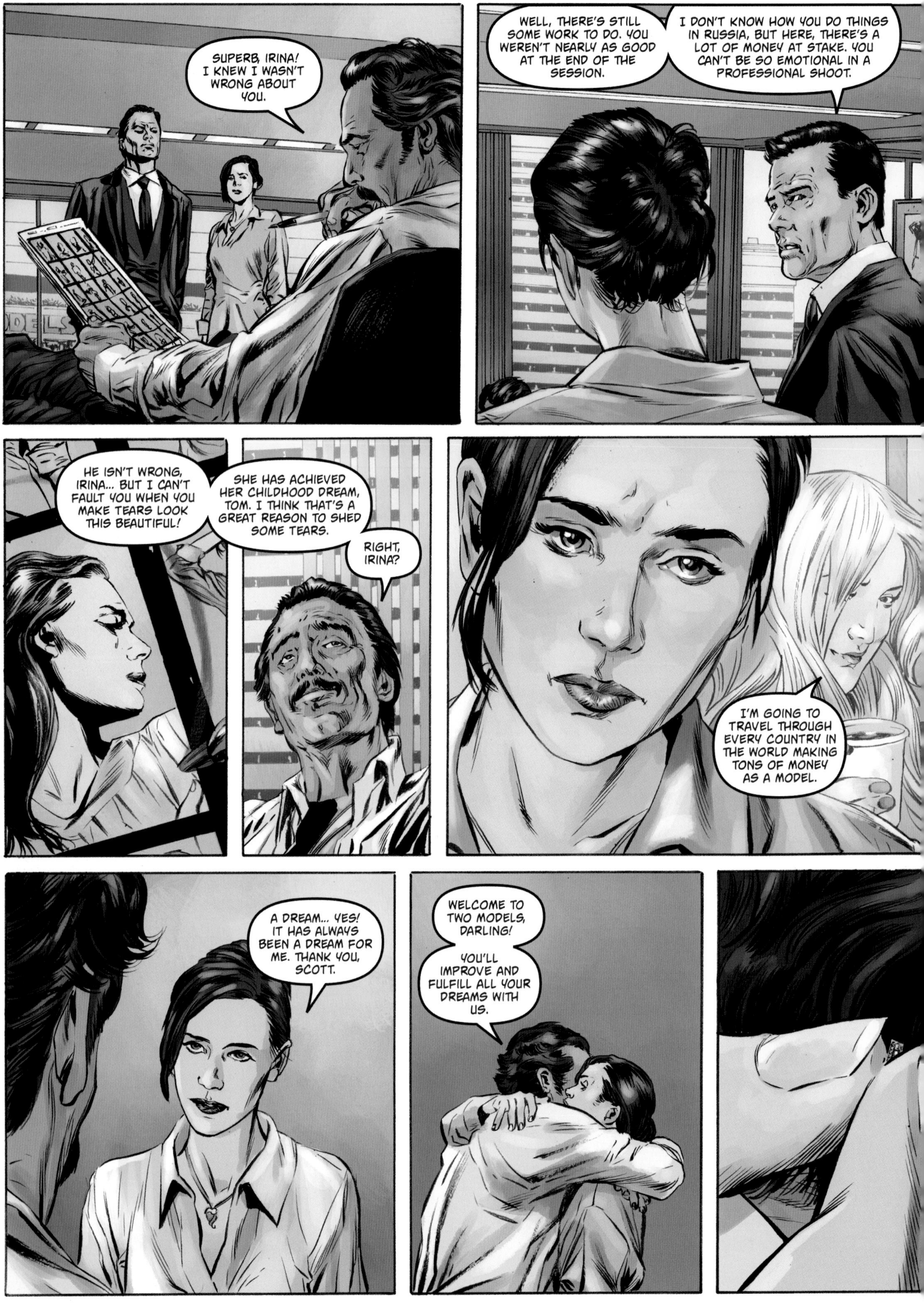
SUPERB, IRINA! I KNEW I WASN'T WRONG ABOUT YOU.
WELL, THERE'S STILL SOME WORK TO DO. YOU WEREN'T NEARLY AS GOOD AT THE END OF THE SESSION.
I DON'T KNOW HOW YOU DO THINGS IN RUSSIA, BUT HERE, THERE'S A LOT OF MONEY AT STAKE. YOU CAN'T BE SO EMOTIONAL IN A PROFESSIONAL SHOOT.
HE ISN'T WRONG, IRINA... BUT I CAN'T FAULT YOU WHEN YOU MAKE TEARS LOOK THIS BEAUTIFUL!
SHE HAS ACHIEVED HER CHILDHOOD DREAM, TOM. I THINK THAT'S A GREAT REASON TO SHED SOME TEARS.
RIGHT, IRINA?
I'M GOING TO TRAVEL THROUGH EVERY COUNTRY IN THE WORLD MAKING TONS OF MONEY AS A MODEL.
A DREAM... YES! IT HAS ALWAYS BEEN A DREAM FOR ME. THANK YOU, SCOTT.
WELCOME TO TWO MODELS, DARLING!
YOU'LL IMPROVE AND FULFILL ALL YOUR DREAMS WITH US.

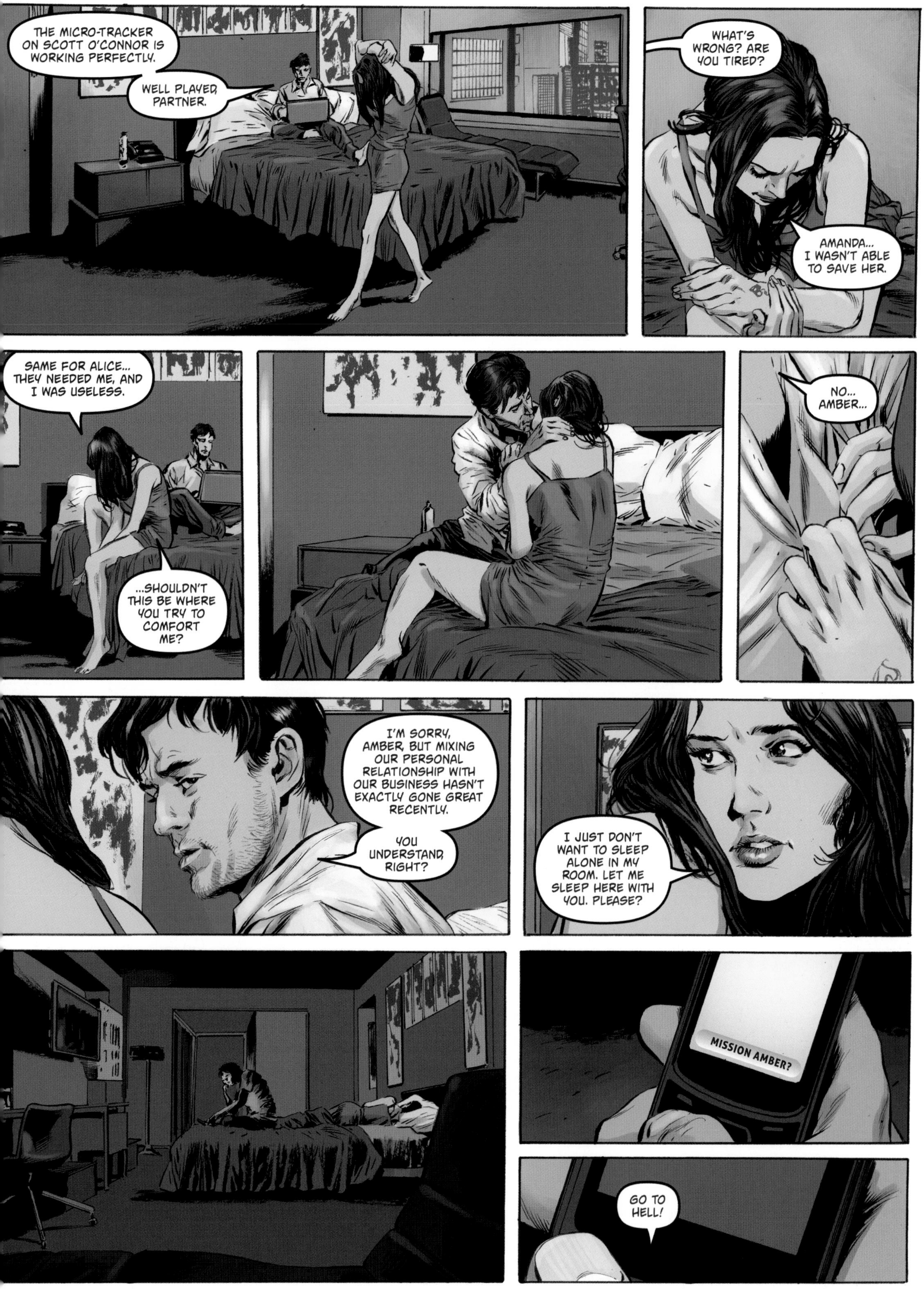
THE MICRO-TRACKER ON SCOTT O'CONNOR IS WORKING PERFECTLY.
WELL PLAYED, PARTNER.
WHAT'S WRONG? ARE YOU TIRED?
AMANDA... I WASN'T ABLE TO SAVE HER.
SAME FOR ALICE... THEY NEEDED ME, AND I WAS USELESS.
...SHOULDN'T THIS BE WHERE YOU TRY TO COMFORT ME?
NO... AMBER...
I'M SORRY, AMBER, BUT MIXING OUR PERSONAL RELATIONSHIP WITH OUR BUSINESS HASN'T EXACTLY GONE GREAT RECENTLY.
YOU UNDERSTAND, RIGHT?
I JUST DON'T WANT TO SLEEP ALONE IN MY ROOM. LET ME SLEEP HERE WITH YOU. PLEASE?
MISSION AMBER?
GO TO HELL!

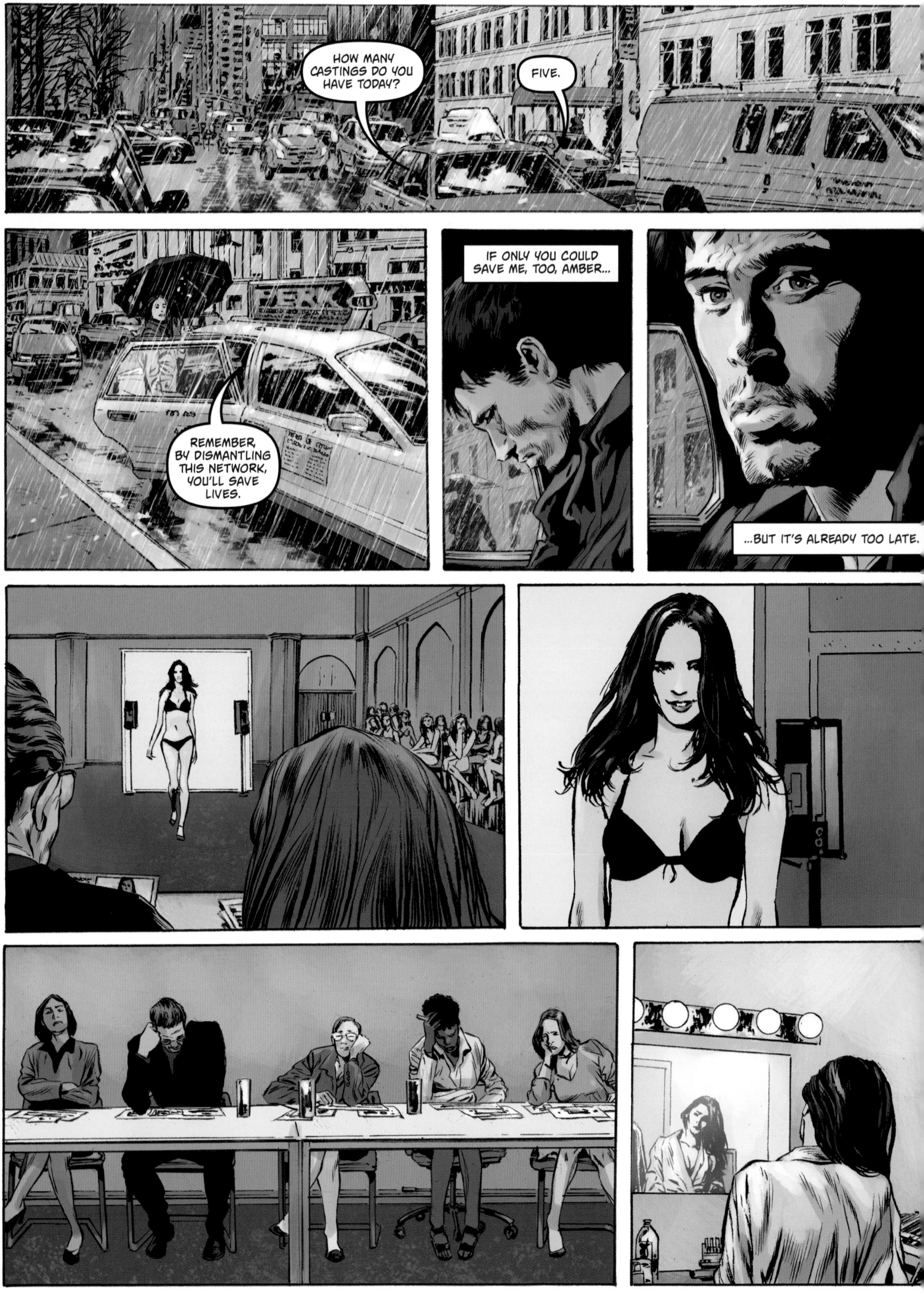
HOW MANY CASTINGS DO YOU HAVE TODAY?
FIVE.
REMEMBER, BY DISMANTLING THIS NETWORK, YOU'LL SAVE LIVES.
IF ONLY YOU COULD SAVE ME, TOO, AMBER...
...BUT IT'S ALREADY TOO LATE.

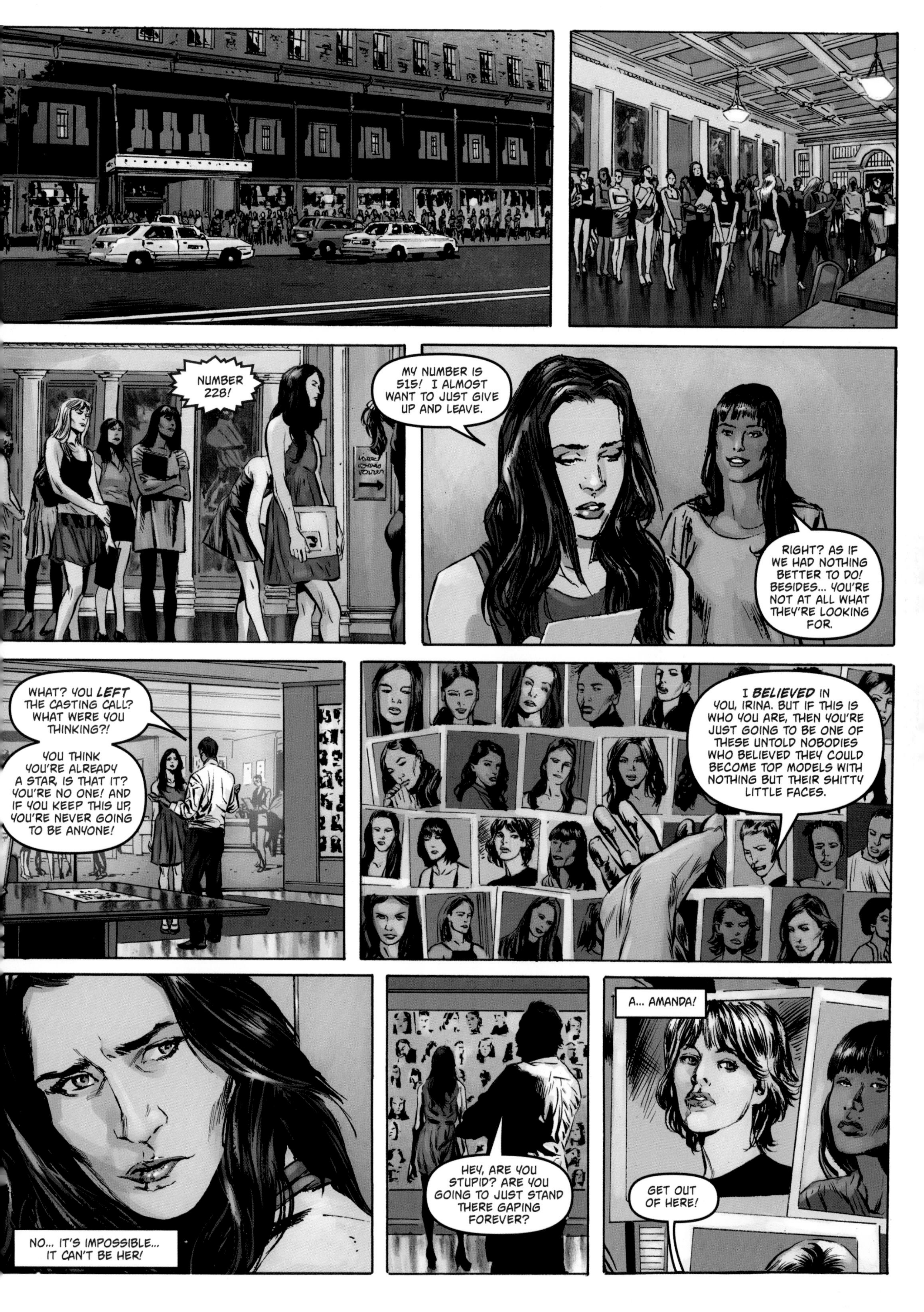
NUMBER 228!
MY NUMBER IS 515! I ALMOST WANT TO JUST GIVE UP AND LEAVE.
RIGHT? AS IF WE HAD NOTHING BETTER TO DO! BESIDES... YOU'RE NOT AT ALL WHAT THEY'RE LOOKING FOR.
WHAT? YOU *LEFT* THE CASTING CALL? WHAT WERE YOU THINKING?!
YOU THINK YOU'RE ALREADY A STAR, IS THAT IT? YOU'RE NO ONE! AND IF YOU KEEP THIS UP, YOU'RE NEVER GOING TO BE ANYONE!
I *BELIEVED* IN YOU, IRINA. BUT IF THIS IS WHO YOU ARE, THEN YOU'RE JUST GOING TO BE ONE OF THESE UNTOLD NOBODIES WHO BELIEVED THEY COULD BECOME TOP MODELS WITH NOTHING BUT THEIR SHITTY LITTLE FACES.
NO... IT'S IMPOSSIBLE... IT CAN'T BE HER!
HEY, ARE YOU STUPID? ARE YOU GOING TO JUST STAND THERE GAPING FOREVER?
A... AMANDA!
GET OUT OF HERE!

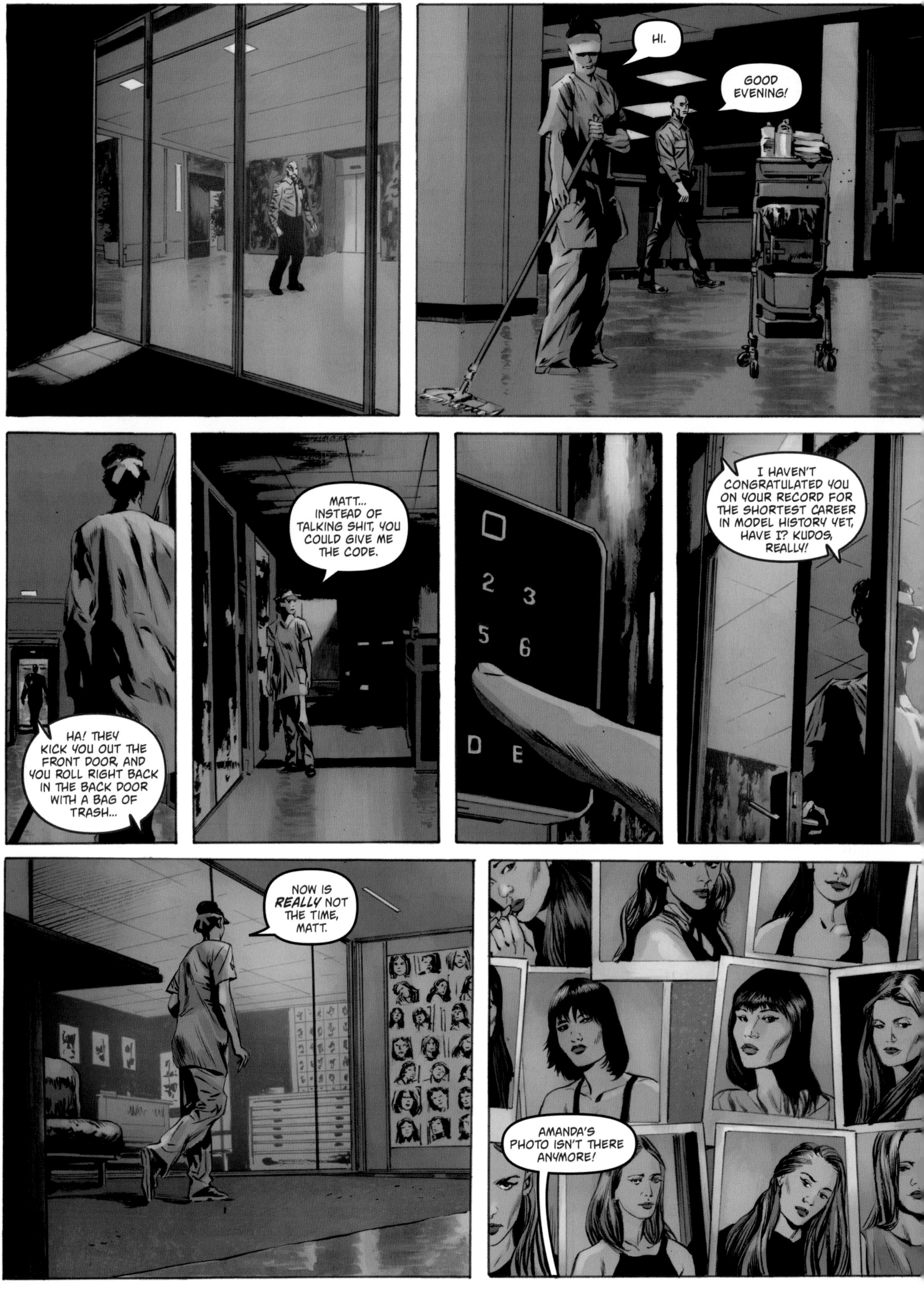
HI.
GOOD EVENING!
HA! THEY KICK YOU OUT THE FRONT DOOR, AND YOU ROLL RIGHT BACK IN THE BACK DOOR WITH A BAG OF TRASH...
MATT... INSTEAD OF TALKING SHIT, YOU COULD GIVE ME THE CODE.
2 3
5 6
D E
I HAVEN'T CONGRATULATED YOU ON YOUR RECORD FOR THE SHORTEST CAREER IN MODEL HISTORY YET, HAVE I? KUDOS, REALLY!
NOW IS REALLY NOT THE TIME, MATT.
AMANDA'S PHOTO ISN'T THERE ANYMORE!

I TOLD YOU. YOU MUST HAVE IMAGINED IT. THERE'S NO WAY THEY COULD HAVE AMANDA'S PHOTO THERE.

I DIDN'T IMAGINE ANYTHING! I'LL PROVE IT TO YOU!

THAT'S GOING TO HAVE TO WAIT! WE HAVE WORK TO DO—OR AT LEAST *I* DO, EVEN IF YOU DON'T. TURN ON HIS COMPUTER.

²Models

ALL RIGHT! I'LL THROW IN A LITTLE PROGRAM CALLED GHOST TAKER, WHICH WILL LET ME TAKE CONTROL OF HIS GEAR...

...AND JUST LIKE THAT, IT'S AS IF I'M RIGHT THERE WITH YOU IN THIS WANKER'S OFFICE.

SCOTT O'CONNOR, YOUR SECRETS ARE MINE!

HUH, THIS WANKER IS SURPRISINGLY ARROGANT. WORKS FOR ME! HE HASN'T PROTECTED ANYTHING.

BINGO! I'VE FOUND THE FILE LISTING HIS PROSTITUTES. LOOKS LIKE HE HAS A REAL ARMY OF THEM OUT THERE.

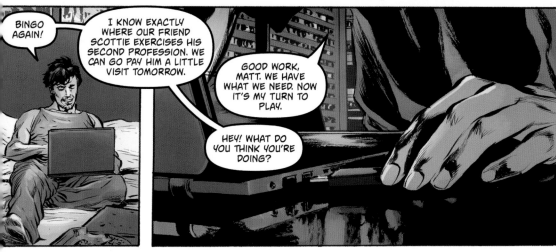

BINGO AGAIN!

I KNOW EXACTLY WHERE OUR FRIEND SCOTTIE EXERCISES HIS SECOND PROFESSION. WE CAN GO PAY HIM A LITTLE VISIT TOMORROW.

GOOD WORK, MATT. WE HAVE WHAT WE NEED. NOW IT'S MY TURN TO PLAY.

HEY! WHAT DO YOU THINK YOU'RE DOING?

WHAT DID YOU JUST PLUG INTO HIS COMPUTER?

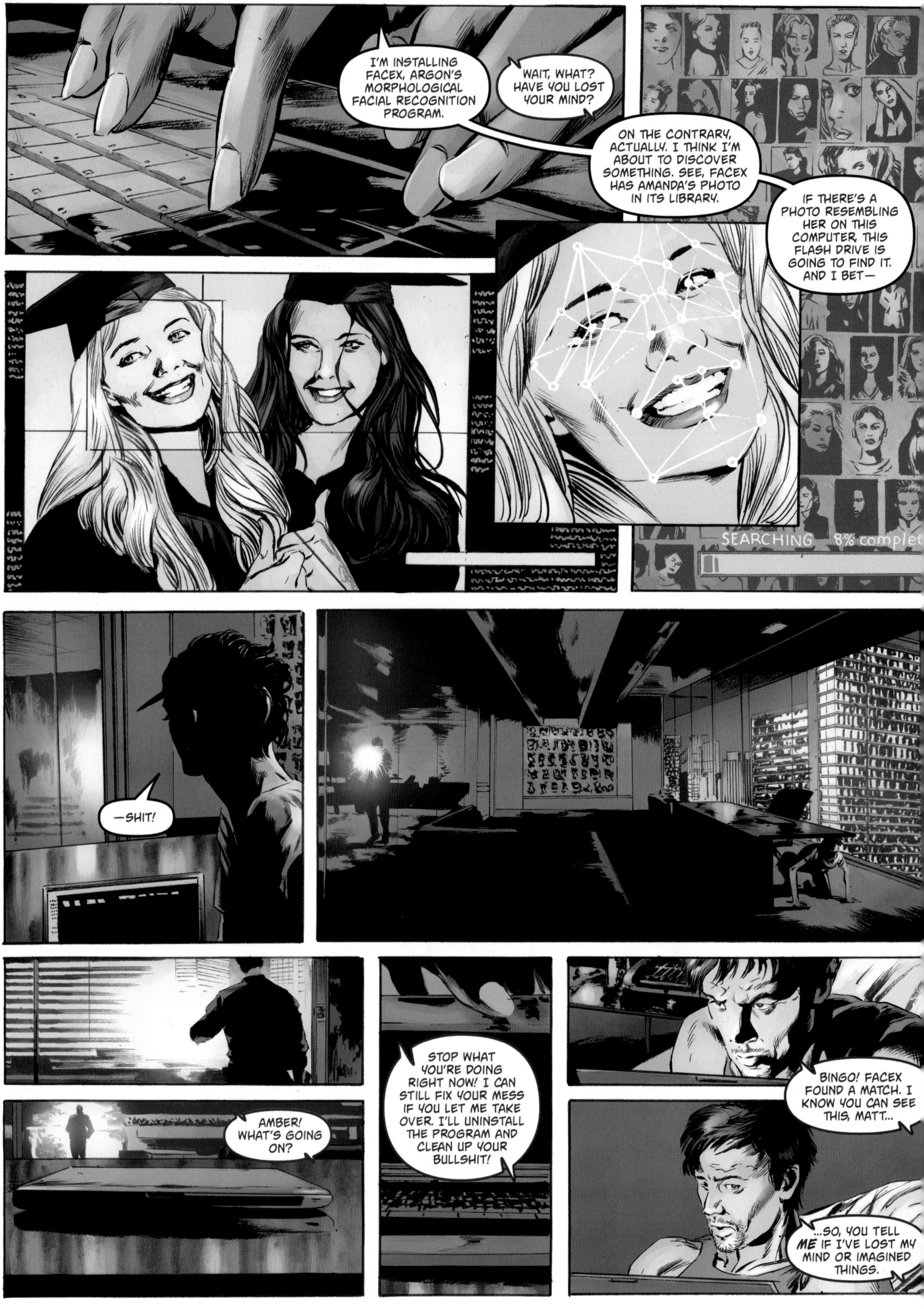
I'M INSTALLING FACEX, ARGON'S MORPHOLOGICAL FACIAL RECOGNITION PROGRAM.
WAIT, WHAT? HAVE YOU LOST YOUR MIND?
ON THE CONTRARY, ACTUALLY. I THINK I'M ABOUT TO DISCOVER SOMETHING. SEE, FACEX HAS AMANDA'S PHOTO IN ITS LIBRARY.
IF THERE'S A PHOTO RESEMBLING HER ON THIS COMPUTER, THIS FLASH DRIVE IS GOING TO FIND IT. AND I BET—
SEARCHING 8% complet
—SHIT!
AMBER! WHAT'S GOING ON?
STOP WHAT YOU'RE DOING RIGHT NOW! I CAN STILL FIX YOUR MESS IF YOU LET ME TAKE OVER. I'LL UNINSTALL THE PROGRAM AND CLEAN UP YOUR BULLSHIT!
BINGO! FACEX FOUND A MATCH. I KNOW YOU CAN SEE THIS, MATT...
...SO, YOU TELL ME IF I'VE LOST MY MIND OR IMAGINED THINGS.

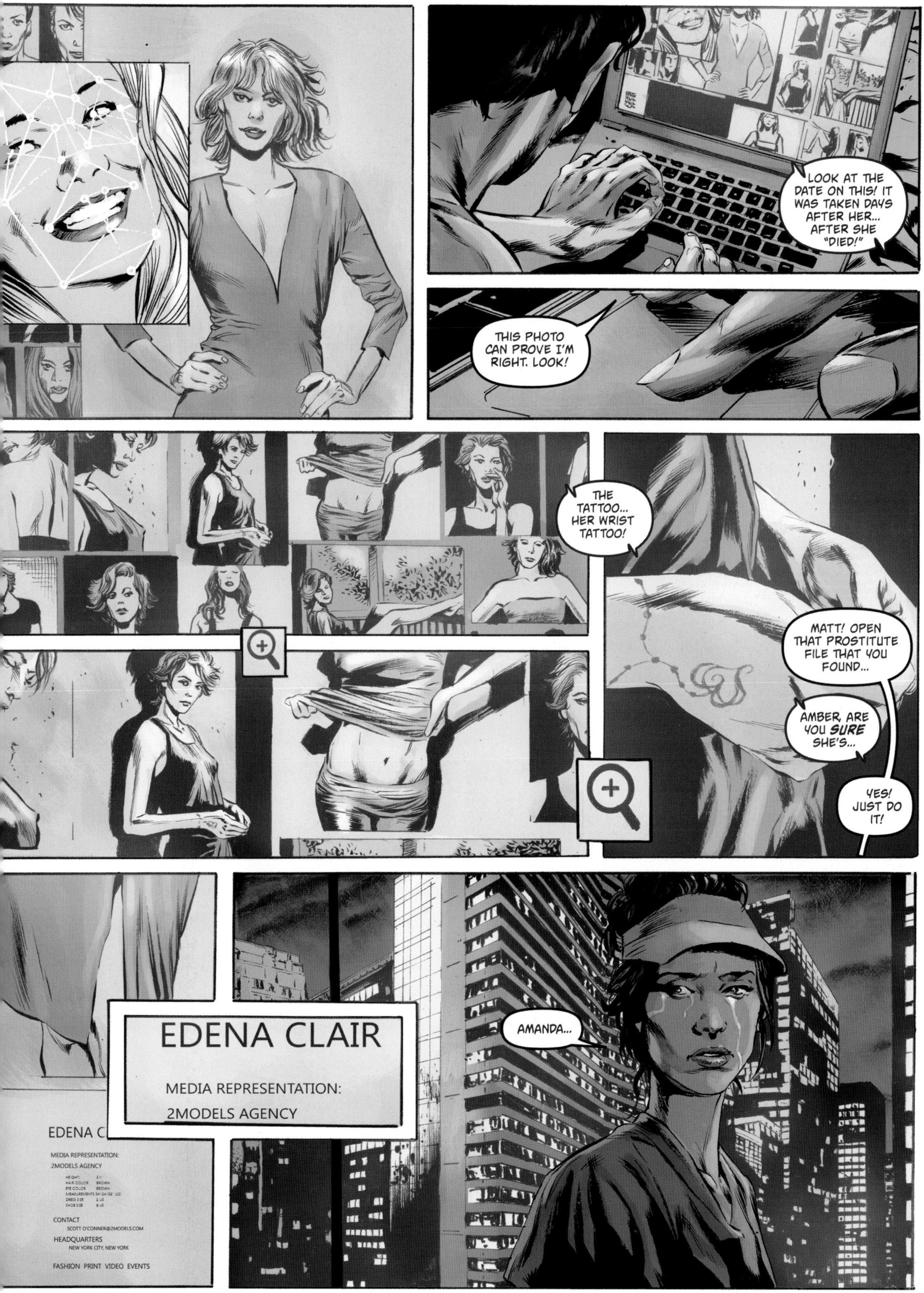
LOOK AT THE DATE ON THIS! IT WAS TAKEN DAYS AFTER HER... AFTER SHE "DIED!"
THIS PHOTO CAN PROVE I'M RIGHT. LOOK!
THE TATTOO... HER WRIST TATTOO!
MATT! OPEN THAT PROSTITUTE FILE THAT YOU FOUND...
AMBER, ARE YOU SURE SHE'S...
YES! JUST DO IT!
EDENA CLAIR
MEDIA REPRESENTATION:
2MODELS AGENCY
MEDIA REPRESENTATION:
2MODELS AGENCY
CONTACT
SCOTT O'CONNER@2MODELS.COM
HEADQUARTERS
NEW YORK CITY, NEW YORK
FASHION PRINT VIDEO EVENTS
AMANDA...

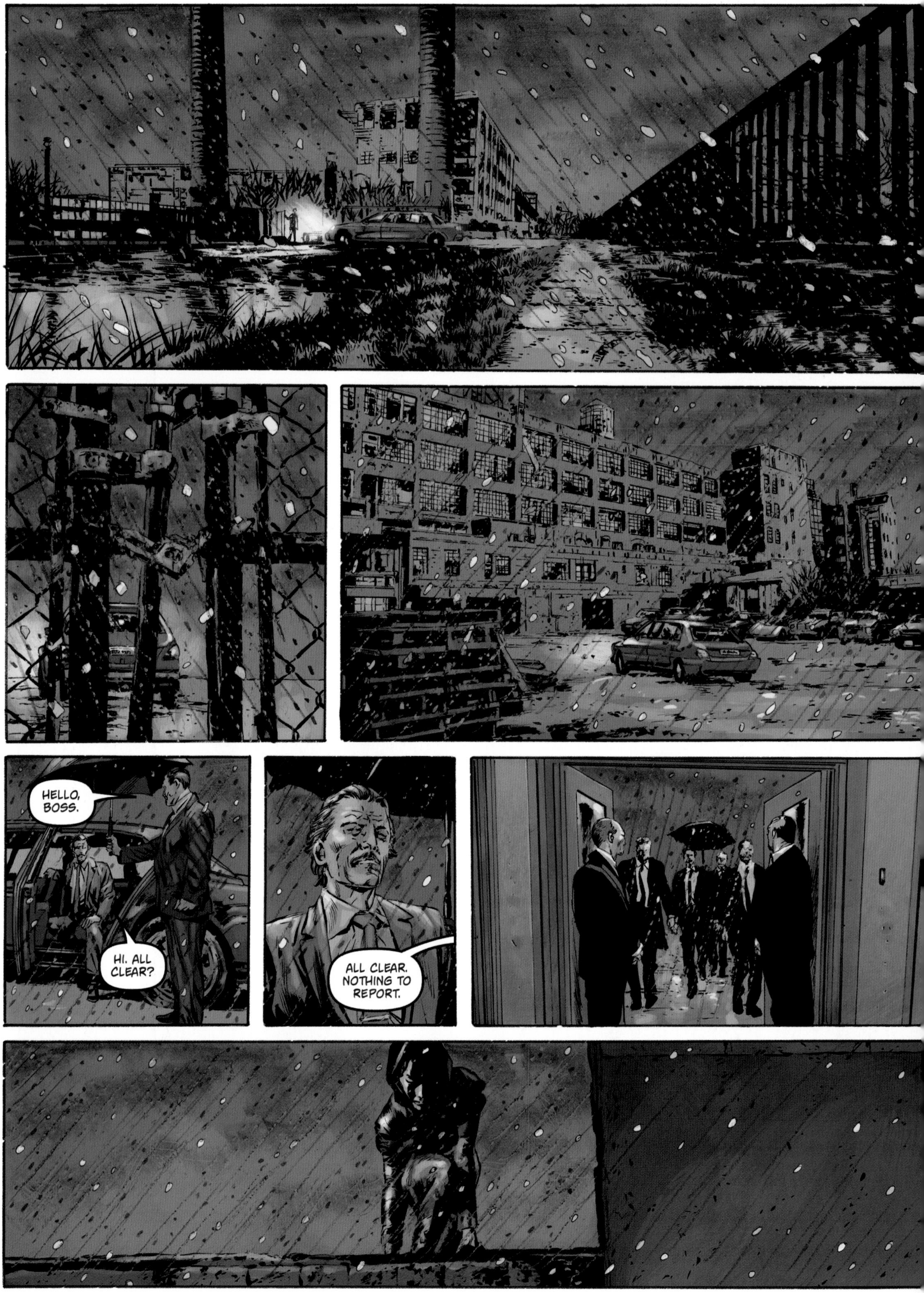
HELLO, BOSS.
HI. ALL CLEAR?
ALL CLEAR. NOTHING TO REPORT.

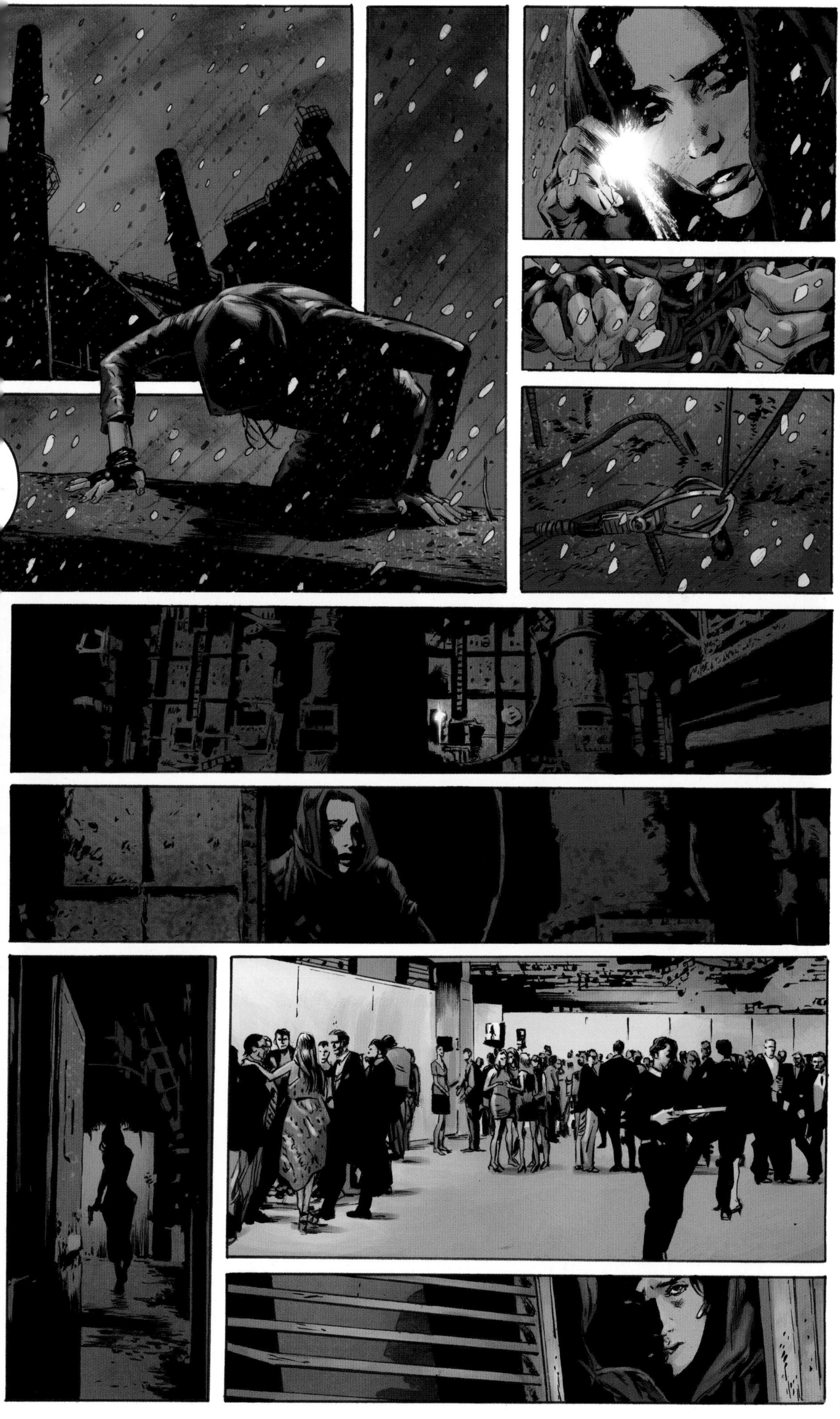

I HAVE EYES ON HIM.

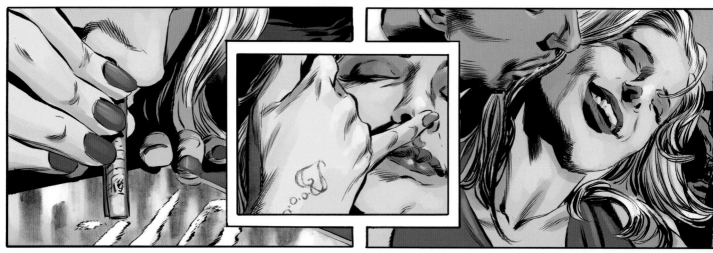

AMBER, ARE YOU OKAY?

I KNOW SEEING HER LIKE THIS IS ROUGH, BUT... YOU **HAVE** TO CONCENTRATE ON THE MISSION. DO YOU HEAR ME? AMBER?

AMBER! NO!

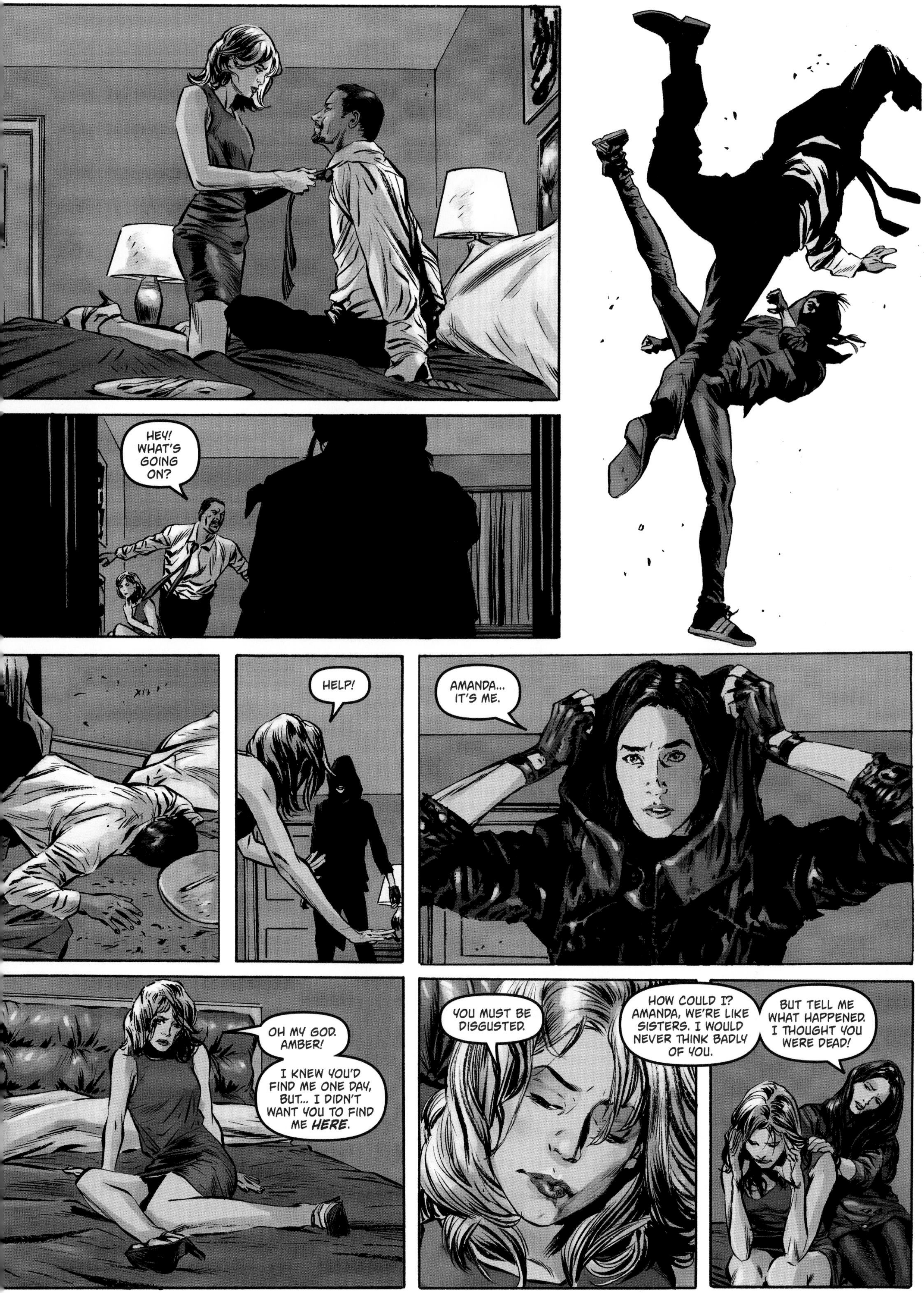
HEY! WHAT'S GOING ON?
HELP!
AMANDA... IT'S ME.
OH MY GOD. AMBER!
I KNEW YOU'D FIND ME ONE DAY, BUT... I DIDN'T WANT YOU TO FIND ME HERE.
YOU MUST BE DISGUSTED.
HOW COULD I? AMANDA, WE'RE LIKE SISTERS. I WOULD NEVER THINK BADLY OF YOU.
BUT TELL ME WHAT HAPPENED. I THOUGHT YOU WERE DEAD!

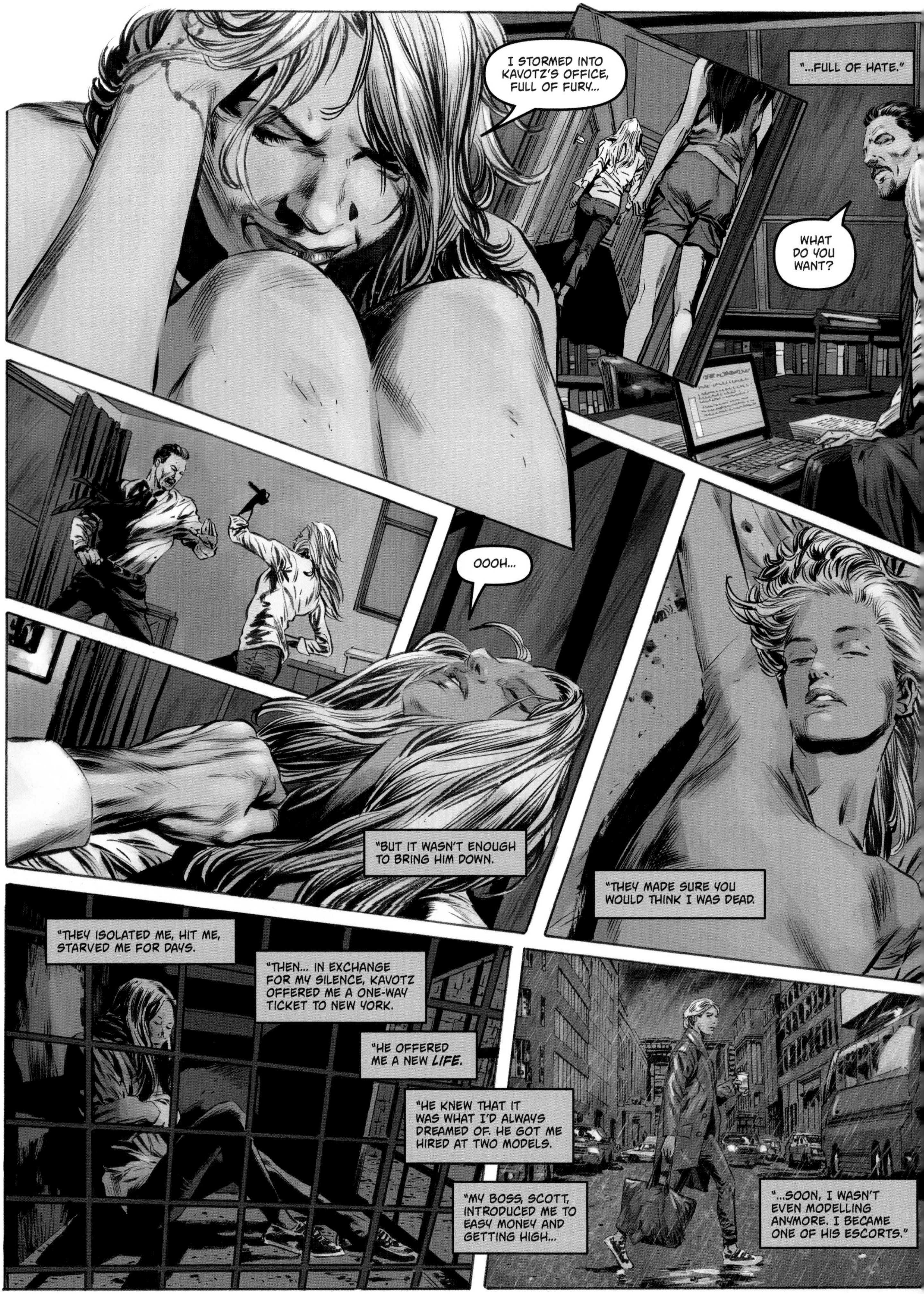
I STORMED INTO KAVOTZ'S OFFICE, FULL OF FURY...
"...FULL OF HATE."
WHAT DO YOU WANT?
OOOH...
"BUT IT WASN'T ENOUGH TO BRING HIM DOWN.
"THEY MADE SURE YOU WOULD THINK I WAS DEAD.
"THEY ISOLATED ME, HIT ME, STARVED ME FOR DAYS.
"THEN... IN EXCHANGE FOR MY SILENCE, KAVOTZ OFFERED ME A ONE-WAY TICKET TO NEW YORK.
"HE OFFERED ME A NEW *LIFE*.
"HE KNEW THAT IT WAS WHAT I'D ALWAYS DREAMED OF. HE GOT ME HIRED AT TWO MODELS.
"MY BOSS, SCOTT, INTRODUCED ME TO EASY MONEY AND GETTING HIGH...
"...SOON, I WASN'T EVEN MODELLING ANYMORE. I BECAME ONE OF HIS ESCORTS."

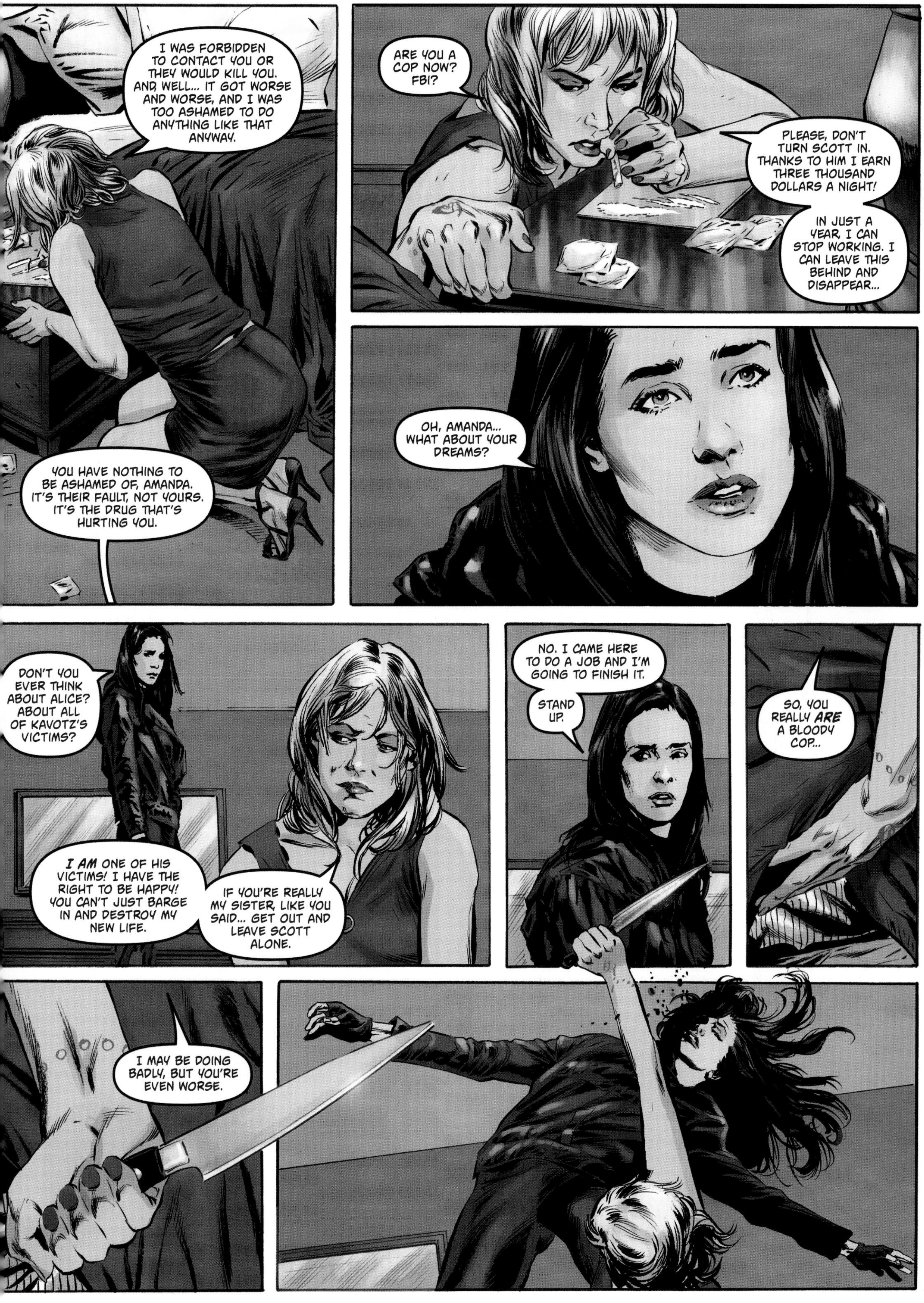
I WAS FORBIDDEN TO CONTACT YOU OR THEY WOULD KILL YOU. AND, WELL... IT GOT WORSE AND WORSE, AND I WAS TOO ASHAMED TO DO ANYTHING LIKE THAT ANYWAY.
YOU HAVE NOTHING TO BE ASHAMED OF, AMANDA. IT'S THEIR FAULT, NOT YOURS. IT'S THE DRUG THAT'S HURTING YOU.
ARE YOU A COP NOW? FBI?
PLEASE, DON'T TURN SCOTT IN. THANKS TO HIM I EARN THREE THOUSAND DOLLARS A NIGHT!
IN JUST A YEAR, I CAN STOP WORKING. I CAN LEAVE THIS BEHIND AND DISAPPEAR...
OH, AMANDA... WHAT ABOUT YOUR DREAMS?
DON'T YOU EVER THINK ABOUT ALICE? ABOUT ALL OF KAVOTZ'S VICTIMS?
*I AM* ONE OF HIS VICTIMS! I HAVE THE RIGHT TO BE HAPPY! YOU CAN'T JUST BARGE IN AND DESTROY MY NEW LIFE.
IF YOU'RE REALLY MY SISTER, LIKE YOU SAID... GET OUT AND LEAVE SCOTT ALONE.
NO. I CAME HERE TO DO A JOB AND I'M GOING TO FINISH IT.
STAND UP.
SO, YOU REALLY *ARE* A BLOODY COP...
I MAY BE DOING BADLY, BUT YOU'RE EVEN WORSE.

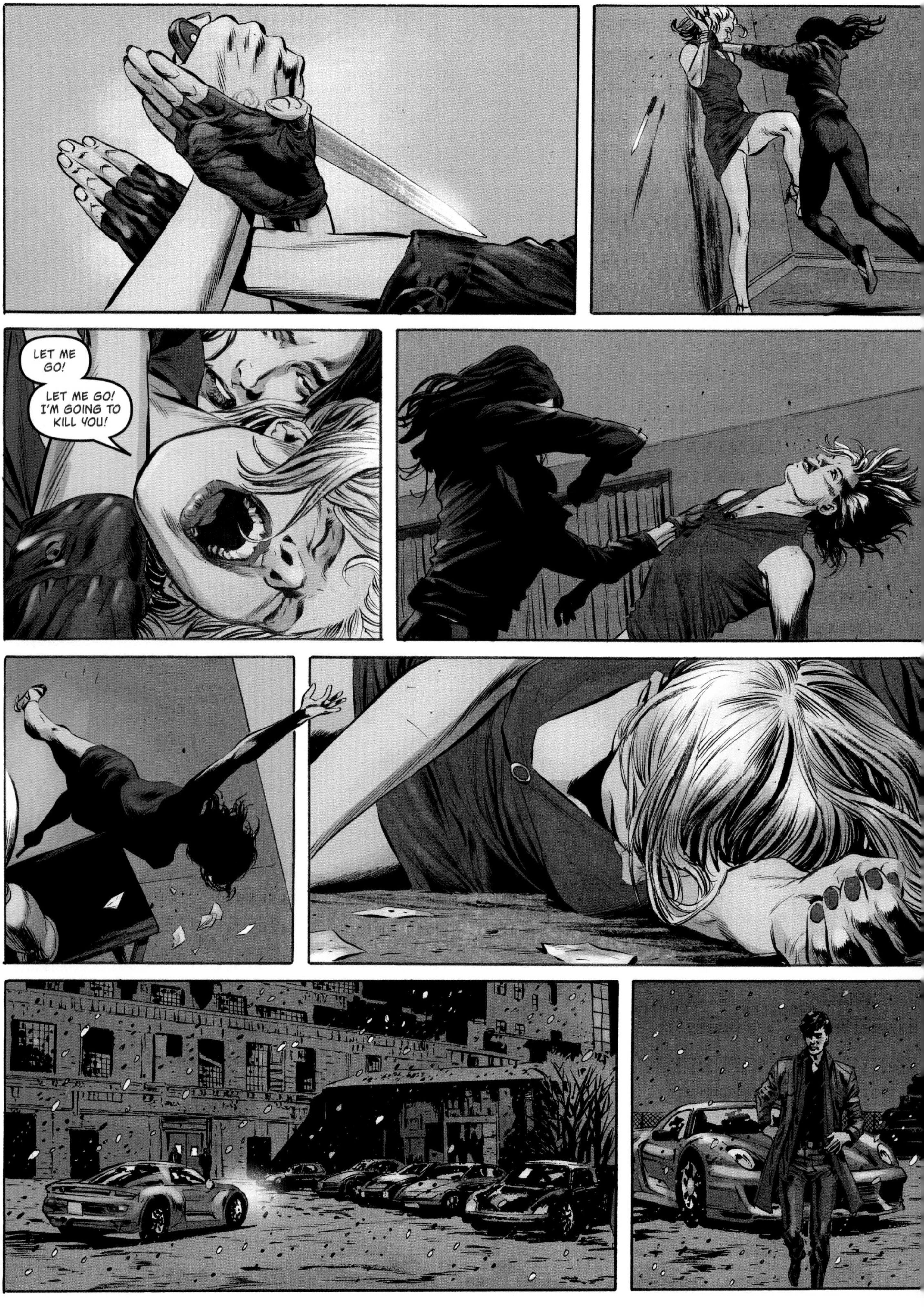
LET ME GO!
LET ME GO! I'M GOING TO KILL YOU!

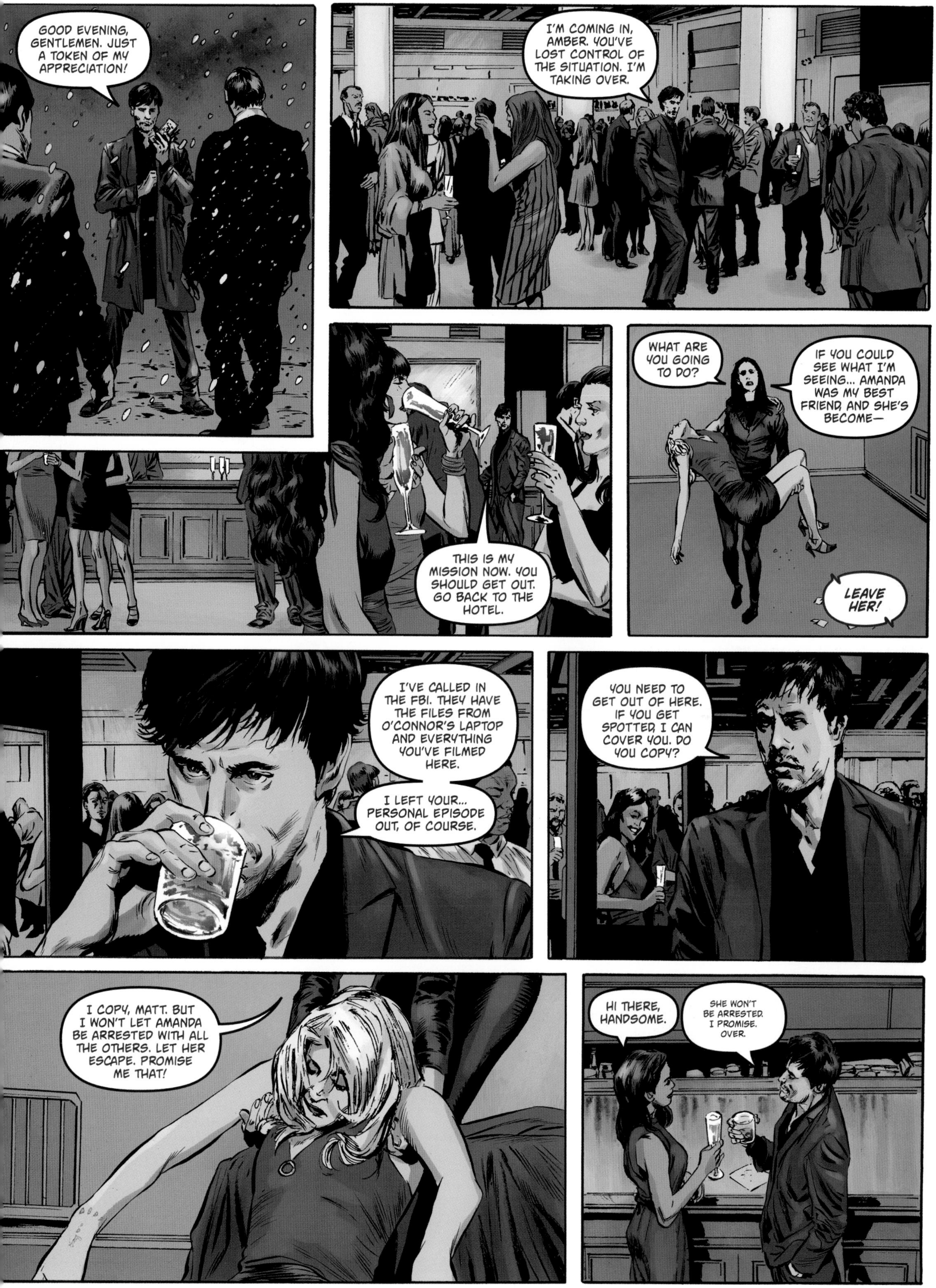
GOOD EVENING, GENTLEMEN. JUST A TOKEN OF MY APPRECIATION!
I'M COMING IN, AMBER. YOU'VE LOST CONTROL OF THE SITUATION. I'M TAKING OVER.
THIS IS MY MISSION NOW. YOU SHOULD GET OUT. GO BACK TO THE HOTEL.
WHAT ARE YOU GOING TO DO?
IF YOU COULD SEE WHAT I'M SEEING... AMANDA WAS MY BEST FRIEND AND SHE'S BECOME—
LEAVE HER!
I'VE CALLED IN THE FBI. THEY HAVE THE FILES FROM O'CONNOR'S LAPTOP AND EVERYTHING YOU'VE FILMED HERE.
I LEFT YOUR... PERSONAL EPISODE OUT, OF COURSE.
YOU NEED TO GET OUT OF HERE. IF YOU GET SPOTTED, I CAN COVER YOU. DO YOU COPY?
I COPY, MATT. BUT I WON'T LET AMANDA BE ARRESTED WITH ALL THE OTHERS. LET HER ESCAPE. PROMISE ME THAT!
HI THERE, HANDSOME.
SHE WON'T BE ARRESTED. I PROMISE. OVER.

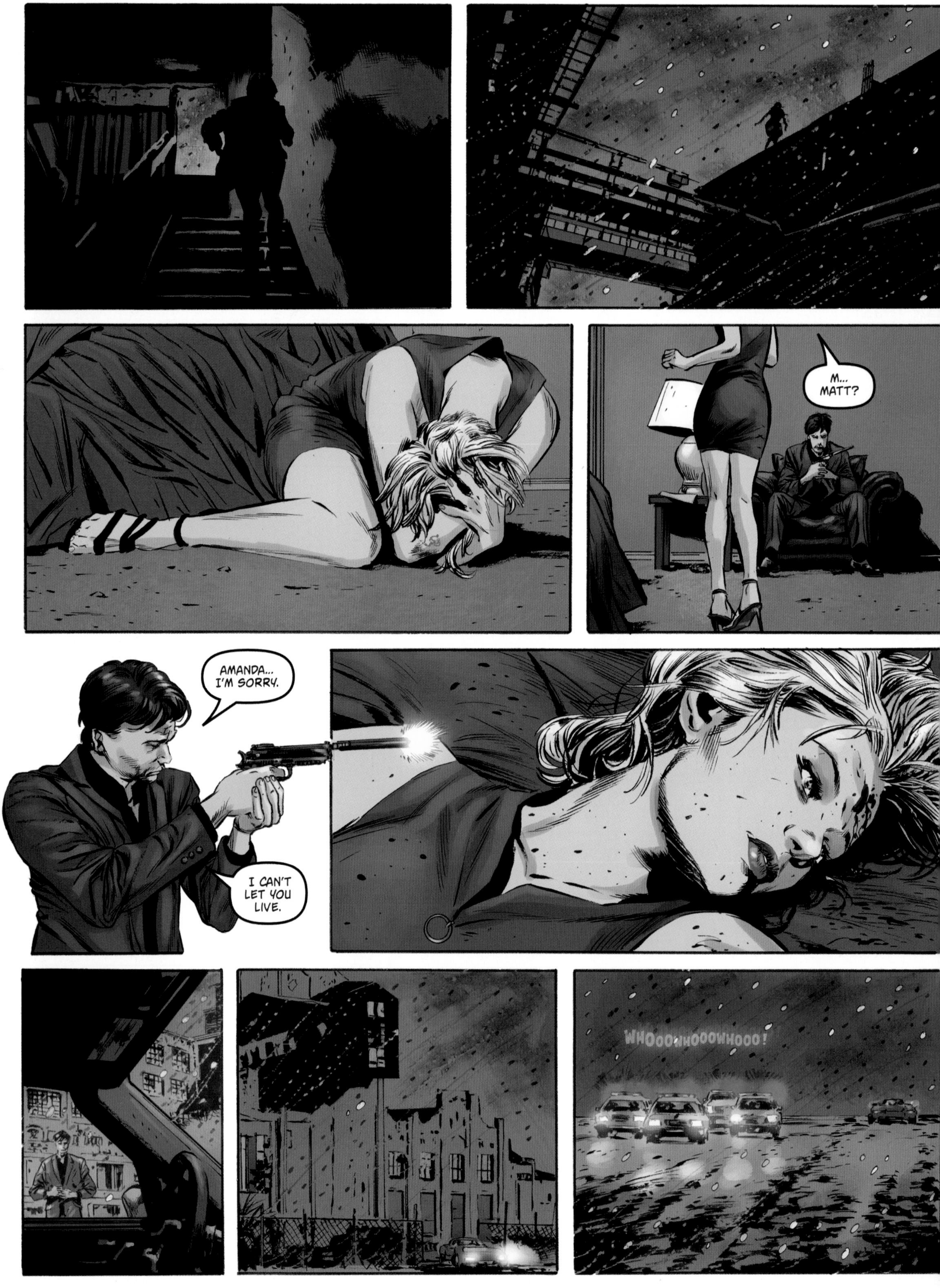
M... MATT?
AMANDA... I'M SORRY.
I CAN'T LET YOU LIVE.
WHOOOWHOOOWHOOO!

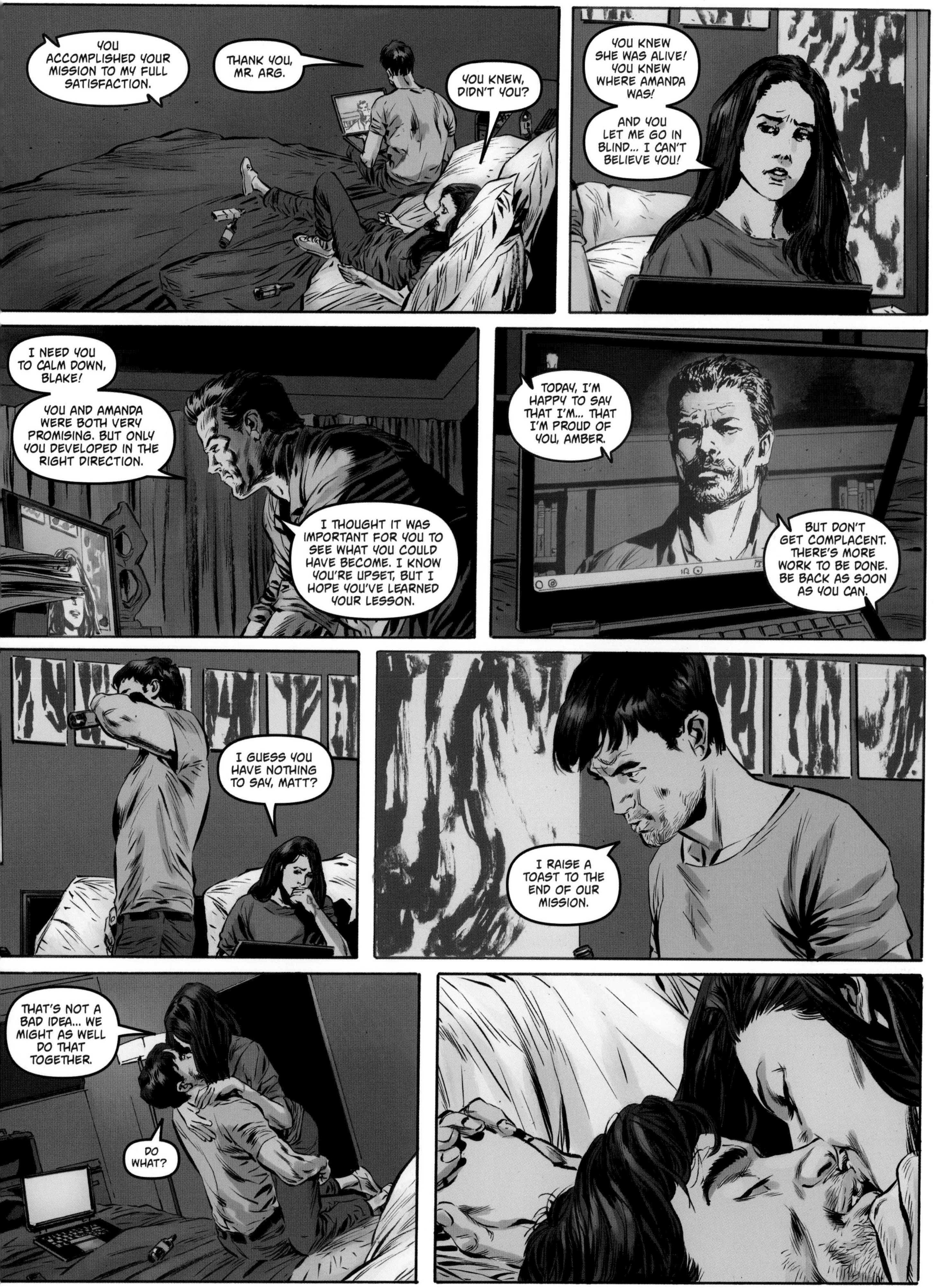
YOU ACCOMPLISHED YOUR MISSION TO MY FULL SATISFACTION.
THANK YOU, MR. ARG.
YOU KNEW, DIDN'T YOU?
YOU KNEW SHE WAS ALIVE! YOU KNEW WHERE AMANDA WAS!
AND YOU LET ME GO IN BLIND... I CAN'T BELIEVE YOU!
I NEED YOU TO CALM DOWN, BLAKE!
YOU AND AMANDA WERE BOTH VERY PROMISING. BUT ONLY YOU DEVELOPED IN THE RIGHT DIRECTION.
I THOUGHT IT WAS IMPORTANT FOR YOU TO SEE WHAT YOU COULD HAVE BECOME. I KNOW YOU'RE UPSET, BUT I HOPE YOU'VE LEARNED YOUR LESSON.
TODAY, I'M HAPPY TO SAY THAT I'M... THAT I'M PROUD OF YOU, AMBER.
BUT DON'T GET COMPLACENT. THERE'S MORE WORK TO BE DONE. BE BACK AS SOON AS YOU CAN.
I GUESS YOU HAVE NOTHING TO SAY, MATT?
I RAISE A TOAST TO THE END OF OUR MISSION.
THAT'S NOT A BAD IDEA... WE MIGHT AS WELL DO THAT TOGETHER.
DO WHAT?

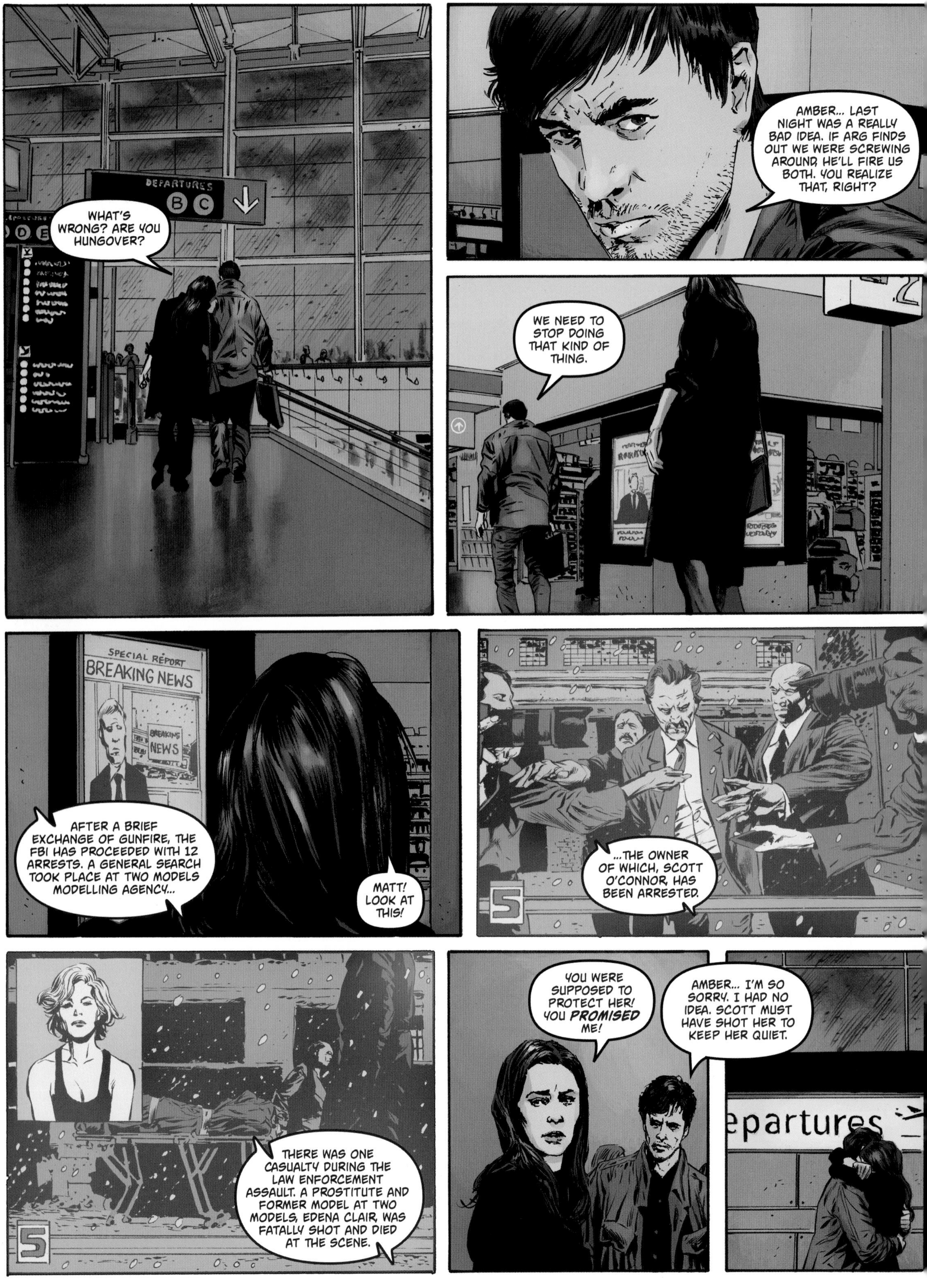
DEPARTURES
B C
WHAT'S WRONG? ARE YOU HUNGOVER?
AMBER... LAST NIGHT WAS A REALLY BAD IDEA. IF ARG FINDS OUT WE WERE SCREWING AROUND, HE'LL FIRE US BOTH. YOU REALIZE THAT, RIGHT?
WE NEED TO STOP DOING THAT KIND OF THING.
SPECIAL REPORT
BREAKING NEWS
BREAKING NEWS
AFTER A BRIEF EXCHANGE OF GUNFIRE, THE FBI HAS PROCEEDED WITH 12 ARRESTS. A GENERAL SEARCH TOOK PLACE AT TWO MODELS MODELLING AGENCY...
MATT! LOOK AT THIS!
...THE OWNER OF WHICH, SCOTT O'CONNOR, HAS BEEN ARRESTED.
5
THERE WAS ONE CASUALTY DURING THE LAW ENFORCEMENT ASSAULT. A PROSTITUTE AND FORMER MODEL AT TWO MODELS, EDENA CLAIR, WAS FATALLY SHOT AND DIED AT THE SCENE.
5
YOU WERE SUPPOSED TO PROTECT HER! YOU PROMISED ME!
AMBER... I'M SO SORRY. I HAD NO IDEA. SCOTT MUST HAVE SHOT HER TO KEEP HER QUIET.
epartures

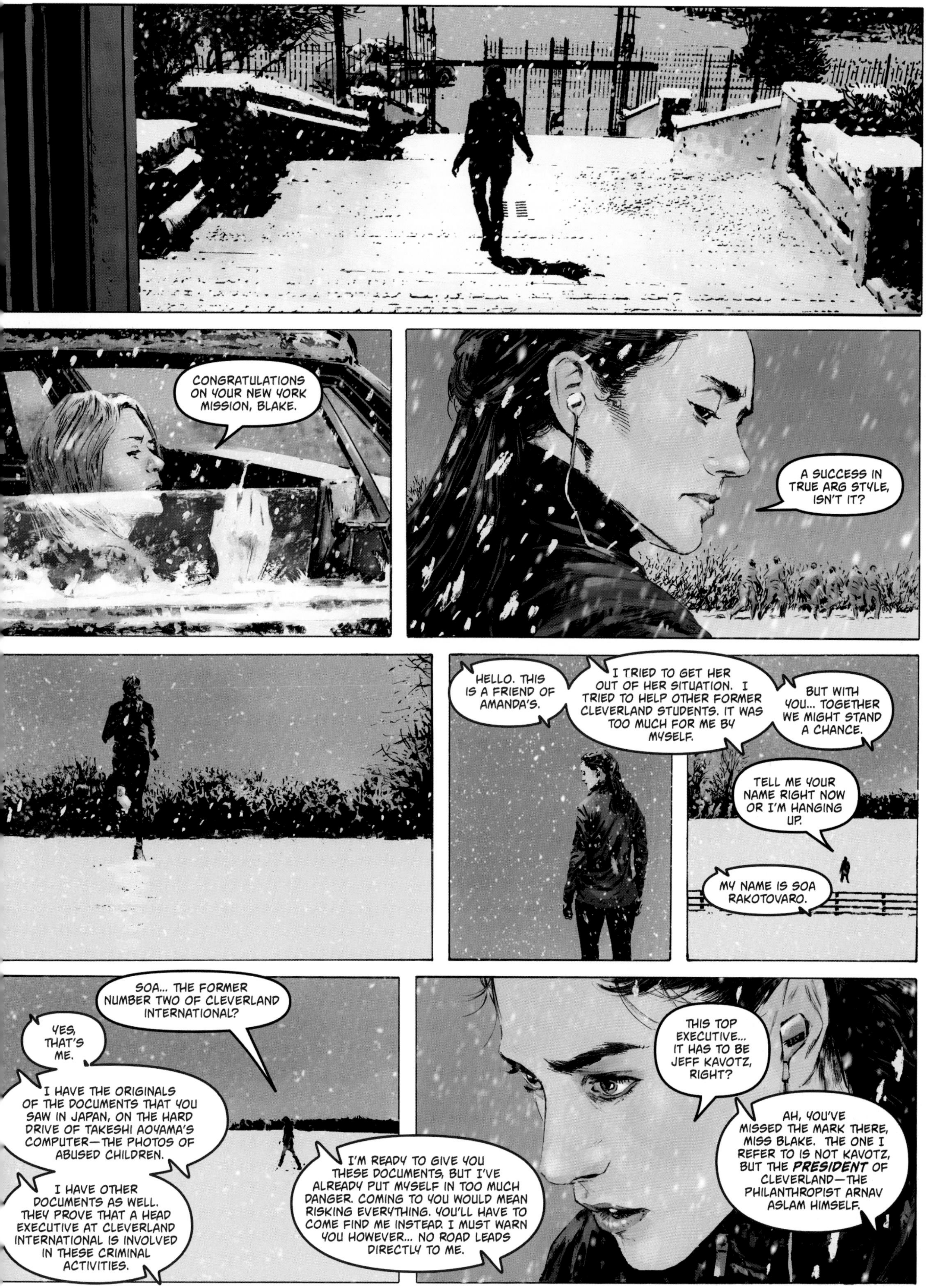
CONGRATULATIONS ON YOUR NEW YORK MISSION, BLAKE.
A SUCCESS IN TRUE ARG STYLE, ISN'T IT?
HELLO. THIS IS A FRIEND OF AMANDA'S.
I TRIED TO GET HER OUT OF HER SITUATION. I TRIED TO HELP OTHER FORMER CLEVERLAND STUDENTS. IT WAS TOO MUCH FOR ME BY MYSELF.
BUT WITH YOU... TOGETHER WE MIGHT STAND A CHANCE.
TELL ME YOUR NAME RIGHT NOW OR I'M HANGING UP.
MY NAME IS SOA RAKOTOVARO.
SOA... THE FORMER NUMBER TWO OF CLEVERLAND INTERNATIONAL?
YES, THAT'S ME.
I HAVE THE ORIGINALS OF THE DOCUMENTS THAT YOU SAW IN JAPAN, ON THE HARD DRIVE OF TAKESHI AOYAMA'S COMPUTER—THE PHOTOS OF ABUSED CHILDREN.
I HAVE OTHER DOCUMENTS AS WELL. THEY PROVE THAT A HEAD EXECUTIVE AT CLEVERLAND INTERNATIONAL IS INVOLVED IN THESE CRIMINAL ACTIVITIES.
I'M READY TO GIVE YOU THESE DOCUMENTS, BUT I'VE ALREADY PUT MYSELF IN TOO MUCH DANGER. COMING TO YOU WOULD MEAN RISKING EVERYTHING. YOU'LL HAVE TO COME FIND ME INSTEAD. I MUST WARN YOU HOWEVER... NO ROAD LEADS DIRECTLY TO ME.
THIS TOP EXECUTIVE... IT HAS TO BE JEFF KAVOTZ, RIGHT?
AH, YOU'VE MISSED THE MARK THERE, MISS BLAKE. THE ONE I REFER TO IS NOT KAVOTZ, BUT THE *PRESIDENT* OF CLEVERLAND—THE PHILANTHROPIST ARNAV ASLAM HIMSELF.

DON'T GET TOO EXCITED OVER THIS. IT SOUNDS LIKE SOMEONE IS MESSING WITH YOU... OR WORSE, IT COULD BE A TRAP.

SOA RAKOTOVARO RETIRED FOUR YEARS AGO DUE TO A SERIOUS ILLNESS.

AND WHERE DID HE GO?

NO IDEA. WE'LL HAVE TO FIND HIM OURSELVES. WITH FACEX, WE SHOULD HAVE A SHOT.

AMBER... YOU *KNOW* WHAT I THINK ABOUT USING ARGON'S RESOURCES FOR YOUR OWN PURPOSES.

MY PURPOSES ARE JUST, MATT. WE CAN SAVE *THOUSANDS* OF CHILDREN! PETER ARG WILL HAVE TO ACKNOWLEDGE THAT.

IT'LL TAKE *DAYS*, JUST LIKE YOUR SEARCH FOR KAVOTZ. AND JUST LIKE WITH KAVOTZ, WE'LL GAIN NOTHING.

BUT SUIT YOURSELF. BYE.

SEARCH
1.067%

SEARCH
100.00%

FINALLY! IT FOUND SOMETHING!

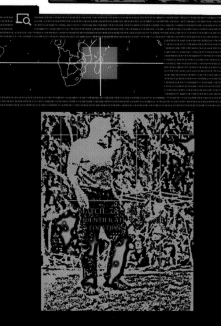

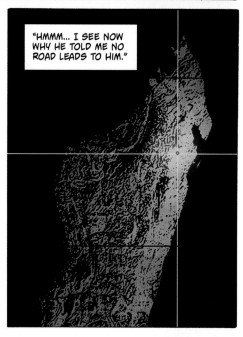

"HMMM... I SEE NOW WHY HE TOLD ME NO ROAD LEADS TO HIM."

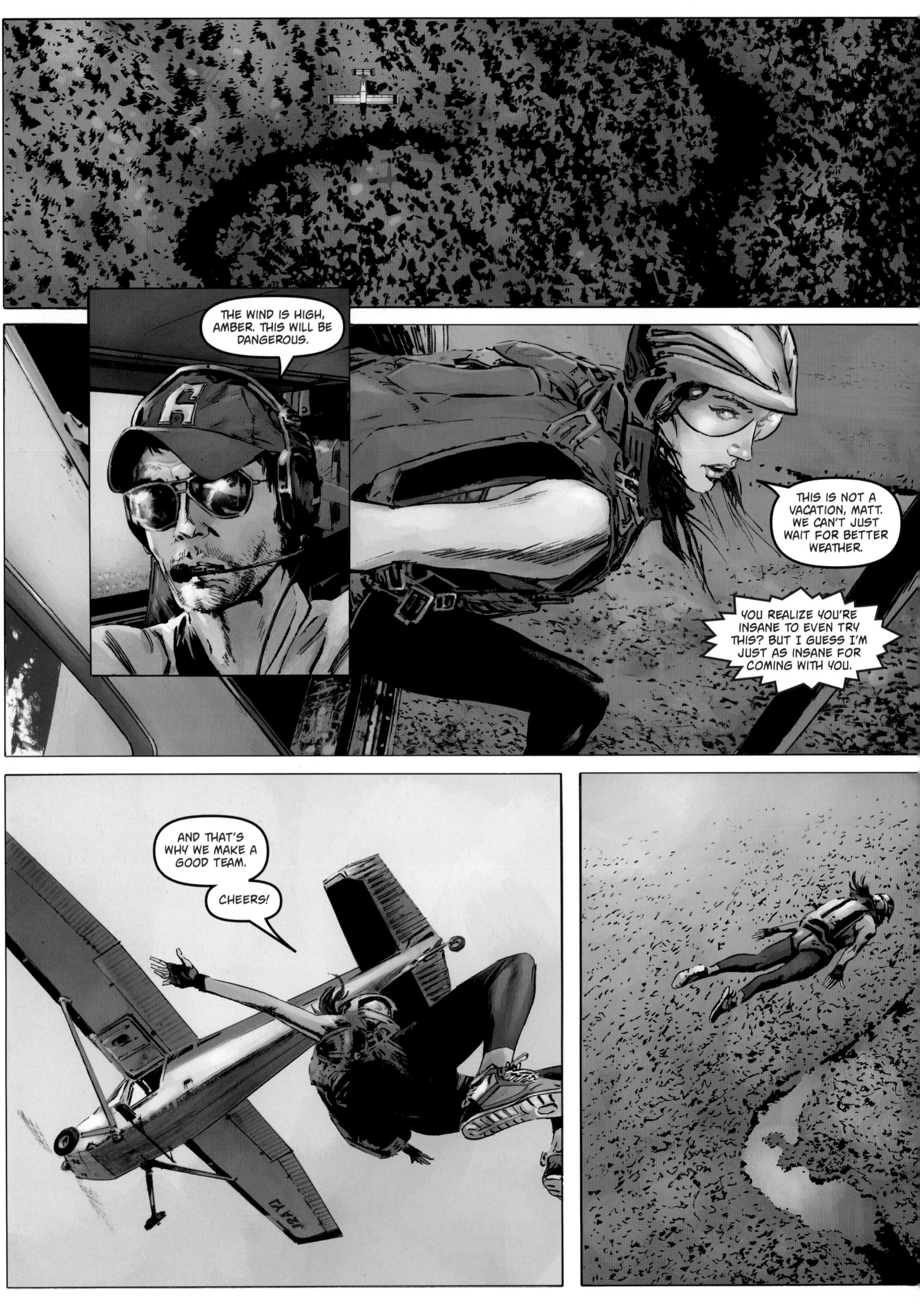
THE WIND IS HIGH, AMBER. THIS WILL BE DANGEROUS.
THIS IS NOT A VACATION, MATT. WE CAN'T JUST WAIT FOR BETTER WEATHER.
YOU REALIZE YOU'RE INSANE TO EVEN TRY THIS? BUT I GUESS I'M JUST AS INSANE FOR COMING WITH YOU.
AND THAT'S WHY WE MAKE A GOOD TEAM.
CHEERS!

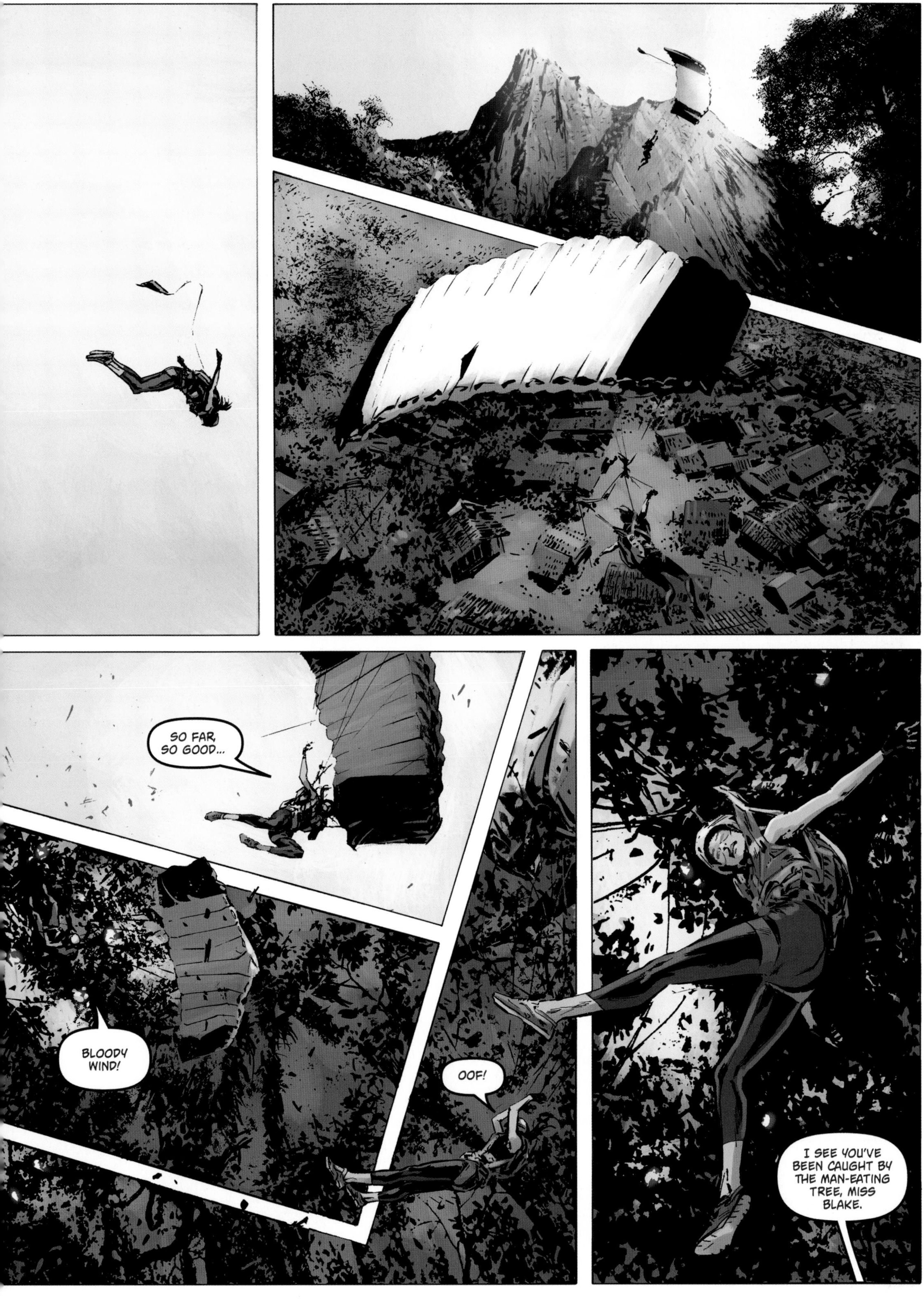
SO FAR, SO GOOD...
BLOODY WIND!
OOF!
I SEE YOU'VE BEEN CAUGHT BY THE MAN-EATING TREE, MISS BLAKE.

THE MAN-EATING TREE?

A LEGEND CREATED BY THE WHITE PEOPLE A LONG TIME AGO HAS IT THAT THIS TREE EATS PEOPLE.

I HOPE YOU HAVE SOMETHING MORE FOR ME THAN LEGENDS FROM LONG AGO.

CLEVERLAND... IT'S THE FIGHT OF MY LIFE.

WHEN ASLAM REALIZED I WASN'T GOING TO JUST SILENTLY WATCH AS HE ABUSED CHILDREN, HE PUT OUT A CONTRACT ON MY HEAD. THEY GOT ME WITH A CAR BOMB, BUT... BY SOME MIRACLE, I ESCAPED AND THEY THOUGHT I WAS DEAD.

I'VE BEEN HIDING HERE FOR FOUR YEARS NOW.

NOW, THANKS TO YOUR EFFORTS, I FINALLY HAVE THE MEANS TO TAKE DOWN ASLAM AND HIS ACCOMPLICES.

FOUR YEARS... MR. RAKOTOVARO, IT TOOK YOU A LONG TIME TO DECIDE TO ACT.

TOO LONG, PERHAPS. TO THINK OF THE DAMAGE DONE TO THE CHILDREN DURING THIS TIME...

BUT, AT LAST, ASLAM WILL PAY FOR EVERYTHING HE HAS DONE.

WE HAVE TO EXPOSE HIM IN PUBLIC SO HE CAN'T JUST SILENCE US. I KNOW THE PERFECT MOMENT TO DO IT: AT THE NEXT CONVENTION OF CLEVERLAND INTERNATIONAL, IN MUMBAI NEXT WEEK, WE WILL PUBLICLY DISPLAY THE DOCUMENTS YOU'VE SECURED.

THEN THE WHOLE PLANET WILL KNOW THE TRUTH, AND WE CAN ERADICATE THIS FILTH ONCE AND FOR ALL.

CAMILA DOREGO!

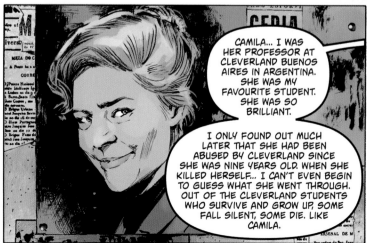

CAMILA... I WAS HER PROFESSOR AT CLEVERLAND BUENOS AIRES IN ARGENTINA. SHE WAS MY FAVOURITE STUDENT. SHE WAS SO BRILLIANT.

I ONLY FOUND OUT MUCH LATER THAT SHE HAD BEEN ABUSED BY CLEVERLAND SINCE SHE WAS NINE YEARS OLD. WHEN SHE KILLED HERSELF... I CAN'T EVEN BEGIN TO GUESS WHAT SHE WENT THROUGH. OUT OF THE CLEVERLAND STUDENTS WHO SURVIVE AND GROW UP, SOME FALL SILENT, SOME DIE. LIKE CAMILA.

"THE OTHERS... BECOME KILLERS."

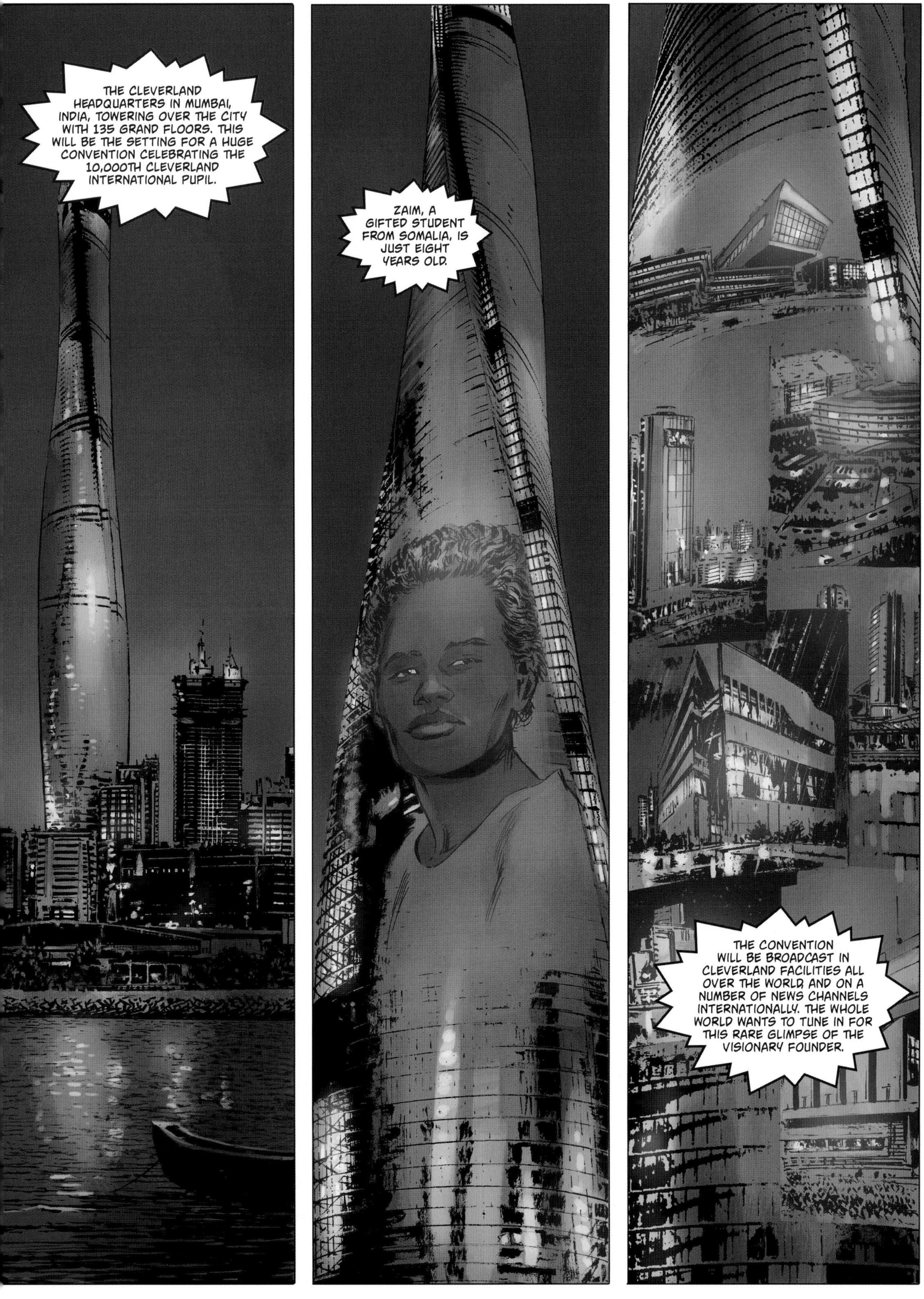
THE CLEVERLAND HEADQUARTERS IN MUMBAI, INDIA, TOWERING OVER THE CITY WITH 135 GRAND FLOORS. THIS WILL BE THE SETTING FOR A HUGE CONVENTION CELEBRATING THE 10,000TH CLEVERLAND INTERNATIONAL PUPIL.
ZAIM, A GIFTED STUDENT FROM SOMALIA, IS JUST EIGHT YEARS OLD.
THE CONVENTION WILL BE BROADCAST IN CLEVERLAND FACILITIES ALL OVER THE WORLD AND ON A NUMBER OF NEWS CHANNELS INTERNATIONALLY. THE WHOLE WORLD WANTS TO TUNE IN FOR THIS RARE GLIMPSE OF THE VISIONARY FOUNDER.

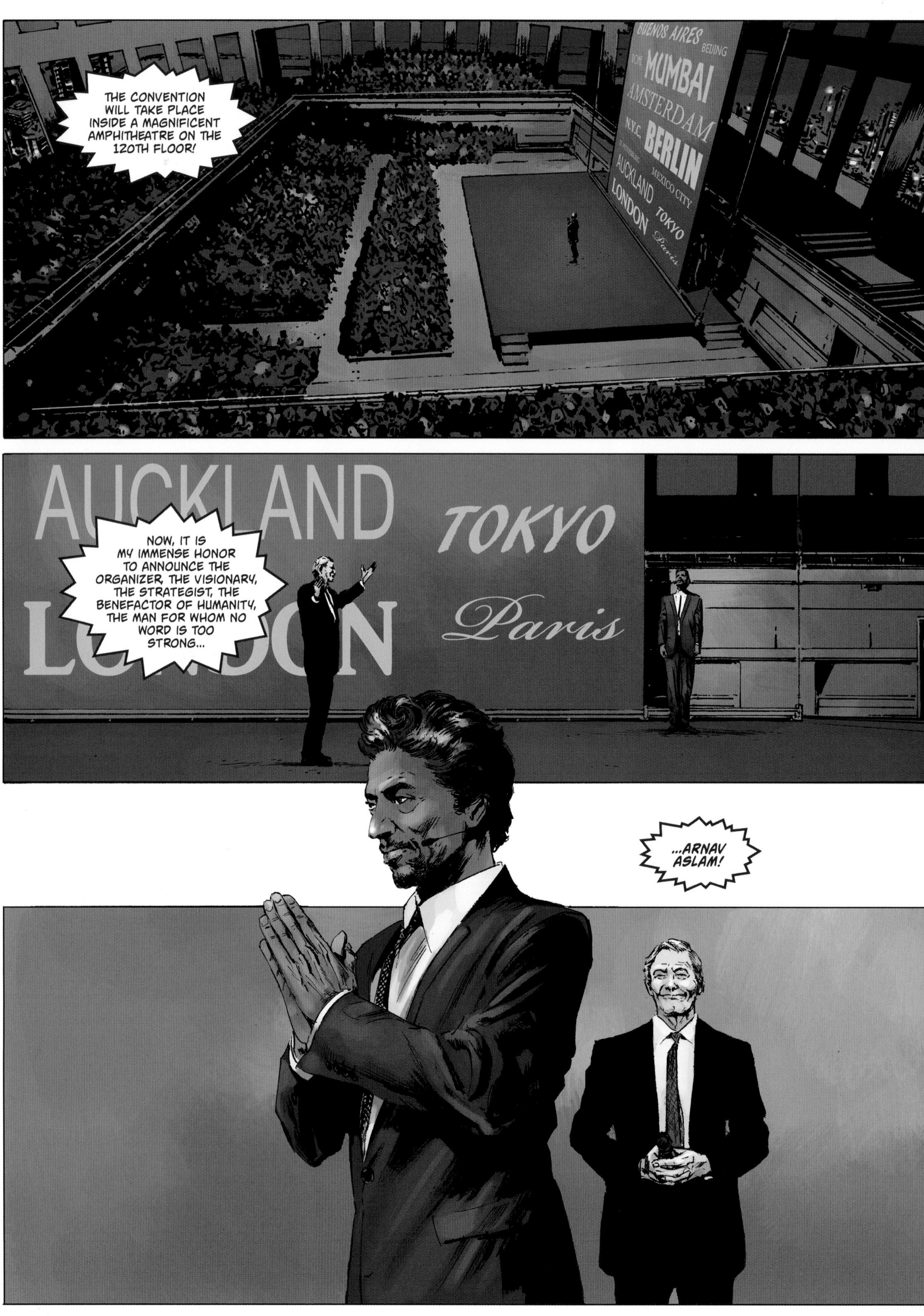
THE CONVENTION WILL TAKE PLACE INSIDE A MAGNIFICENT AMPHITHEATRE ON THE 120TH FLOOR!
BUENOS AIRES
BEIJING
ROME
MUMBAI
AMSTERDAM
N.Y.C.
BERLIN
MEXICO CITY
AUCKLAND
LONDON
TOKYO
Paris
NOW, IT IS MY IMMENSE HONOR TO ANNOUNCE THE ORGANIZER, THE VISIONARY, THE STRATEGIST, THE BENEFACTOR OF HUMANITY, THE MAN FOR WHOM NO WORD IS TOO STRONG...
...ARNAV ASLAM!

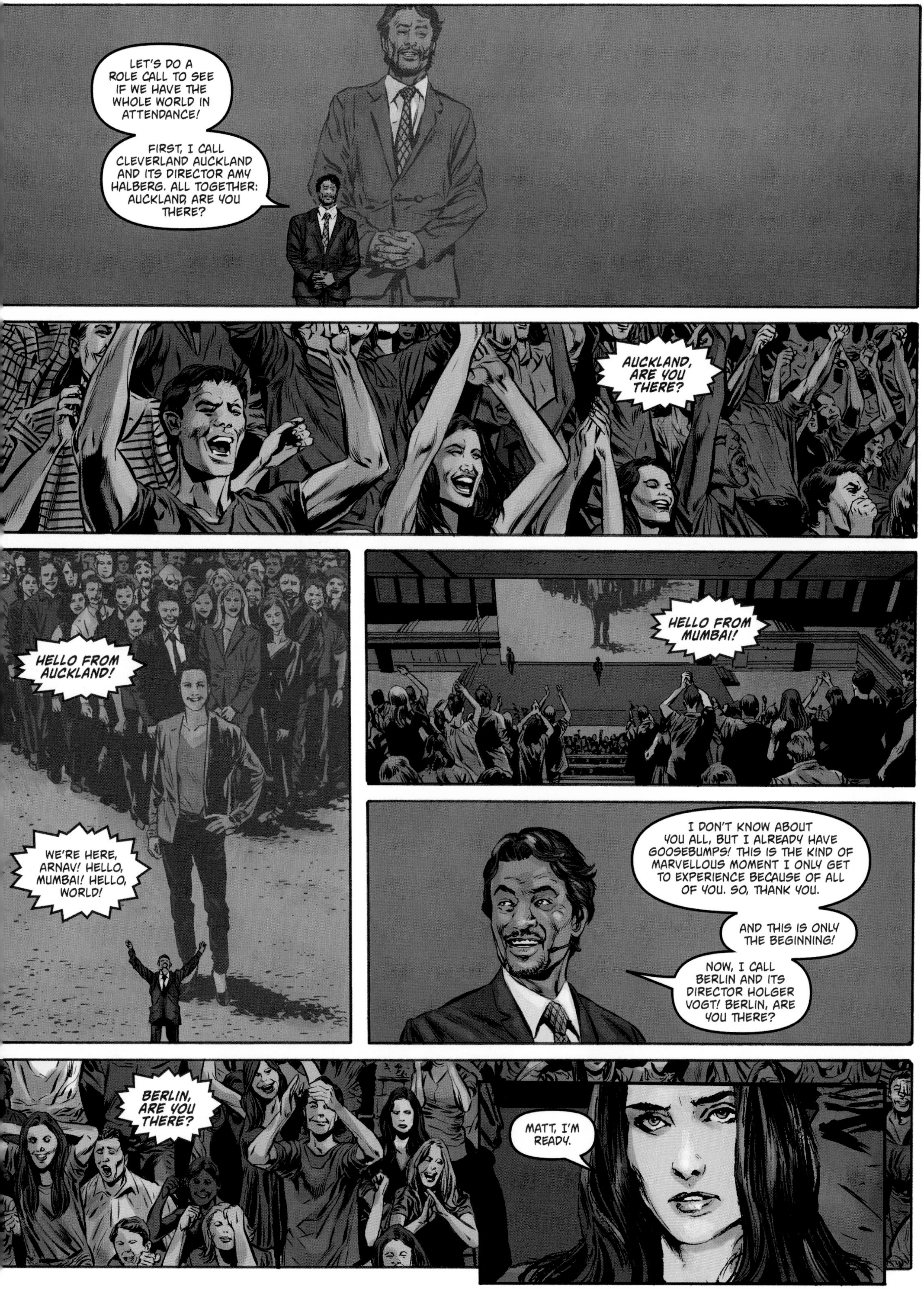

LET'S DO A ROLE CALL TO SEE IF WE HAVE THE WHOLE WORLD IN ATTENDANCE!
FIRST, I CALL CLEVERLAND AUCKLAND AND ITS DIRECTOR AMY HALBERG. ALL TOGETHER: AUCKLAND, ARE YOU THERE?
AUCKLAND, ARE YOU THERE?
HELLO FROM AUCKLAND!
WE'RE HERE, ARNAV! HELLO, MUMBAI! HELLO, WORLD!
HELLO FROM MUMBAI!
I DON'T KNOW ABOUT YOU ALL, BUT I ALREADY HAVE GOOSEBUMPS! THIS IS THE KIND OF MARVELLOUS MOMENT I ONLY GET TO EXPERIENCE BECAUSE OF ALL OF YOU. SO, THANK YOU.
AND THIS IS ONLY THE BEGINNING!
NOW, I CALL BERLIN AND ITS DIRECTOR HOLGER VOGT! BERLIN, ARE YOU THERE?
BERLIN, ARE YOU THERE?
MATT, I'M READY.

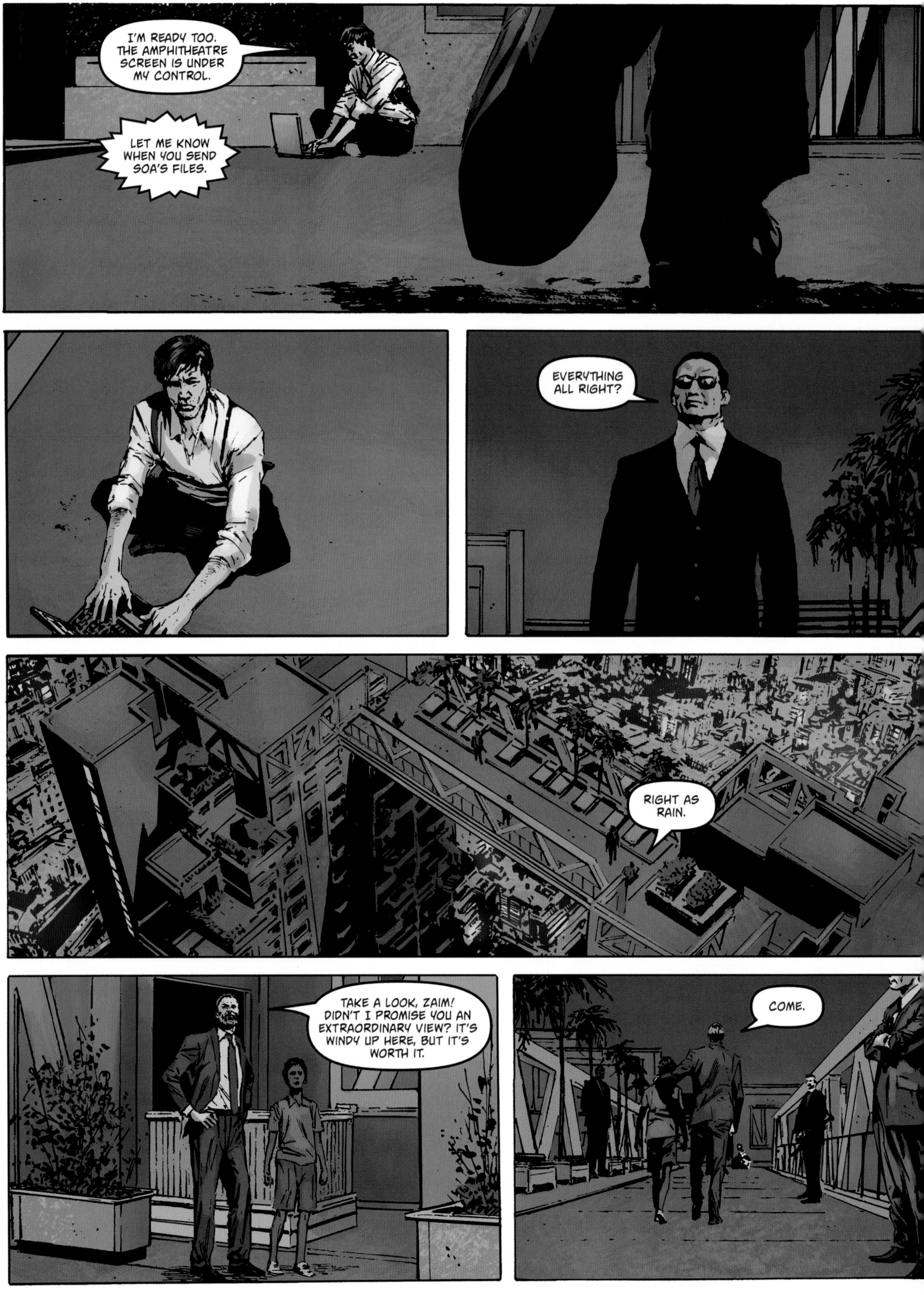
I'M READY TOO. THE AMPHITHEATRE SCREEN IS UNDER MY CONTROL.
LET ME KNOW WHEN YOU SEND SOA'S FILES.
EVERYTHING ALL RIGHT?
RIGHT AS RAIN.
TAKE A LOOK, ZAIM! DIDN'T I PROMISE YOU AN EXTRAORDINARY VIEW? IT'S WINDY UP HERE, BUT IT'S WORTH IT.
COME.

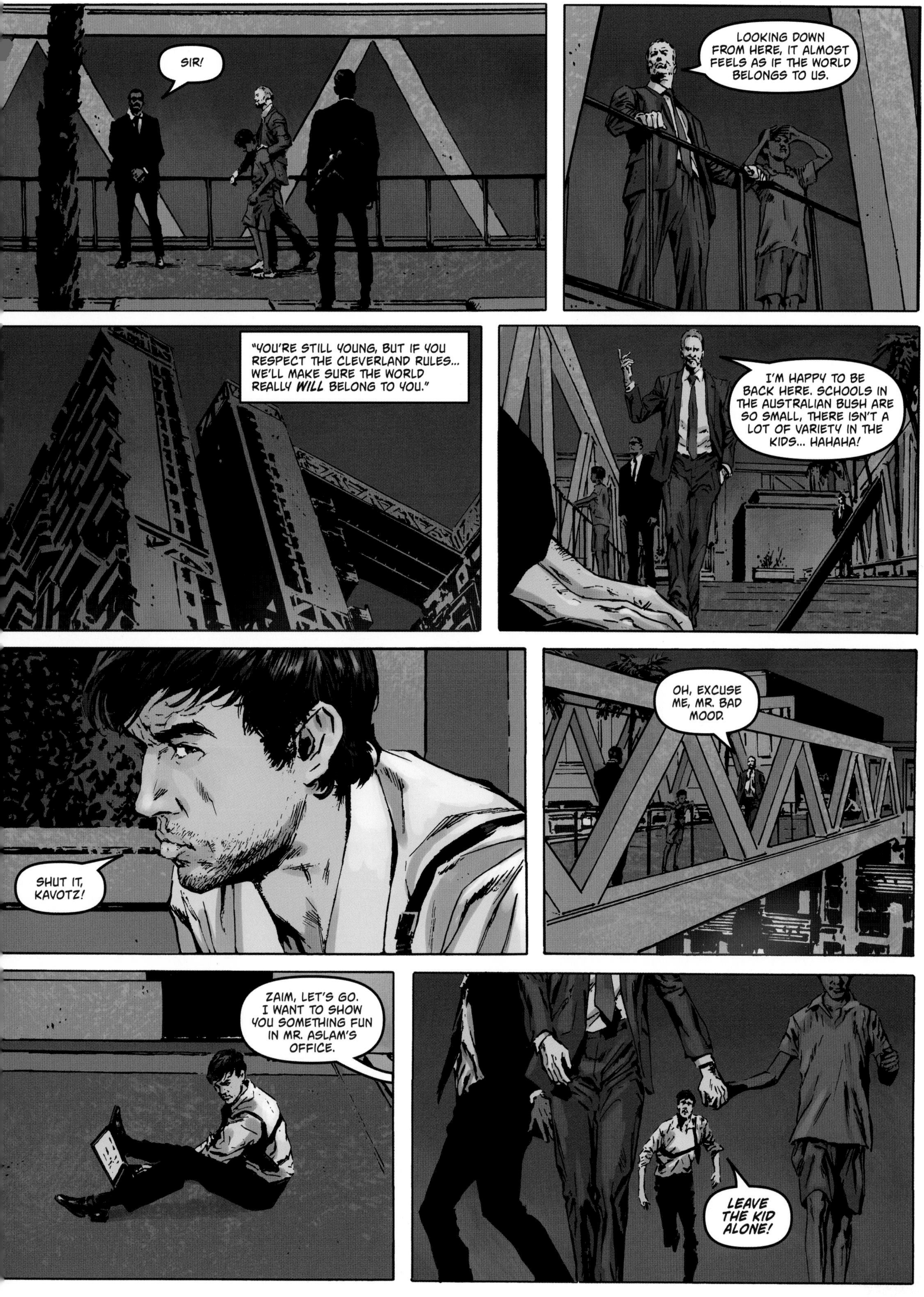
SIR!
LOOKING DOWN FROM HERE, IT ALMOST FEELS AS IF THE WORLD BELONGS TO US.
"YOU'RE STILL YOUNG, BUT IF YOU RESPECT THE CLEVERLAND RULES... WE'LL MAKE SURE THE WORLD REALLY WILL BELONG TO YOU."
I'M HAPPY TO BE BACK HERE. SCHOOLS IN THE AUSTRALIAN BUSH ARE SO SMALL, THERE ISN'T A LOT OF VARIETY IN THE KIDS... HAHAHA!
SHUT IT, KAVOTZ!
OH, EXCUSE ME, MR. BAD MOOD.
ZAIM, LET'S GO. I WANT TO SHOW YOU SOMETHING FUN IN MR. ASLAM'S OFFICE.
LEAVE THE KID ALONE!

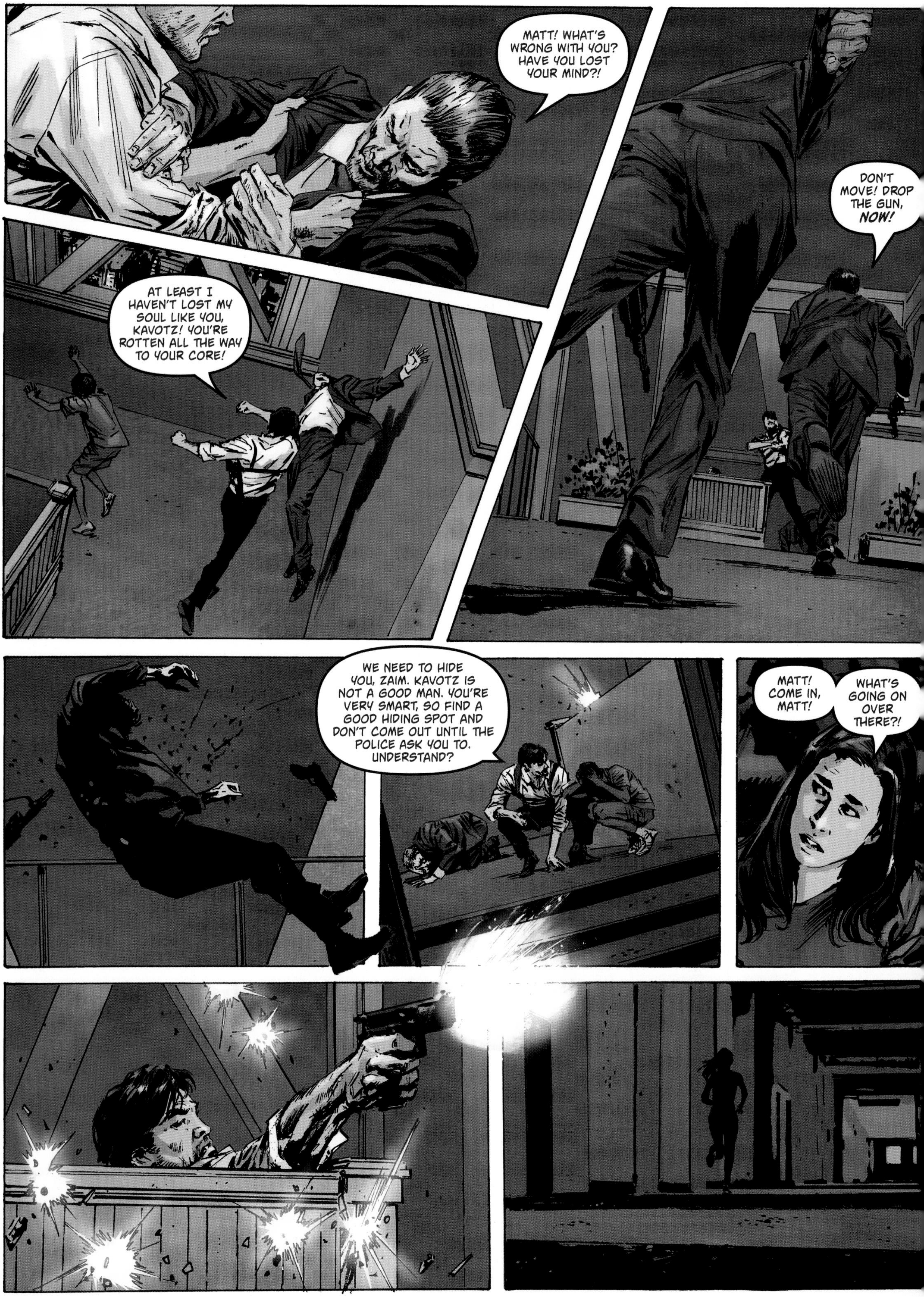
MATT! WHAT'S WRONG WITH YOU? HAVE YOU LOST YOUR MIND?!
DON'T MOVE! DROP THE GUN, **NOW!**
AT LEAST I HAVEN'T LOST MY SOUL LIKE YOU, KAVOTZ! YOU'RE ROTTEN ALL THE WAY TO YOUR CORE!
WE NEED TO HIDE YOU, ZAIM. KAVOTZ IS NOT A GOOD MAN. YOU'RE VERY SMART, SO FIND A GOOD HIDING SPOT AND DON'T COME OUT UNTIL THE POLICE ASK YOU TO. UNDERSTAND?
MATT! COME IN, MATT!
WHAT'S GOING ON OVER THERE?!

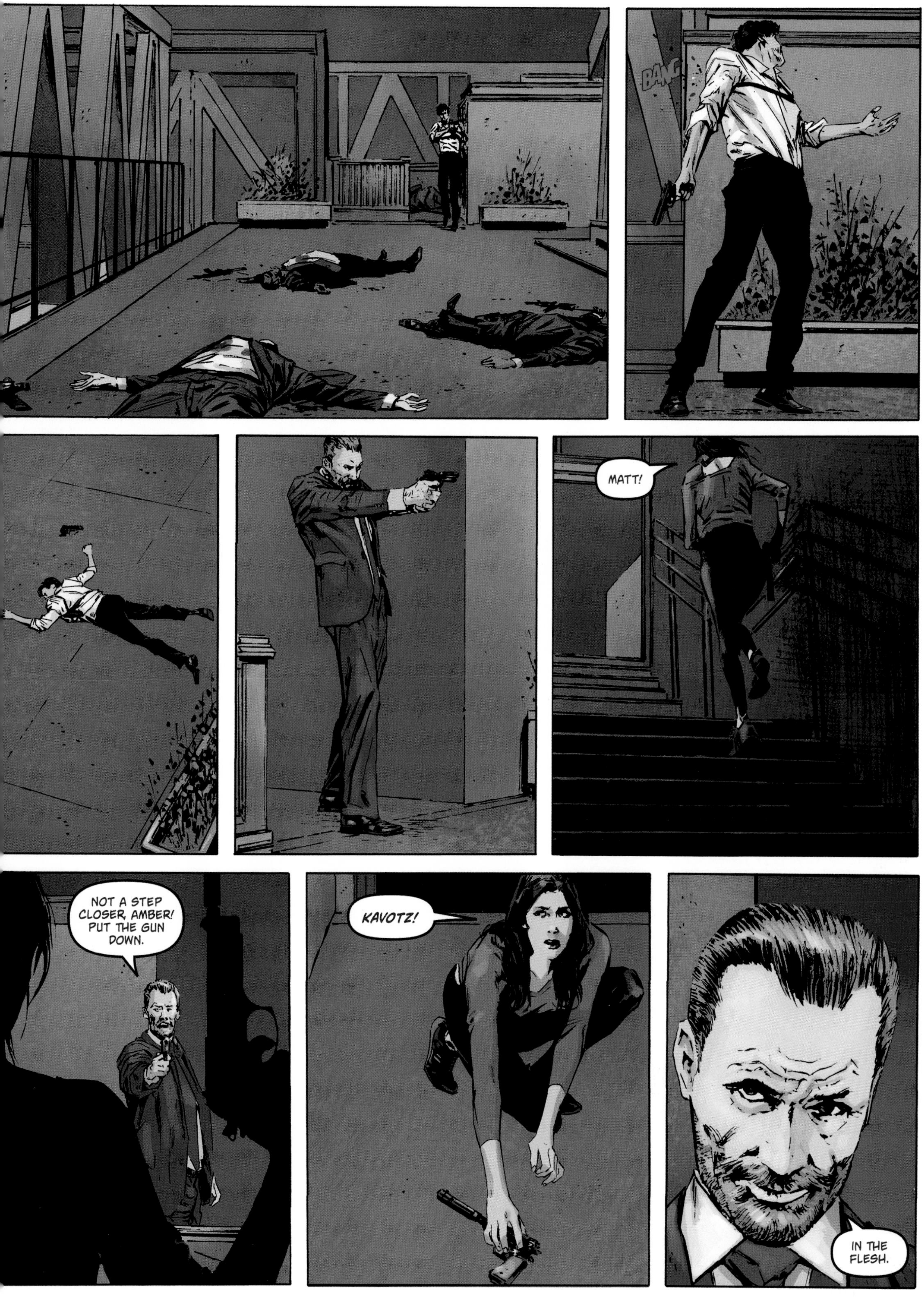
BANG
MATT!
NOT A STEP CLOSER, AMBER! PUT THE GUN DOWN.
KAVOTZ!
IN THE FLESH.

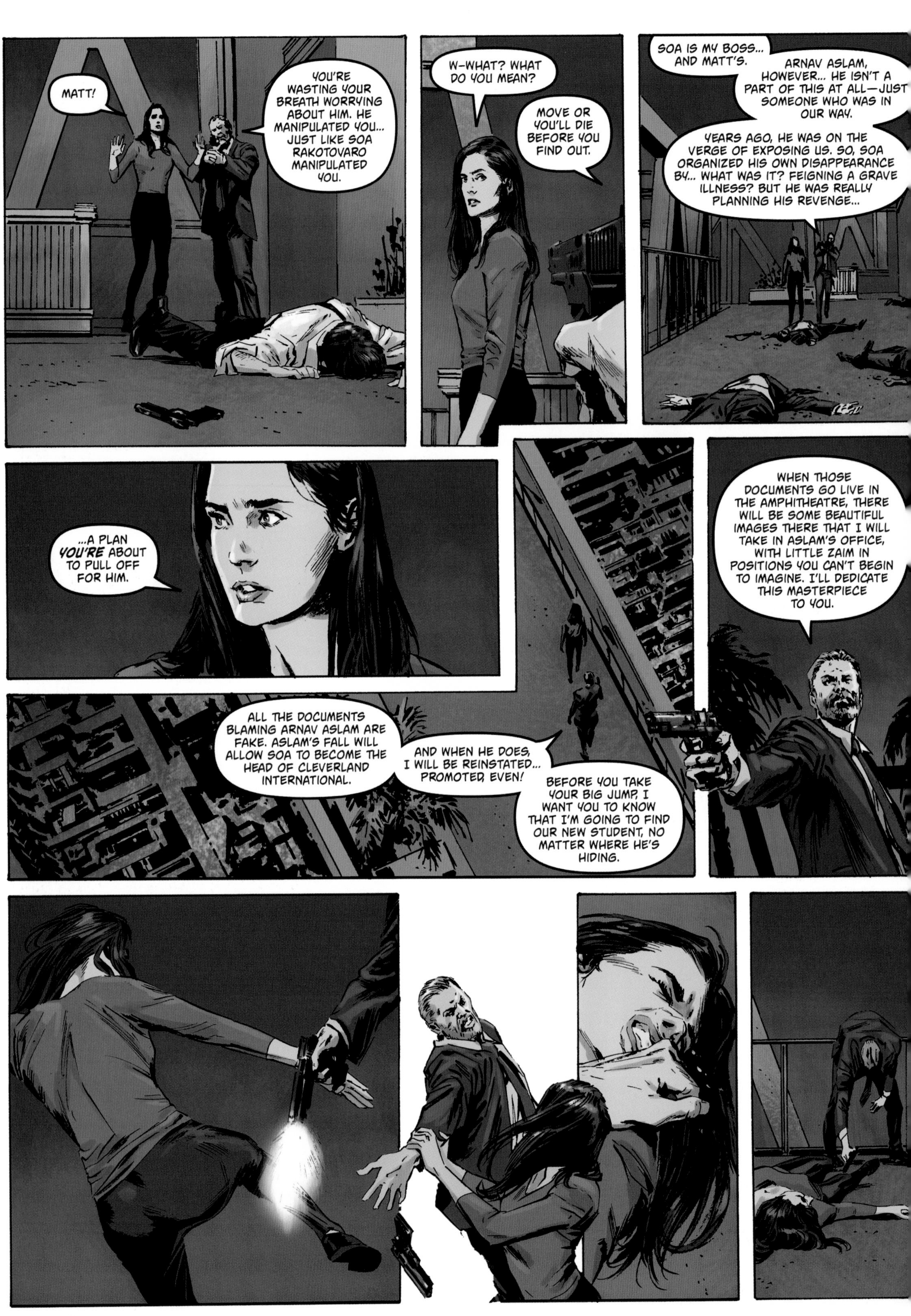

MATT!
YOU'RE WASTING YOUR BREATH WORRYING ABOUT HIM. HE MANIPULATED YOU... JUST LIKE SOA RAKOTOVARO MANIPULATED YOU.
W-WHAT? WHAT DO YOU MEAN?
MOVE OR YOU'LL DIE BEFORE YOU FIND OUT.
SOA IS MY BOSS... AND MATT'S.
ARNAV ASLAM, HOWEVER... HE ISN'T A PART OF THIS AT ALL—JUST SOMEONE WHO WAS IN OUR WAY.
YEARS AGO, HE WAS ON THE VERGE OF EXPOSING US. SO, SOA ORGANIZED HIS OWN DISAPPEARANCE BY... WHAT WAS IT? FEIGNING A GRAVE ILLNESS? BUT HE WAS REALLY PLANNING HIS REVENGE...
...A PLAN YOU'RE ABOUT TO PULL OFF FOR HIM.
ALL THE DOCUMENTS BLAMING ARNAV ASLAM ARE FAKE. ASLAM'S FALL WILL ALLOW SOA TO BECOME THE HEAD OF CLEVERLAND INTERNATIONAL.
AND WHEN HE DOES, I WILL BE REINSTATED... PROMOTED, EVEN!
WHEN THOSE DOCUMENTS GO LIVE IN THE AMPHITHEATRE, THERE WILL BE SOME BEAUTIFUL IMAGES THERE THAT I WILL TAKE IN ASLAM'S OFFICE, WITH LITTLE ZAIM IN POSITIONS YOU CAN'T BEGIN TO IMAGINE. I'LL DEDICATE THIS MASTERPIECE TO YOU.
BEFORE YOU TAKE YOUR BIG JUMP, I WANT YOU TO KNOW THAT I'M GOING TO FIND OUR NEW STUDENT, NO MATTER WHERE HE'S HIDING.

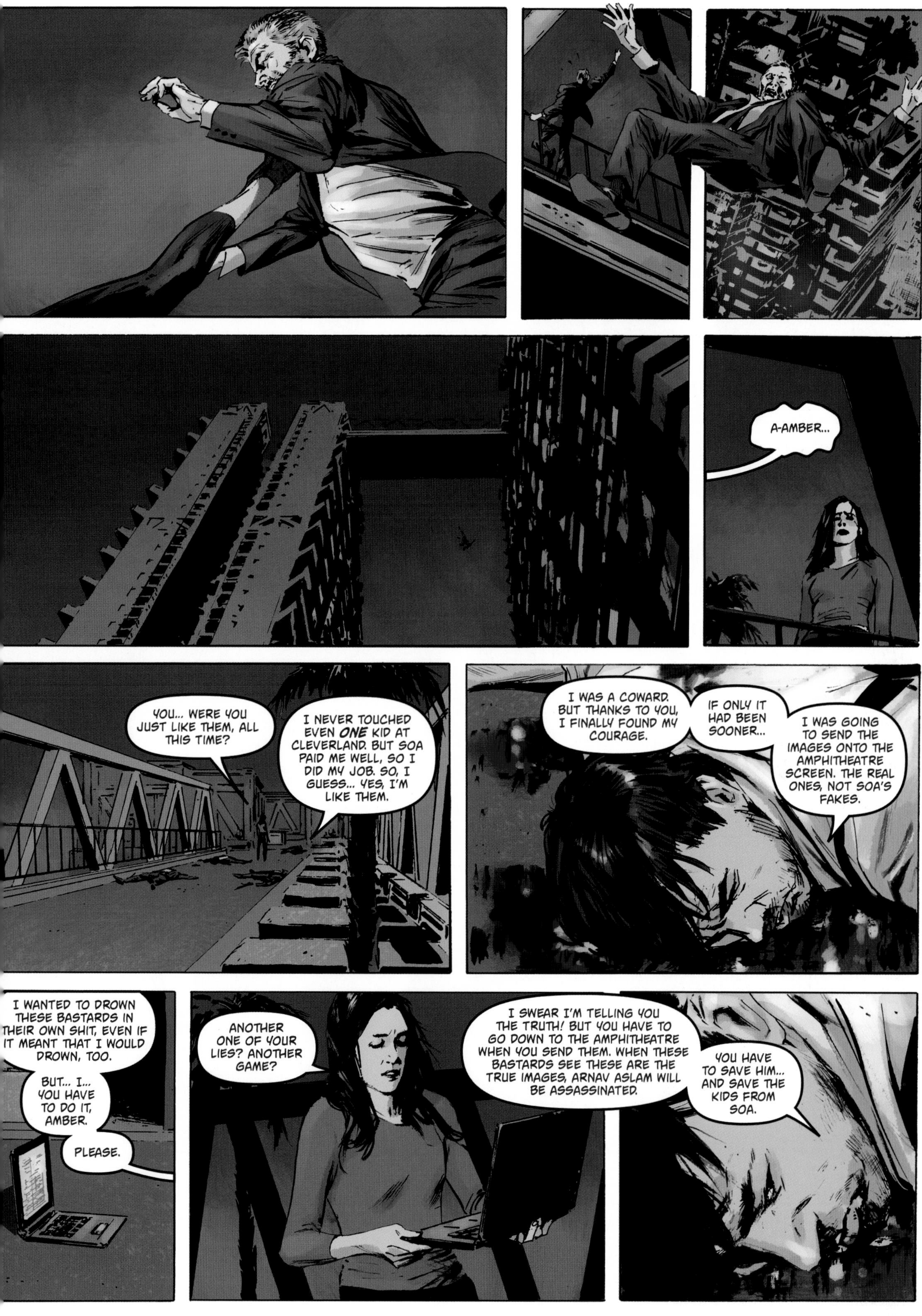
A-AMBER...
YOU... WERE YOU JUST LIKE THEM, ALL THIS TIME?
I NEVER TOUCHED EVEN ONE KID AT CLEVERLAND. BUT SOA PAID ME WELL, SO I DID MY JOB. SO, I GUESS... YES, I'M LIKE THEM.
I WAS A COWARD. BUT THANKS TO YOU, I FINALLY FOUND MY COURAGE.
IF ONLY IT HAD BEEN SOONER...
I WAS GOING TO SEND THE IMAGES ONTO THE AMPHITHEATRE SCREEN. THE REAL ONES, NOT SOA'S FAKES.
I WANTED TO DROWN THESE BASTARDS IN THEIR OWN SHIT, EVEN IF IT MEANT THAT I WOULD DROWN, TOO.
BUT... I... YOU HAVE TO DO IT, AMBER.
PLEASE.
ANOTHER ONE OF YOUR LIES? ANOTHER GAME?
I SWEAR I'M TELLING YOU THE TRUTH! BUT YOU HAVE TO GO DOWN TO THE AMPHITHEATRE WHEN YOU SEND THEM. WHEN THESE BASTARDS SEE THESE ARE THE TRUE IMAGES, ARNAV ASLAM WILL BE ASSASSINATED.
YOU HAVE TO SAVE HIM... AND SAVE THE KIDS FROM SOA.

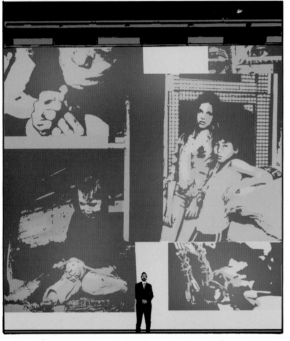

WHAT IS THIS?
WHAT ARE THESE...
HORRORS?

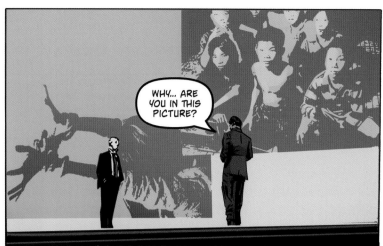

WHY... ARE YOU IN THIS PICTURE?

GET RID OF HIM!

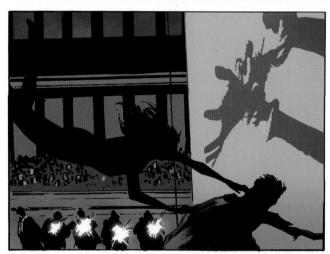

HE SAVED US—WE HAVE TO PROTECT HIM!

COME ON!

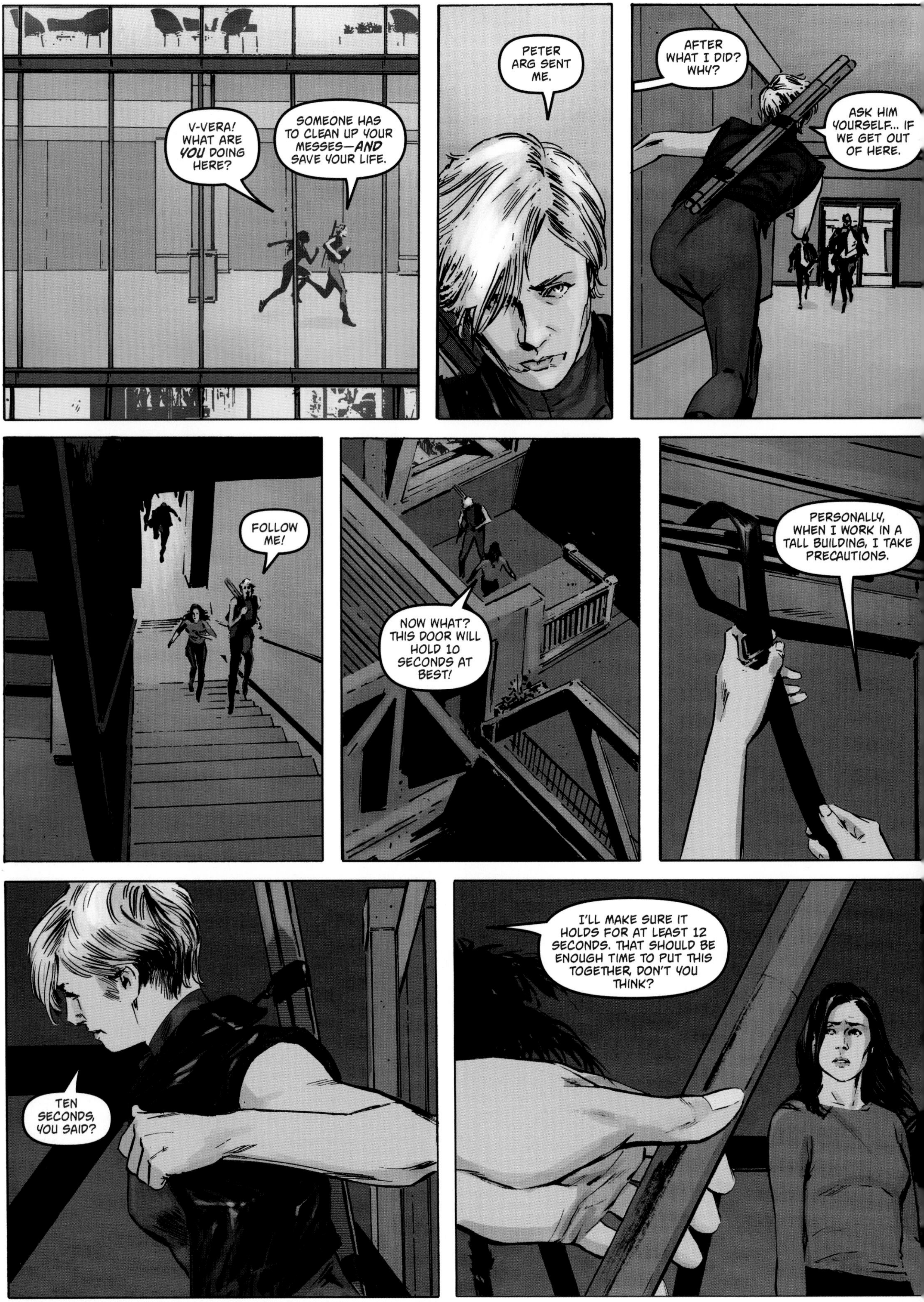
V-VERA! WHAT ARE YOU DOING HERE?
SOMEONE HAS TO CLEAN UP YOUR MESSES—AND SAVE YOUR LIFE.
PETER ARG SENT ME.
AFTER WHAT I DID? WHY?
ASK HIM YOURSELF... IF WE GET OUT OF HERE.
FOLLOW ME!
NOW WHAT? THIS DOOR WILL HOLD 10 SECONDS AT BEST!
PERSONALLY, WHEN I WORK IN A TALL BUILDING, I TAKE PRECAUTIONS.
TEN SECONDS, YOU SAID?
I'LL MAKE SURE IT HOLDS FOR AT LEAST 12 SECONDS. THAT SHOULD BE ENOUGH TIME TO PUT THIS TOGETHER, DON'T YOU THINK?

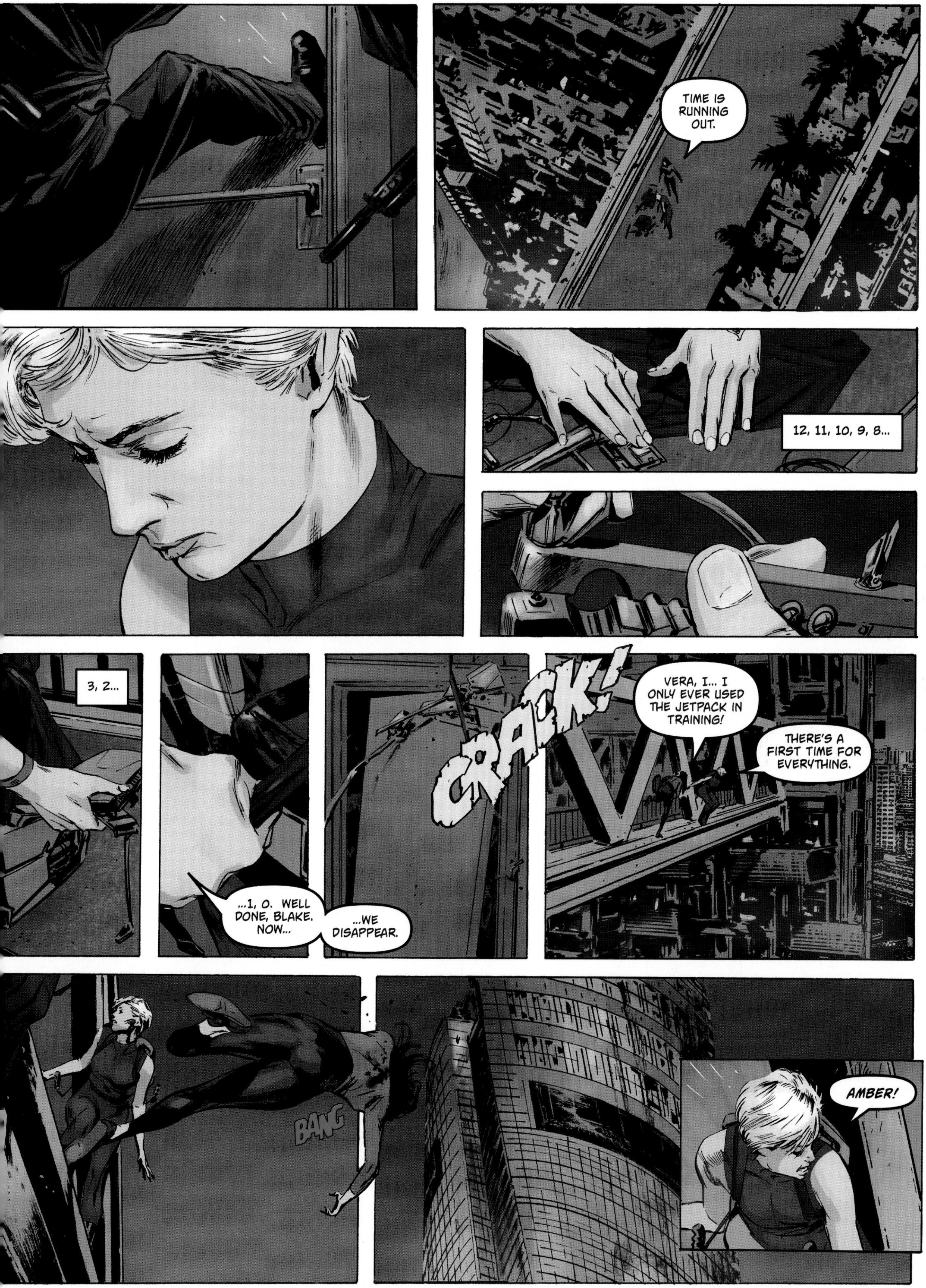
TIME IS RUNNING OUT.
12, 11, 10, 9, 8...
3, 2...
...1, 0. WELL DONE, BLAKE. NOW...
...WE DISAPPEAR.
CRACK!
VERA, I... I ONLY EVER USED THE JETPACK IN TRAINING!
THERE'S A FIRST TIME FOR EVERYTHING.
BANG
AMBER!

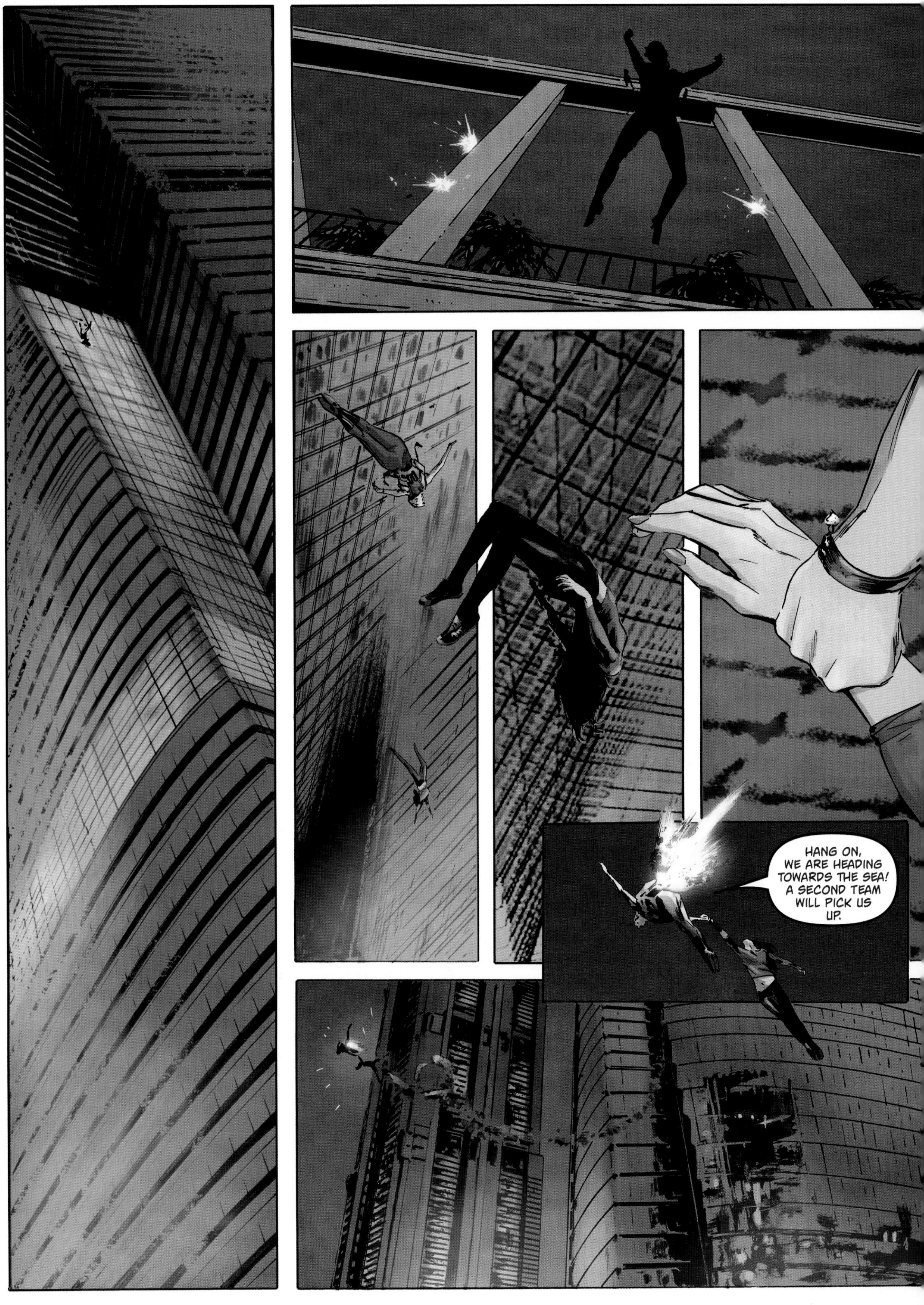
HANG ON, WE ARE HEADING TOWARDS THE SEA! A SECOND TEAM WILL PICK US UP.

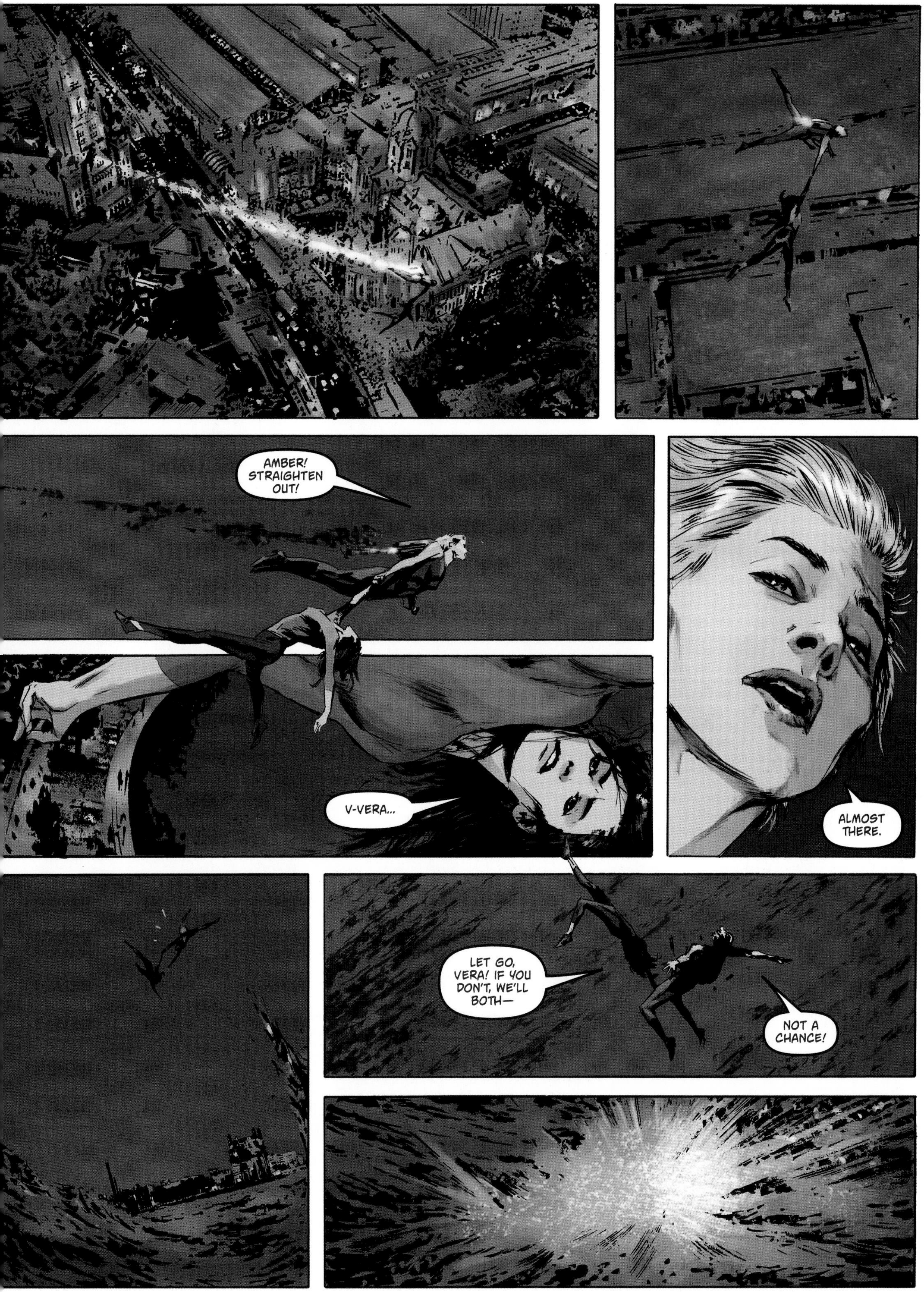
AMBER! STRAIGHTEN OUT!
V-VERA...
ALMOST THERE.
LET GO, VERA! IF YOU DON'T, WE'LL BOTH—
NOT A CHANCE!

LONDON. THREE DAYS LATER.

YOU SAVED HER, VERA.

I WOULD HAVE LIKED TO DO IT *BETTER*.

MOST OF THE MEMBERS OF CLEVERLAND INTERNATIONAL IMPLICATED IN THE SCANDAL REVEALED BY THE MYSTERIOUS YOUNG WOMAN IN MUMBAI HAVE BEEN ARRESTED. THE DIRECTOR, ARNAV ASLAM, HAS PROMISED A THOROUGH CLEANSING OF HIS INSTITUTION ACROSS THE GLOBE.

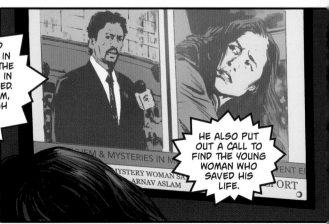

HE ALSO PUT OUT A CALL TO FIND THE YOUNG WOMAN WHO SAVED HIS LIFE.

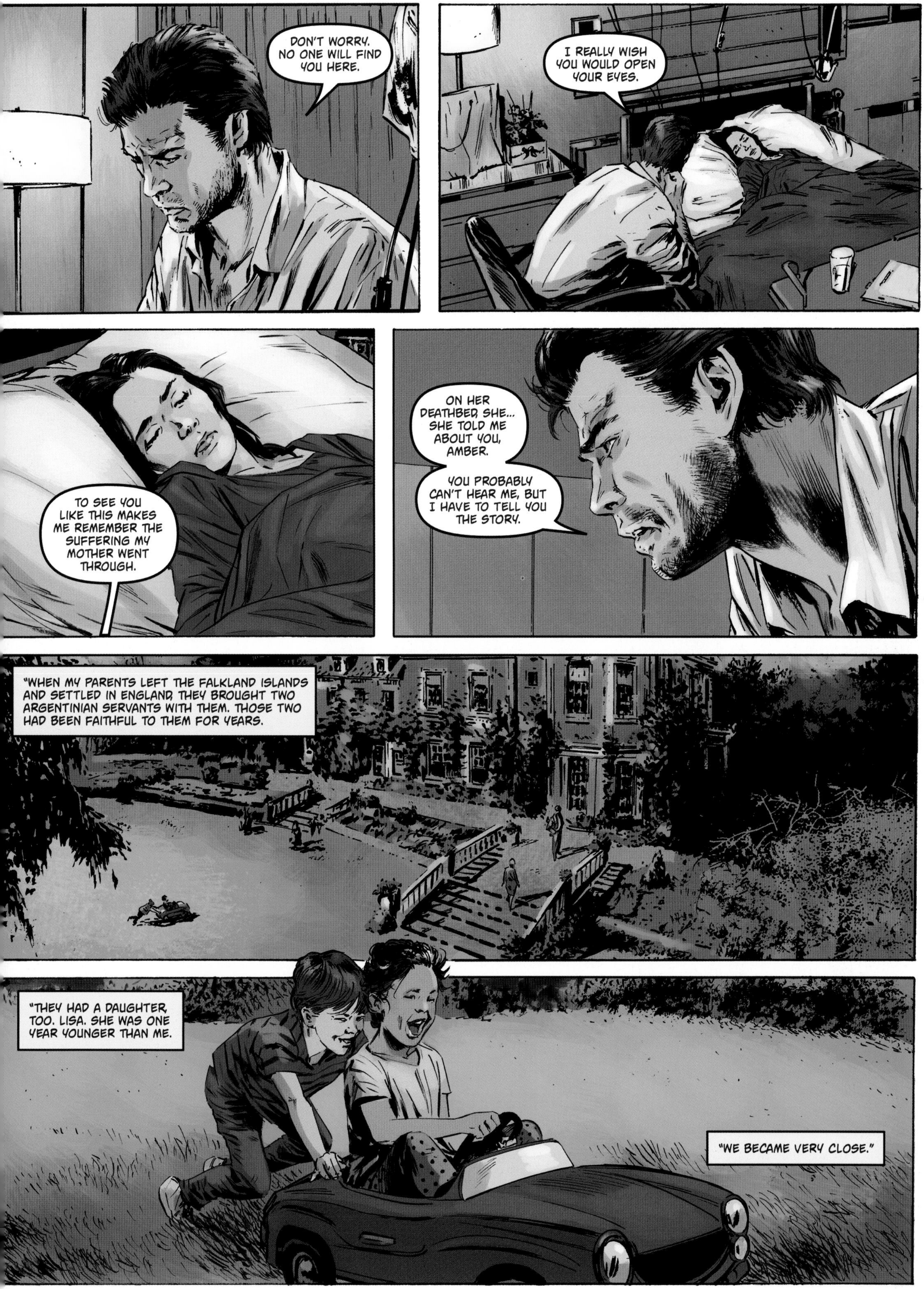
DON'T WORRY. NO ONE WILL FIND YOU HERE.
I REALLY WISH YOU WOULD OPEN YOUR EYES.
TO SEE YOU LIKE THIS MAKES ME REMEMBER THE SUFFERING MY MOTHER WENT THROUGH.
ON HER DEATHBED, SHE... SHE TOLD ME ABOUT YOU, AMBER.
YOU PROBABLY CAN'T HEAR ME, BUT I HAVE TO TELL YOU THE STORY.
"WHEN MY PARENTS LEFT THE FALKLAND ISLANDS AND SETTLED IN ENGLAND, THEY BROUGHT TWO ARGENTINIAN SERVANTS WITH THEM. THOSE TWO HAD BEEN FAITHFUL TO THEM FOR YEARS.
"THEY HAD A DAUGHTER, TOO. LISA. SHE WAS ONE YEAR YOUNGER THAN ME.
"WE BECAME VERY CLOSE."

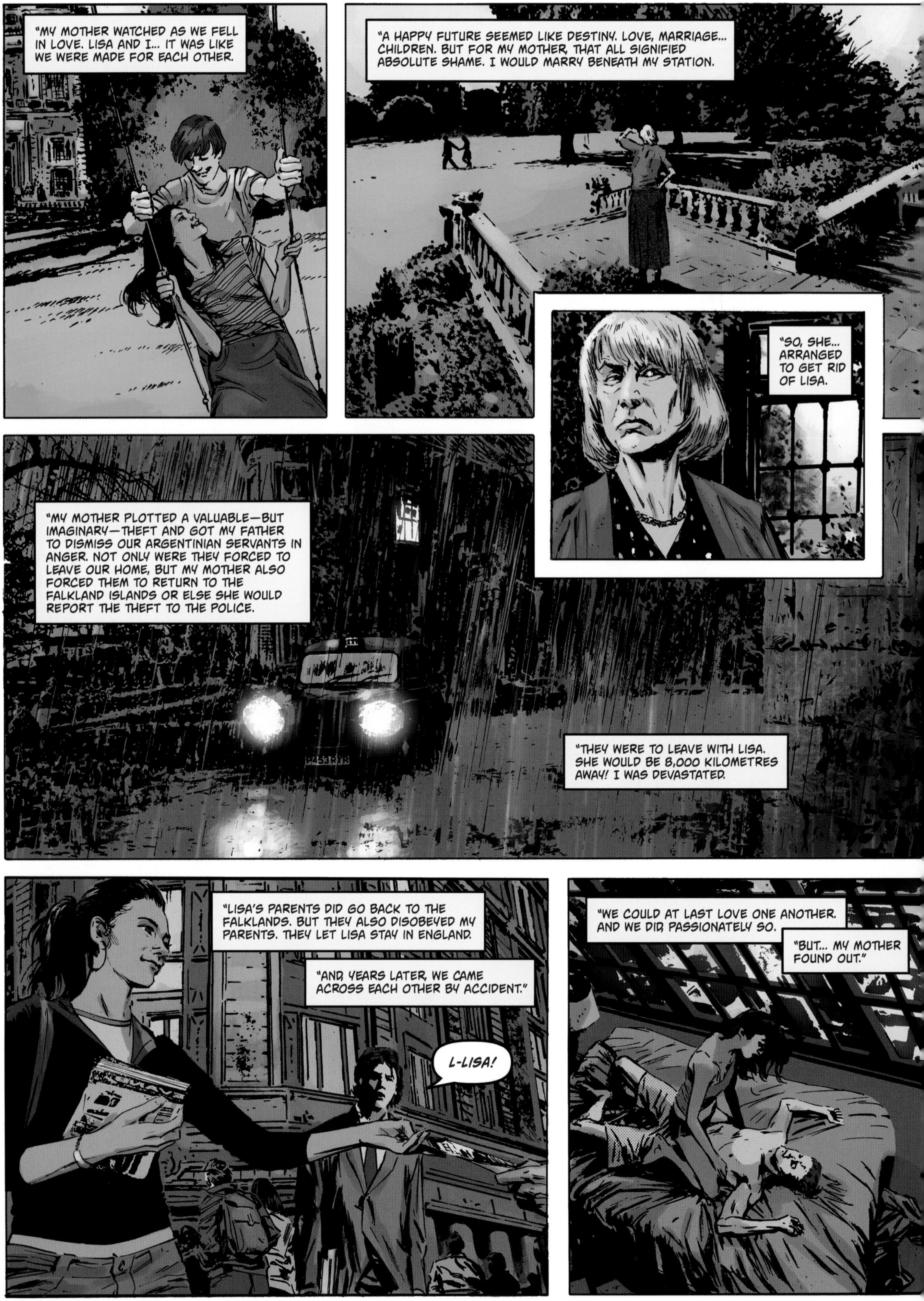
"MY MOTHER WATCHED AS WE FELL IN LOVE. LISA AND I... IT WAS LIKE WE WERE MADE FOR EACH OTHER.
"A HAPPY FUTURE SEEMED LIKE DESTINY. LOVE, MARRIAGE... CHILDREN. BUT FOR MY MOTHER, THAT ALL SIGNIFIED ABSOLUTE SHAME. I WOULD MARRY BENEATH MY STATION.
"SO, SHE... ARRANGED TO GET RID OF LISA.
"MY MOTHER PLOTTED A VALUABLE—BUT IMAGINARY—THEFT AND GOT MY FATHER TO DISMISS OUR ARGENTINIAN SERVANTS IN ANGER. NOT ONLY WERE THEY FORCED TO LEAVE OUR HOME, BUT MY MOTHER ALSO FORCED THEM TO RETURN TO THE FALKLAND ISLANDS OR ELSE SHE WOULD REPORT THE THEFT TO THE POLICE.
"THEY WERE TO LEAVE WITH LISA. SHE WOULD BE 8,000 KILOMETRES AWAY! I WAS DEVASTATED.
"LISA'S PARENTS DID GO BACK TO THE FALKLANDS. BUT THEY ALSO DISOBEYED MY PARENTS. THEY LET LISA STAY IN ENGLAND.
"AND, YEARS LATER, WE CAME ACROSS EACH OTHER BY ACCIDENT."
L-LISA!
"WE COULD AT LAST LOVE ONE ANOTHER. AND WE DID, PASSIONATELY SO.
"BUT... MY MOTHER FOUND OUT."

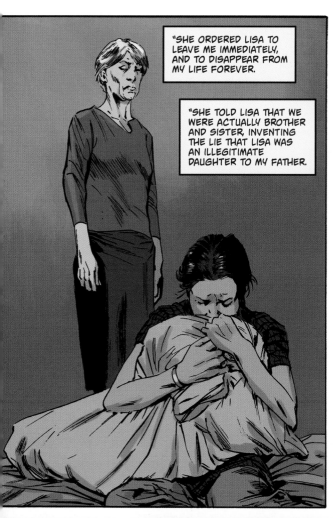

"SHE ORDERED LISA TO LEAVE ME IMMEDIATELY, AND TO DISAPPEAR FROM MY LIFE FOREVER.

"SHE TOLD LISA THAT WE WERE ACTUALLY BROTHER AND SISTER, INVENTING THE LIE THAT LISA WAS AN ILLEGITIMATE DAUGHTER TO MY FATHER.

"LISA BELIEVED HER AND LEFT.

"WE DIDN'T KNOW SHE WAS PREGNANT..."

...WITH YOU.

"SHE GAVE YOU LIFE AND NAMED YOU AMBER.

"THE REST OF HER SHORT LIFE WAS A DESCENT INTO HELL.

"WHEN YOU WERE FIVE, MY MOTHER DECIDED THAT LISA WAS UNFIT TO RAISE YOU. SHE CONVINCED HER TO LEAVE YOU IN AN ORPHANAGE. SHE SAID YOU WERE THE DEGENERATE CHILD OF INCEST.

"THAT'S HOW YOU GOT STRANDED AT MERTON CASTLE."

"MY MOTHER WENT SO FAR AS TO CHOOSE THE WORST HOME FOR YOU. SHE SAID THAT EVEN IF I FOUND OUT ABOUT YOUR EXISTENCE, AND I TRACKED YOU DOWN, YOU WOULD HAVE BECOME SUCH A BAD SEED THAT I WOULDN'T WANT YOU.

"JUST BEFORE DYING, MOTHER NEEDED TO RELIEVE HER CONSCIENCE OF HER CRIMINAL MANUEVERS, WHICH HAD DESTROYED SEVERAL LIVES."

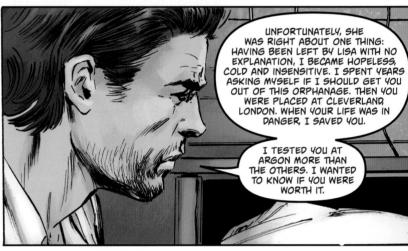

UNFORTUNATELY, SHE WAS RIGHT ABOUT ONE THING: HAVING BEEN LEFT BY LISA WITH NO EXPLANATION, I BECAME HOPELESS, COLD AND INSENSITIVE. I SPENT YEARS ASKING MYSELF IF I SHOULD GET YOU OUT OF THIS ORPHANAGE. THEN YOU WERE PLACED AT CLEVERLAND, LONDON. WHEN YOUR LIFE WAS IN DANGER, I SAVED YOU.

I TESTED YOU AT ARGON MORE THAN THE OTHERS. I WANTED TO KNOW IF YOU WERE WORTH IT.

TODAY, I REGRET THAT, AND I DON'T WANT YOU TO LEAVE ME. I WANT TO CONTINUE WORKING TOGETHER.

YES, I KNOW NOW THAT YOU WERE WORTH IT.

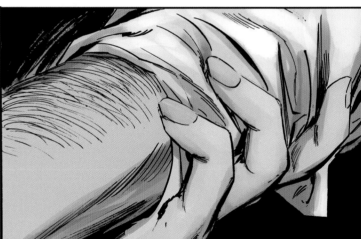

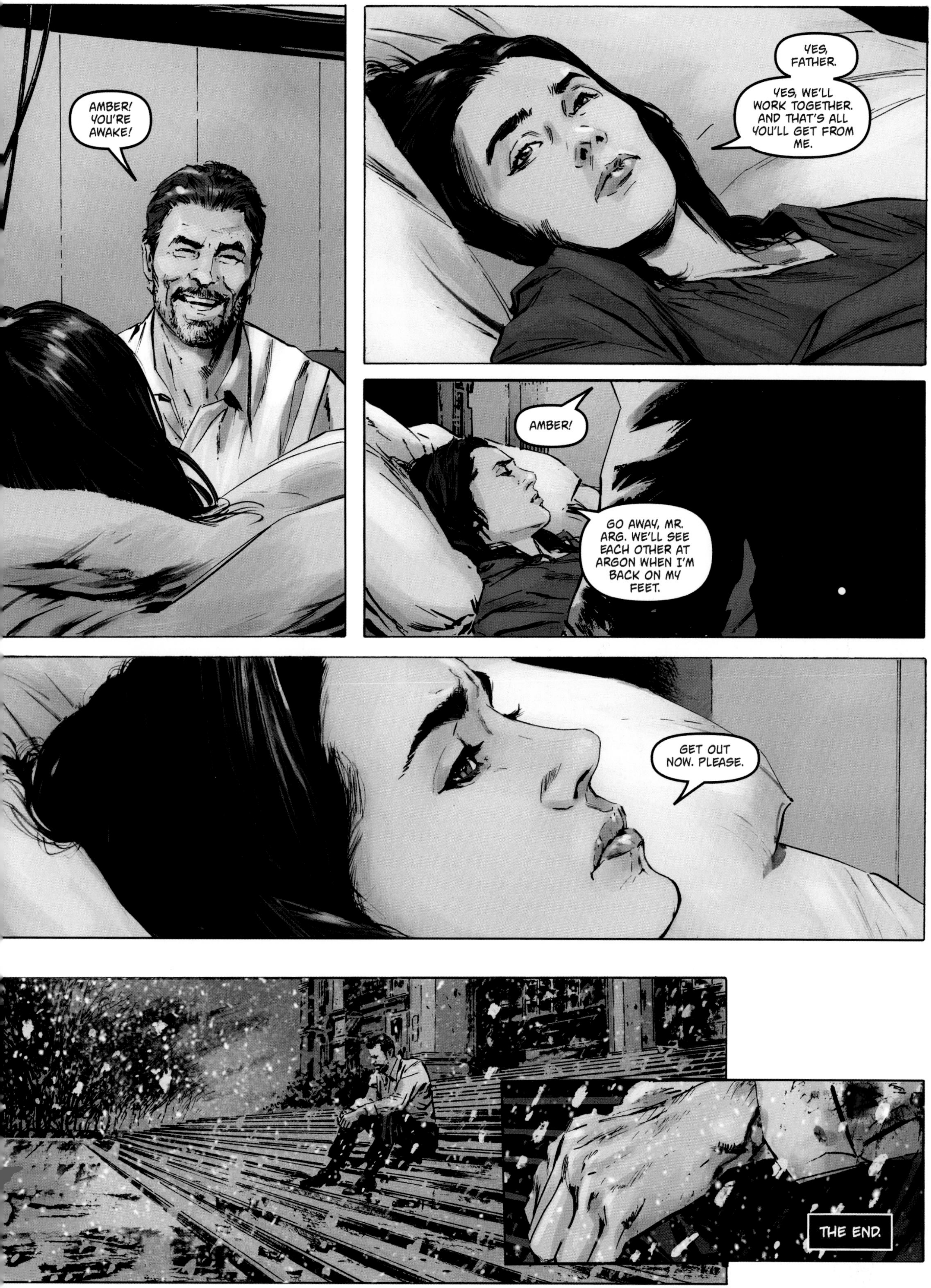
AMBER! YOU'RE AWAKE!
YES, FATHER.
YES, WE'LL WORK TOGETHER. AND THAT'S ALL YOU'LL GET FROM ME.
AMBER!
GO AWAY, MR. ARG. WE'LL SEE EACH OTHER AT ARGON WHEN I'M BACK ON MY FEET.
GET OUT NOW. PLEASE.
THE END.

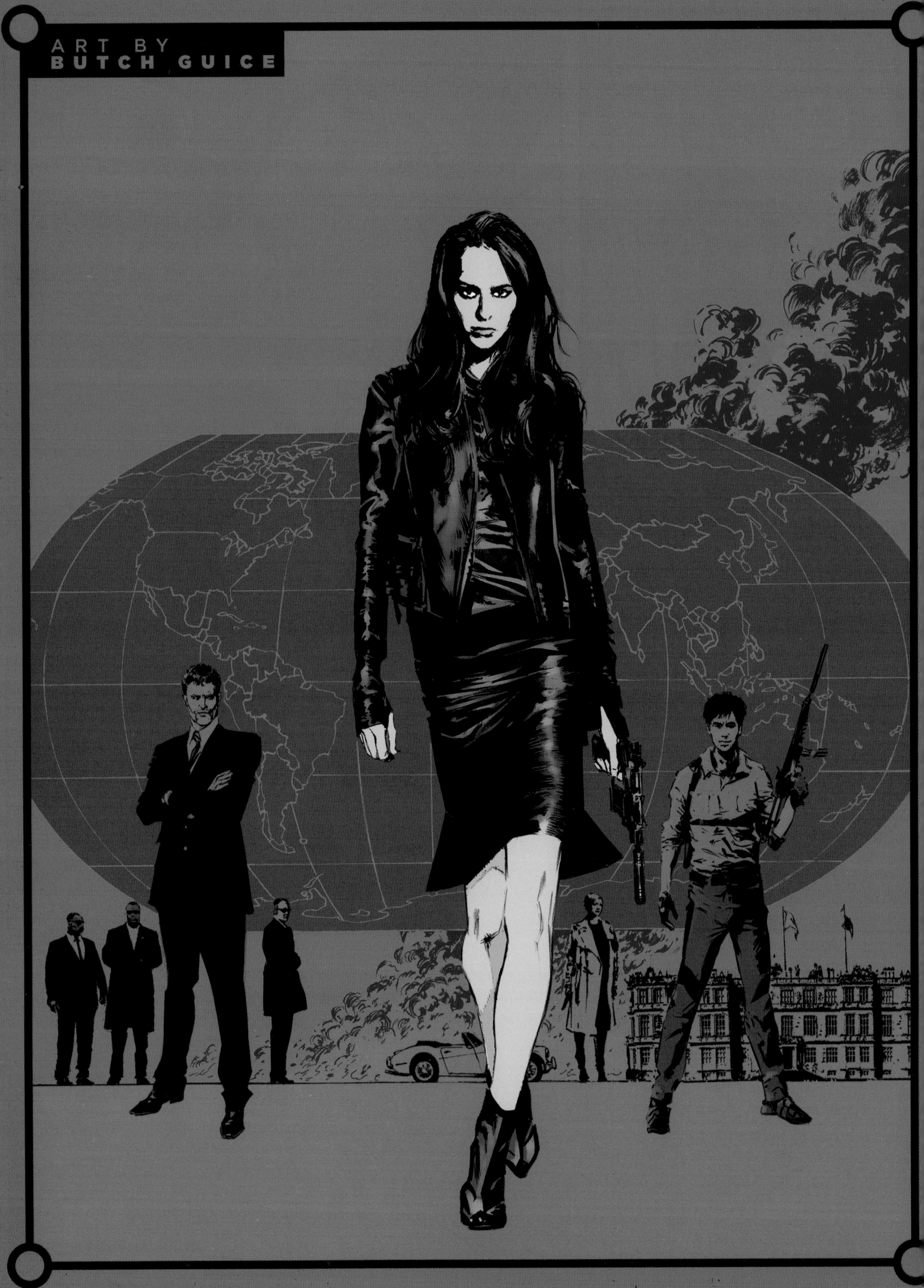

ART BY
BUTCH GUICE

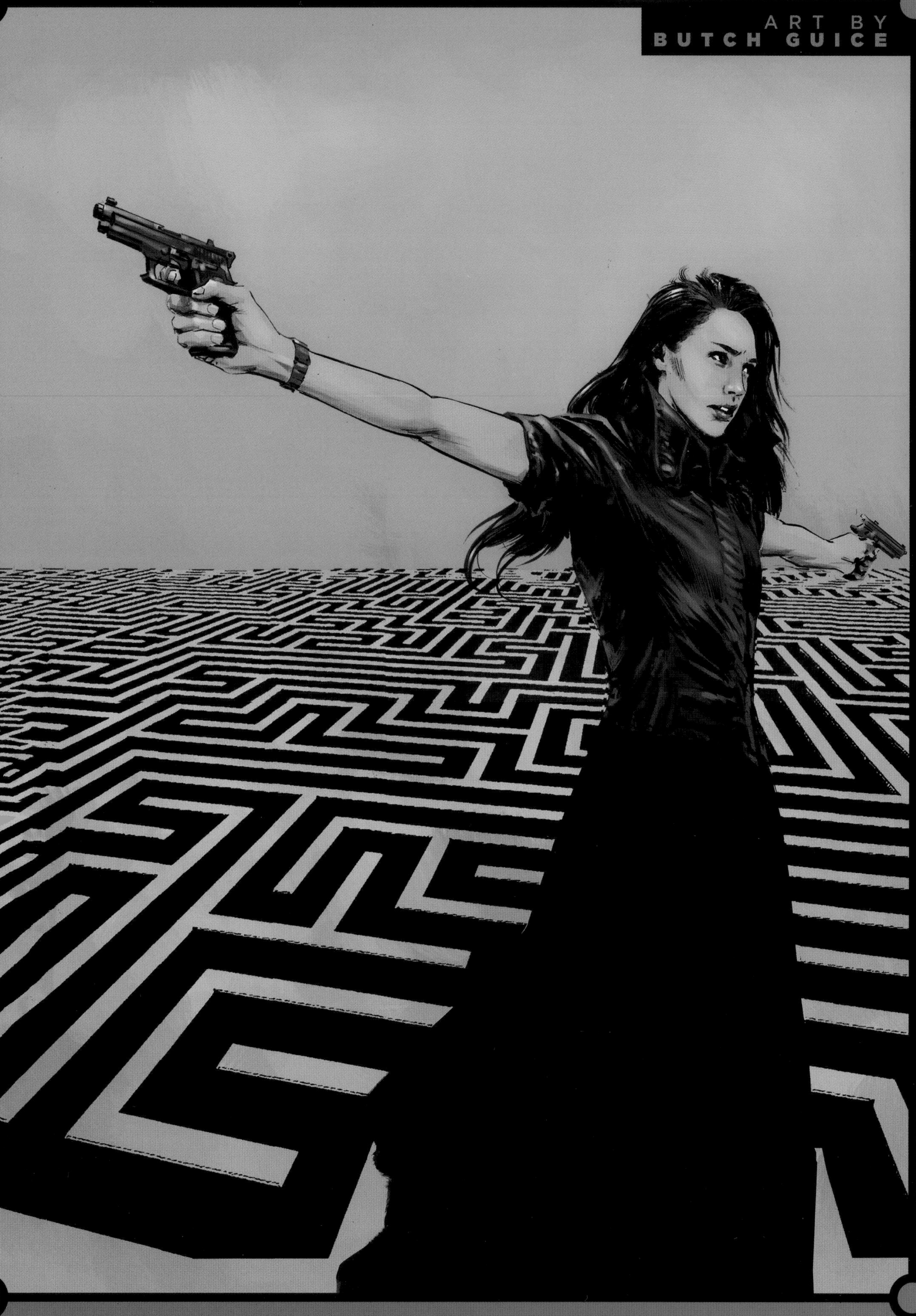
ART BY
BUTCH GUICE

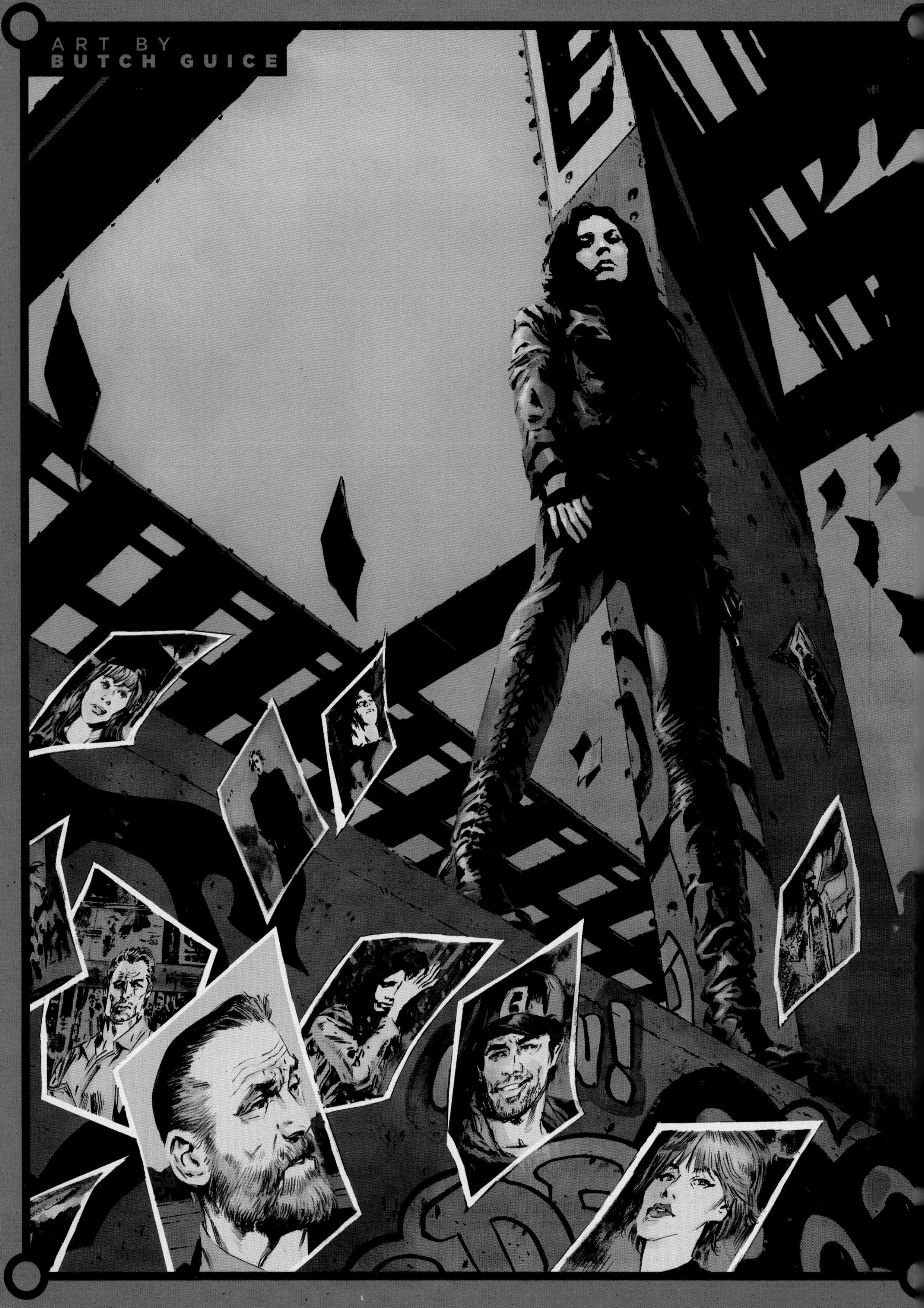
ART BY
BUTCH GUICE

ART BY
BUTCH GUICE

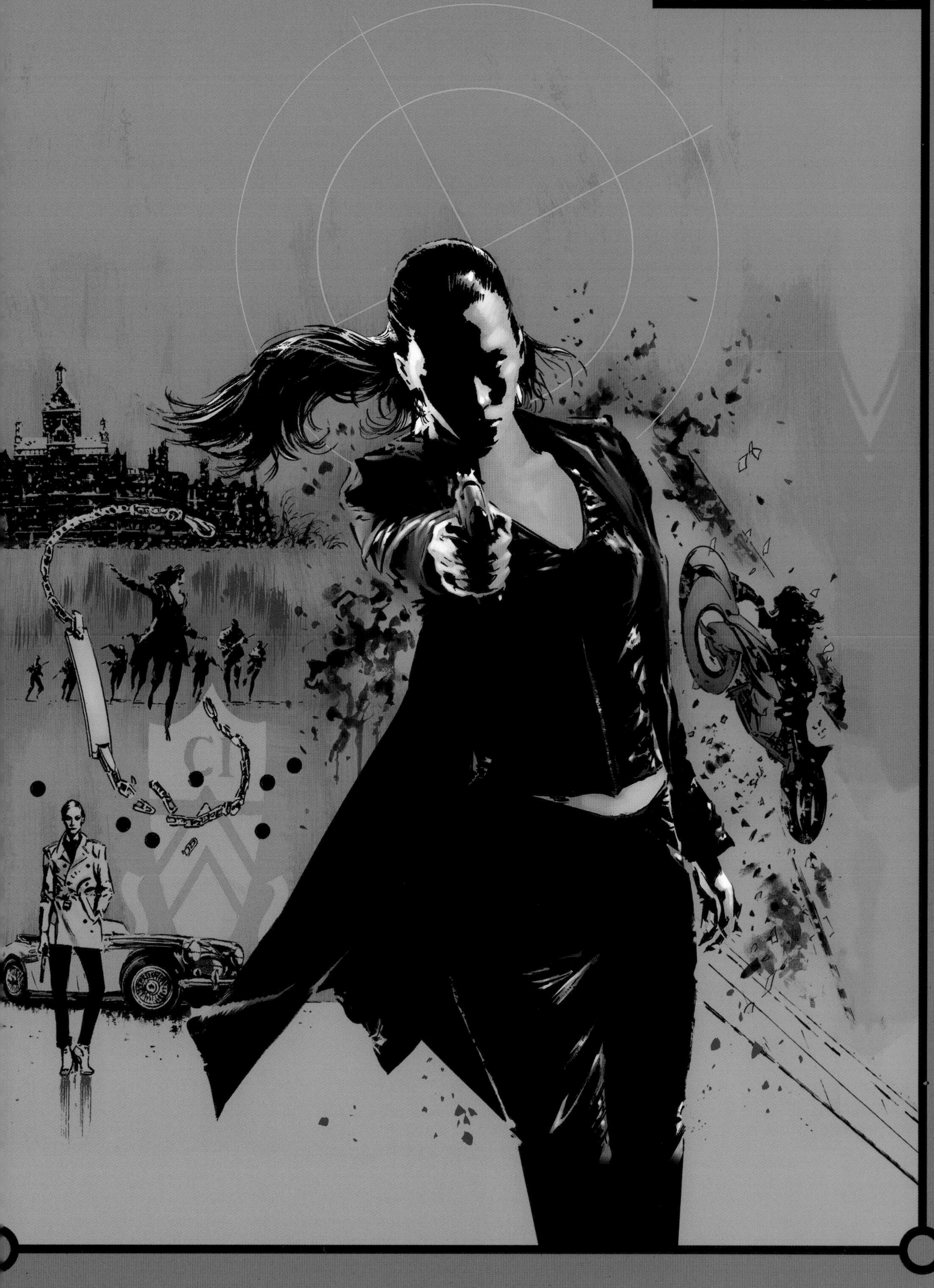

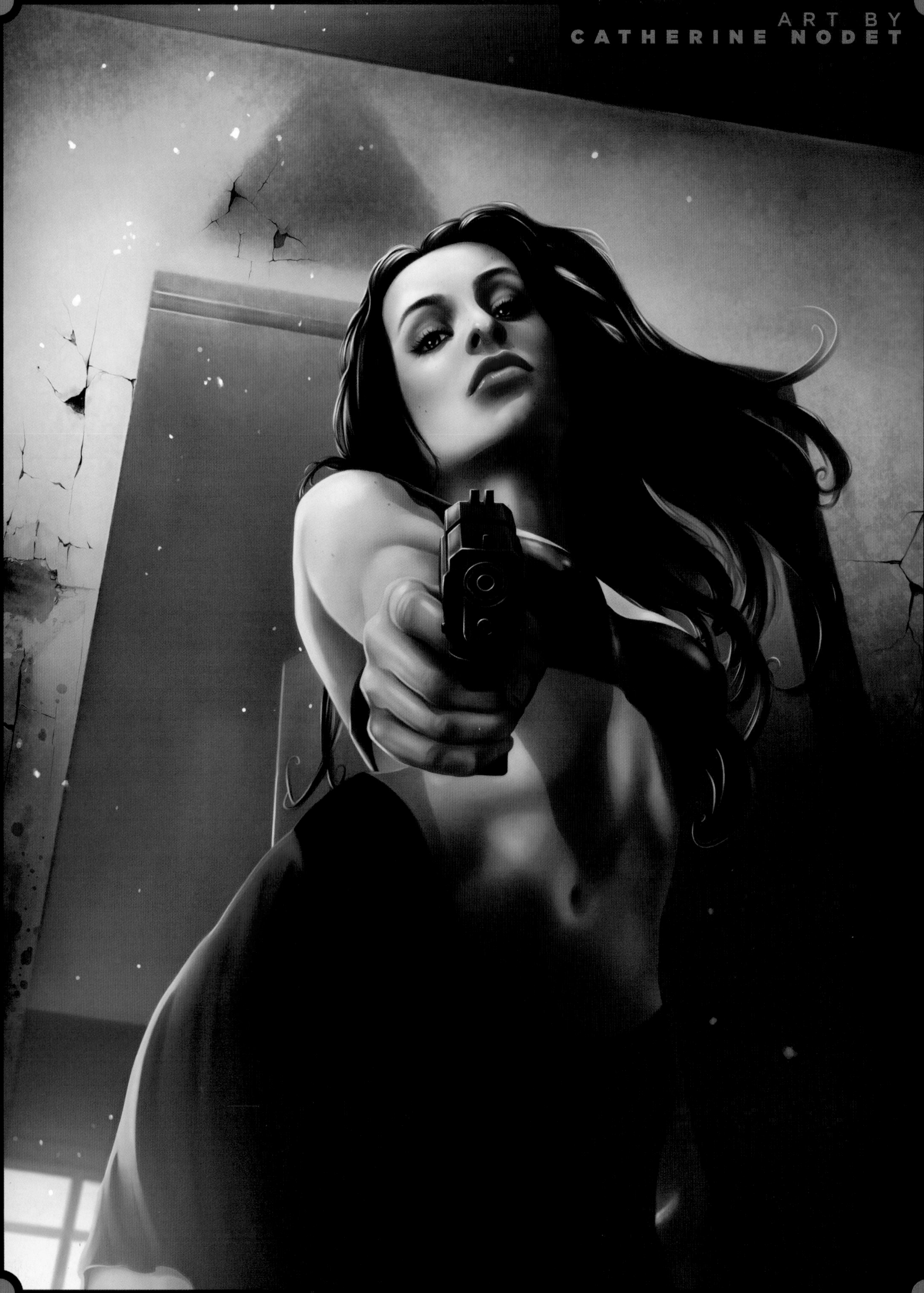
ART BY
CATHERINE NODET

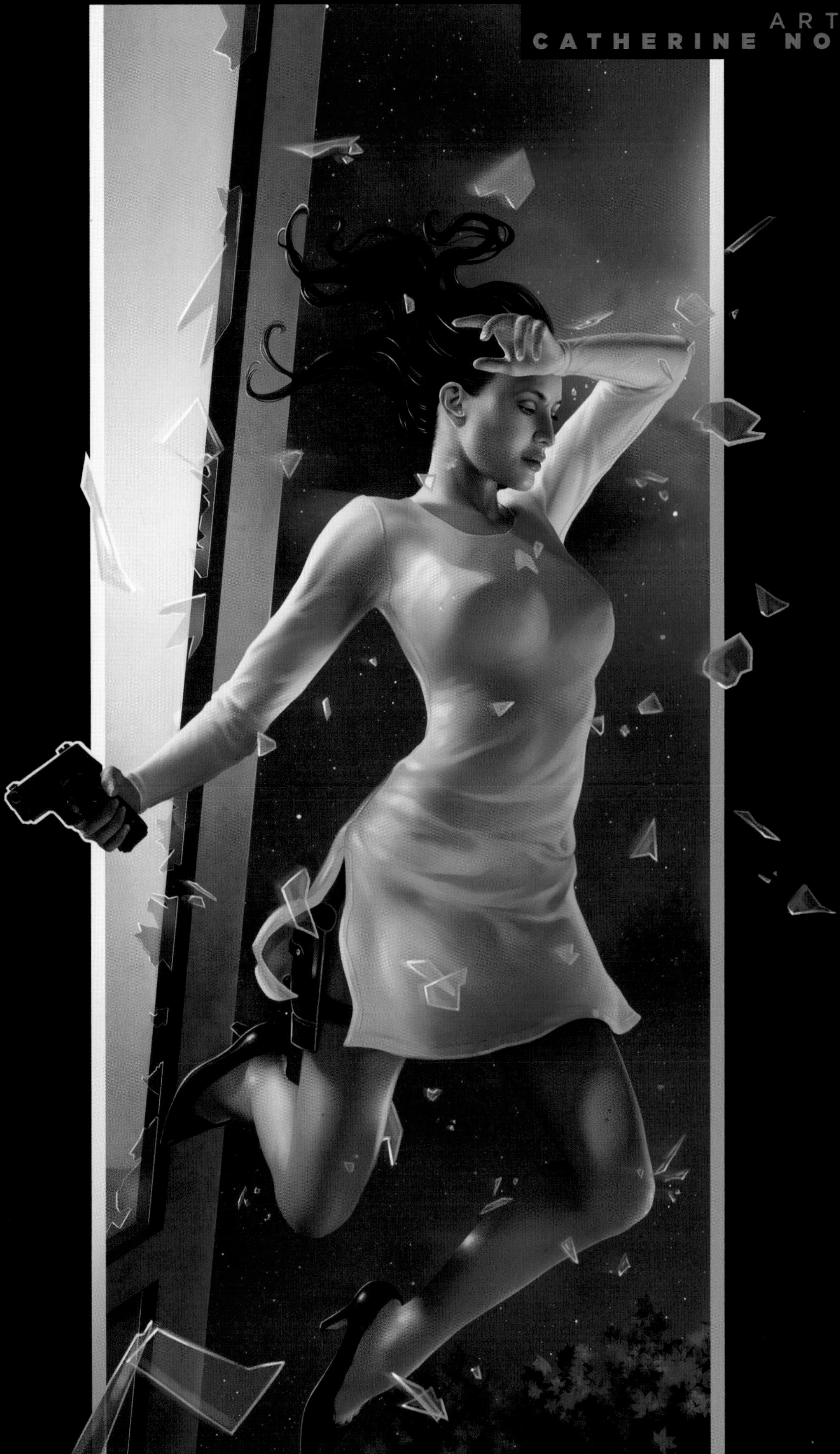

ART BY
CATHERINE NODET

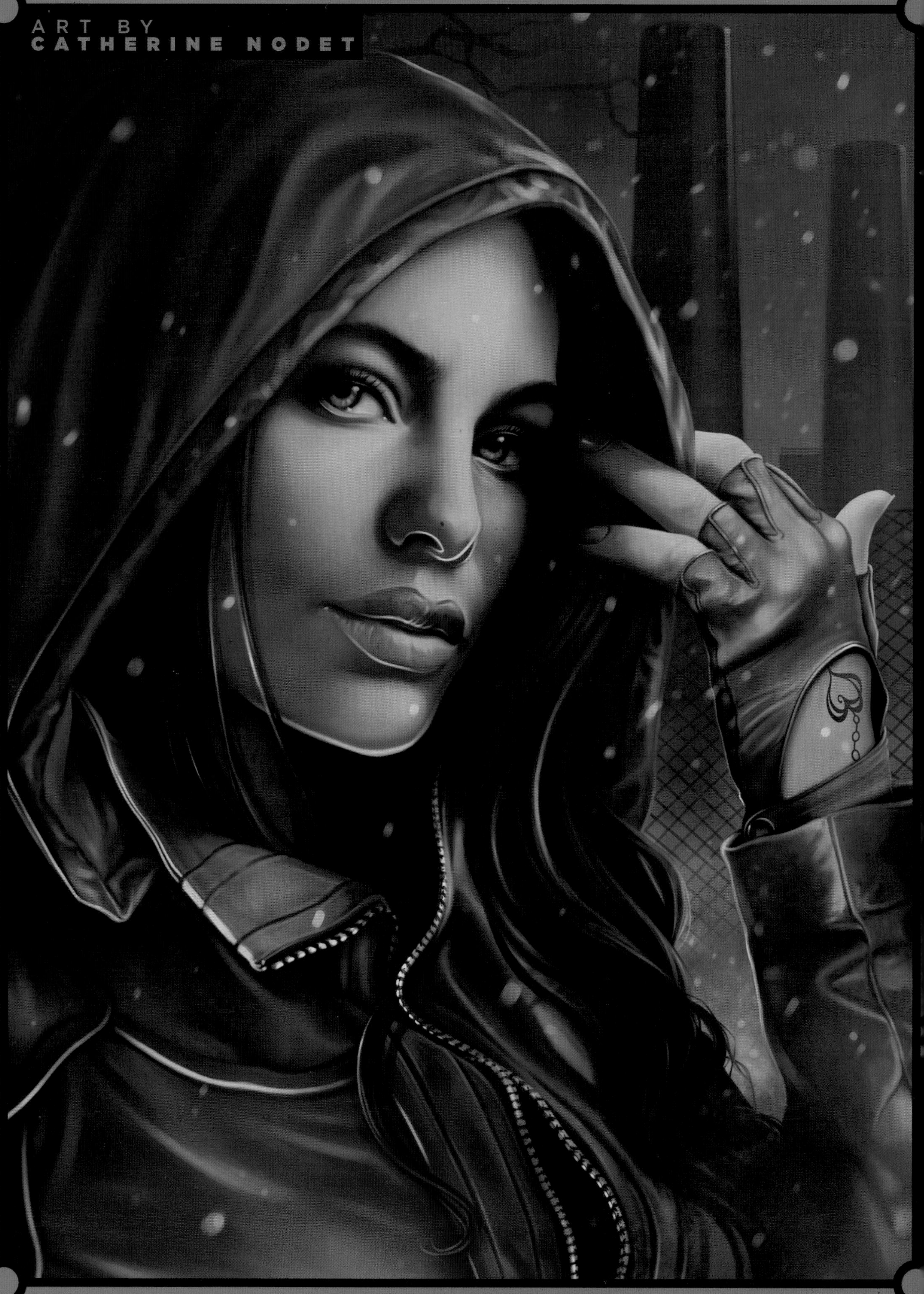
ART BY
CATHERINE NODET

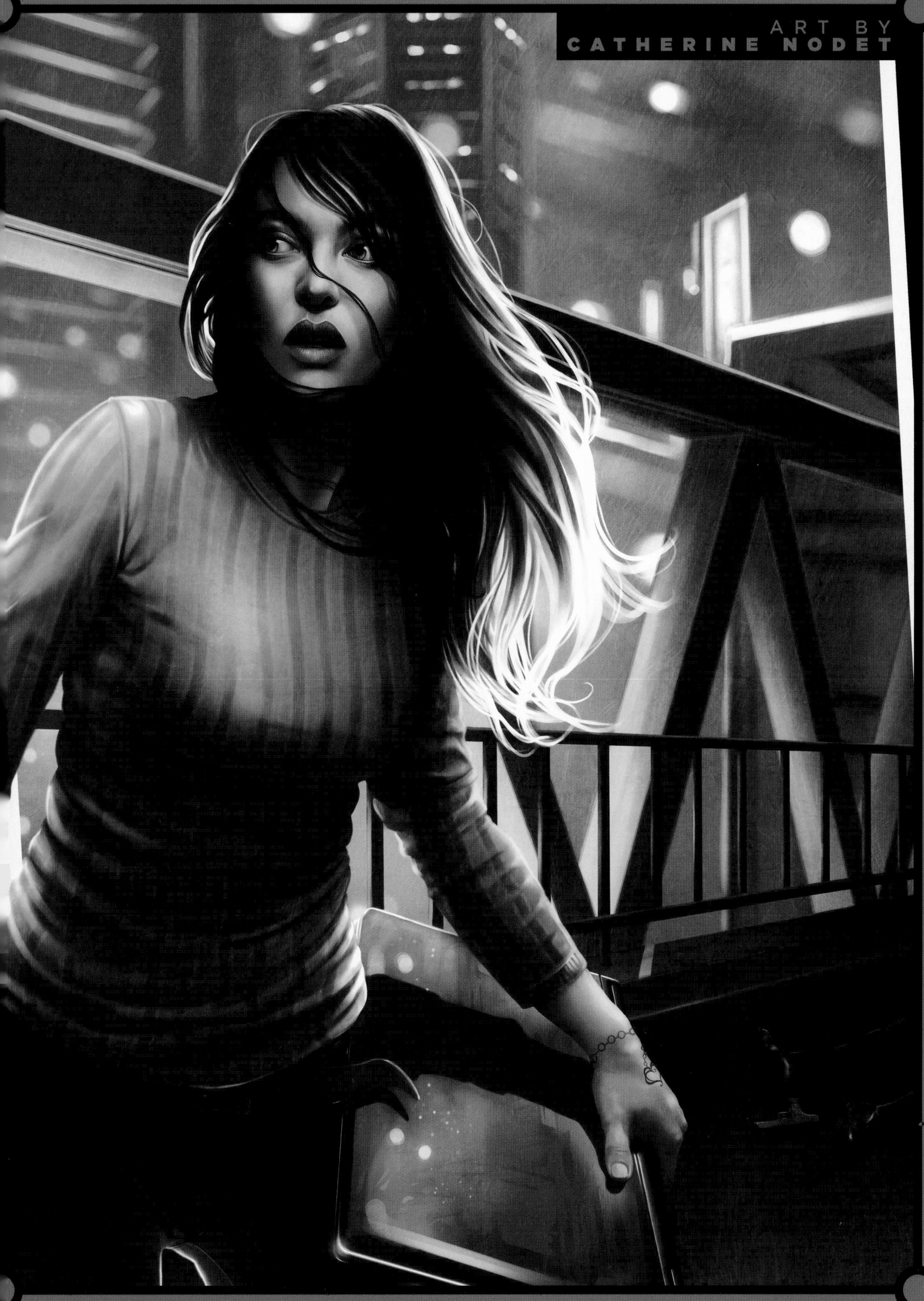
ART BY
CATHERINE NODET

# JADE LAGARDÉRE

Jade Lagardère was born in Belgium and started very early as a model in haute couture and ready-to-wear fashion. At the age of 15, she was involved in a humanitarian mission to Morocco for SOS Children's Villages. At 18, she wrote her first script. At the age of 20, she met, then married Arnaud Lagardère with whom she has three children. During her second pregnancy, Jade returned to her first love by imagining and creating the character of Amber Blake, first published by Glenat in 2017.

# BUTCH GUICE

Jackson "Butch" Guice is a prolific U.S. artist having worked for every major U.S. comic company on titles such as *Captain America*, *Ultimate Origins* (Marvel), *Superman*, *Aquaman: Swords of Atlantis* (DC Comics), *Ruse* (CrossGen), and *William Gibson's Archangel* (IDW). He has been shortlisted twice for the Best Penciller/Inker Eisner Award